His Grace, His Mercy

His Grace, His Mercy

Keshia Dawn

www.urbanchristianonline.net

Urban Books, LLC
97 N18th Street
Wyandanch, NY 11798

ISBN 13: 978-1-60162-768-1
ISBN 10: 1-60162-768-8

First Mass Market Paperback Printing September 2013
First Trade Paperback Printing September 2009
Printed in the United States of America

10 9 8 7 6 5 4 3 2 1

This is a work of fiction. Any references or similarities to actual events, real people, living or dead, or to real locales are intended to give the novel a sense of reality. Any similarity in other names, characters, places, and incidents is entirely coincidental.

Distributed by Kensington Publishing Corp.
Submit Wholesale Orders to:
Kensington Publishing Corp.
C/O Penguin Group (USA) Inc.
Attention: Order Processing
405 Murray Hill Parkway
East Rutherford, NJ 07073-2316
Phone: 1-800-526-0275
Fax: 1-800-227-9604

Dedication

For the love you have allowed me to show you,
and for the innocent love you have given me.

To my number one fan, my dearest Chayse,
Mommy dedicates another beginning to YOU.

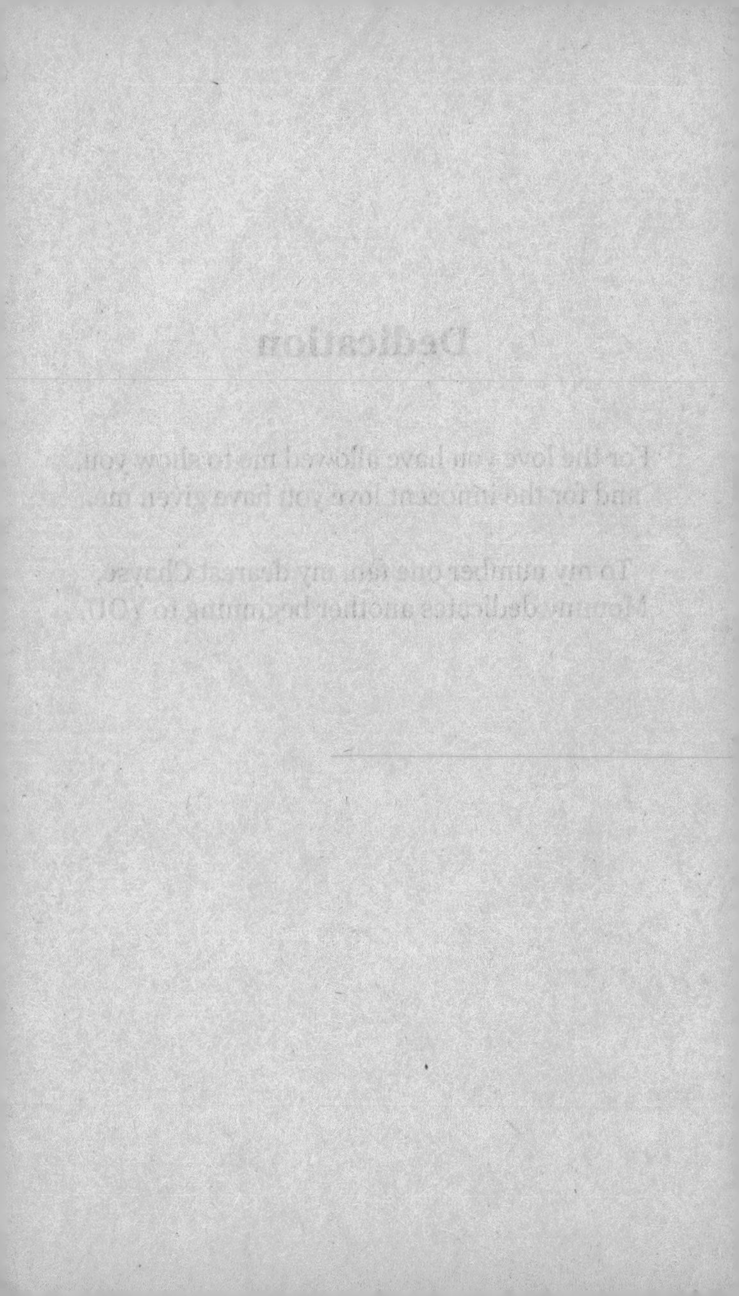

Acknowledgments

As always, it's forever an honor and privilege to give God thanks. Another year, and I'm thankful even the more for the stories that He has aligned in my thoughts, and for the breath, ability, as well as the trials and tribulations that allow me to test myself in Christ. Though I'm not perfect, I strive to be who God says that I shall be.

To my parents: (I must put the names in bold!) To my dad, **Minister Donald Sauls**, and my mother, **Sister Fannie P. Sauls**, thank you for my life. Thank you, Daddy, for being there for thirty-three years when you could have easily been just a drive-by dad. You overcame all the adversities that tried to keep you down, and I thank God for second chances. Thank you, Mama, for bringing me into this world and for always wanting more for your three girls and wanting us to always be family. You're the funniest woman I know, and I'm glad that I inherited my humor from you. Laughing keeps us looking young!

To my sisters, Fanasha and Angel, who definitely took after Momma and left me with Daddy's little legs, thank you two, once again, for being as second mothers to Chayse. I'm happy that you all have finally (well, almost) caught up with me in age. Nonetheless, I'm happy that we've grown closer over the years, and I pray that we will forever stay in each other's corners. Whatever you want, grab it; whatever you need, God has it; and I'll definitely be there to help you hold it down.

To Baby Chayse, who has grown into a very smart, big girl (all of three years' worth), everything I do is and always will be for God to get the glory, then for the completeness of you. Love you, Shoonie! You make Mommy proud already!

To my family and extended family in Dallas, as well as Temple, Texas, on to Paris, Texas, the connection is always deeper than it appears. My cousins, the next generation, never settle for less. Less is way too easy to find. Work hard for things that bring you happiness, but know that happiness begins with God.

There are so many authors that I've met in the industry that I won't even begin to name, but thankfully many of them are online family members. That being said, my gratitude goes out to the online writing groups that I'm grateful to be a part of. The ongoing support that we show one another in the industry is so genuine and unlike anything I've seen in a long time. The Writers Hut, Fiction Folks, BW Christian Literature are the names of a few of the groups that have put up with me from day one. Bless you all and all the information that you share willingly. Being an author is the beginning, having great people behind you makes the difference.

To the readers, book clubs, bookstores, and individuals that made me feel welcome with By the Grace of God, thank you graciously for the push to continue my writing. It's always first for God, then for you. I always pray that you'll take something out of the words I pray to God for. Thanks for the love.

Those at Black Expressions Book Club, thank you tremendously for adding *By the Grace of God* to your lineup. For the readers who left their reviews, thank you all. Do know that your words encourage me even the more. Those on Shelfari, as well as Amazon, I'm grateful for each and every one of you who continue to leave your mark where my writing is concerned. Tyora, Mrs. AAkul turezone.com, thanks for letting me back into your growing world. Rhonda with Mocha Readers, you're awesome.

What can I say? You're truly a hardworking woman. APOOO, Rawsistaz, and Urban Reviewers, thanks for the love. We authors are grateful for the avenue you allow. SORMAG, LaShunda Hoffman, can you get any better? If so, I can't wait to see what you have up your sleeves.

Once again to Kensington/Urban Christian, thank you for the opportunity. All of the authors who have become like family, let's keep this thing rocking and rolling, but let's not forget the tambourines, LOL. Sharon Oliver, you're a gifted and witty writer. Keep it up, lady. And a big thank you to Joylynn for being an honest, God-fearing, and hardworking woman. You've made this sequel even more than what I imagined for it to be. Much continued success.

Surely I have to thank new friends who have become like family to me. Just the encouragement alone pushes me over the top. It's not what you do, but what you say that helps me to stay on track. Next to my mom, you're my biggest promoter. Thank you so very much, Monekia.

Until the pen hits the pad once more, stay blessed.

Keshia Dawn

Prologue

With the overwhelming feel of holding her new baby, the humbled mother allowed her tears to surface from their hiding place. The wisdom that God gives to all mothers was already evident in her being: knowing how to hold, comfort, and love her child.

She had somewhat believed in miracles and blessings, but on the day she was able to deliver a child that she hadn't even prepared for, the meek new mother now knew that God was still in the blessing business. Even for her.

"Don't you go and spoil that baby." The older woman interrupted the youthful mother, standing from the rocking chair that had been placed in the hospital room. "That's my job. Give her here." She pushed up the sleeves on her comfortably worn shirt, held out her washed hands, and opened her arms for the bundle of joy.

Barely peeking up from her infant child's round face, the mother contemplated. "I guess

I'll let you hold her. Isn't she just beautiful? She is my special angel," she said, fighting her joyful tears and releasing her newborn into the visitor's maternal arms.

Agreeing about the beauty of the child, the older woman didn't let the mother forget that her job wasn't complete. "You know you have to name this child before you leave the hospital, don't you? Thought any further?" she asked, keeping her eyes glued to the infant covered in the fluffed pink blanket.

With a stiff motion, she sat herself up in the retractable bed and pushed strands of hair back into her makeshift ponytail. The thirty-something mother exhaled as she thought about naming her child.

"I thought about it, prayed about it, and I have chosen her name. You know it's nothing but God's grace that could allow me to go through so much and make it out with my head up. But for all that I've done, God's mercy is so sufficient." Holding in her cry, the child's mother borrowed a breath before she shared the name that rested well with her.

"Mercy. She's another chance that God has given me to do right with this life that He's given me. Mercy fits her well." Readying her arms to receive the baby, Mercy's mother held a smile that only God could place on her yearning face. With the feel of the baby's soft fingers between her own, the grateful mother closed her heavy eyes and quietly sang the words that came to her heart:

"God's mercy held me, so I wouldn't let go."

Chapter 1

"Ashes to ashes, and dust to dust . . ." was all Gracie heard before her vision blurred and her eyes crossed, leaving her blacked out on the simmering grass underneath her feet. The summer's weather had been plagued with boisterous winds, making the day stretch—the week, for that matter. The stored energy she clung to had finally seeped through her pores, leaving her faint.

Moments before, while standing and mourning along with the outsized crowd, Gracie replayed the painful past in her mind. Vividly, her mind took her on an unwanted reverse of her life with her ex-fiancé, Dillian, and how she dreamed it would be one way, when in fact it had turned out another.

Seven years prior, in the blink of an eye, Gracie's own pending nuptials to Dillian had been halted when she'd found that her fiancé had not only contracted HIV, but had also slept with her best friend, Kendra, leaving her, too, with the lingering disease.

Now, standing with the other mourners sending a farewell to Dillian, Gracie had become overwhelmed with the unburying of her past. With the June summer sun beaming on the crown of her head, Gracie had fallen past her feet, lying on the cracked, waterless ground that crowded beneath her high-heeled shoes.

"Gracie! Honey, are you okay?" Marcus repeated as he hovered over his wife of six and a half years, mother of his six-year-old honeymoon-produced twin boys. Gathering her up in his arms, Marcus made his way out of the crowd and toward the paved parking lot full of vehicles.

"I'm . . . I'm okay, Marcus. I should have eaten something this morning." Finally opening her dim brown eyes, Gracie wanted out of the horrible dream. Placing her hands over her eyes, shielding them from the sun's rays, Gracie remembered the funeral. "Is it over?" she asked, noticing that she had been placed on the backseat of their Tahoe, resting in Marcus's burly arms.

"It's over. Here, drink this water." Holding the clear plastic container in place as he guided the beverage toward her mouth, Marcus helped Gracie position herself. "Do you feel up for the repast back at the church? If not, we—"

"We can go." She looked up into her husband's eyes. "I'd like that. Thank you, sweetheart. I love you for understanding."

"Gracie, we made vows that I wouldn't break even if you twisted my arm. I know how much Dillian meant to you, and I wouldn't stand in the way of your history with him. He was almost your husband . . . remember?"

"Thank you," she concluded with a smirk.

"Cool. You can stay back here, but somebody's gotta drive," he joked and tapped her designer brown–hosed leg that stretched across the seat. "Let me up." He looked through the front windshield, seeing the other vehicles lining up to leave the cemetery. Easing himself out of the backseat, Marcus stood outside of the forest green Tahoe and released himself from his suit jacket. "Here, babe." He handed his grayish-blue Sean John couture jacket to Gracie.

Holding her hand out to take her husband's outerwear, Gracie made eye contact with Marcus. "Honey, I really do love you." Her eyes promised the same as she tilted her head.

With a wink toward his wife, Marcus responded, "I love you too," as he opened the front entrance of the truck and got inside.

Stretching out on the warmed leather seat in the back of their family's vehicle, Gracie tried to relax as much as possible. She hoped to redeem herself and gather enough strength for the comfort she would need to offer a grieving Kendra.

It was just like Marcus, the devoted husband, to know what Gracie truly needed. Right as she closed her eyes to rest, melodies floated throughout the previously silent truck. No words, just gospel music played with musical instruments that sounded as if jazz had landed right in the midst of it. It was the ultimate. Worship was behind the meaning of such an awesome compact disc.

With tears streaming down her previously cried-out and puffed face, Gracie rode silently in the backseat, basking in the glory of God for the many blessings He had allowed to rain down on her life. Not trying to place herself in the "what-if" category, Gracie couldn't help it. What if she'd had to deal with Dillian's death as his significant other? Or even worse, what if she was the one who had—Gracie couldn't even allow her mind to think the word.

Only Oscar-nominated movies could produce a script as delicate as her life had been. If Gracie tried to explain to a stranger everything that had gone on in her less than forty years of living on this earth, she just knew they wouldn't believe her. That's why she never even tried. Gracie never would have guessed the current outcome of her life either. Dillian, the former love of her life, had become one of her best friends, instead of the husband she had once desired.

In a flash is how quickly things had changed. One moment she was the happy fiancée of Dillian McNab, a champion in the weightlifting world. In an instant, the dream of floating down the aisle in an off-the-shoulder wedding gown had been snatched away. The only thing left was the worry of not knowing, wondering if her negative HIV status would ever change to match that of not only Dillian's, but of Kendra's. Gracie was more than thankful to God that it had not.

Six and a half years of no longer being called Dillian's fiancée, but loving every minute of being the wife of Marcus Jeffries, Gracie had finally reacted to the life planted by God. Though no one would ever buy tickets to see her on the big screen, Gracie was certain her life—Dillian's life—had great meaning and purpose. With him laid to rest, Gracie clasped her hands and thanked God for the opportunity to be a part of His plan, His designs on each of their lives. And for some reason, she felt as though God was not finished with her yet, not by far. Feeling her life fulfilled, her husband a Godly man and her children healthy and growing, Gracie placed her hands over her heart and released Dillian.

I'll always love you, Dillian. Always.

With the mindset of giving, Gracie fluttered her eyes completely open once she saw the church in view and knew there was more to be done.

Walking arm in arm beside her husband, Gracie made her way inside the church cafeteria, where food had been prepared especially for Dillian's family and other well-wishers. With a buffet-style spread, Marcus couldn't decide which table to begin with. Macaroni was his favorite, but where he was standing, there were black eyed peas, greens, yams, and even a green pea casserole.

Wondering which table housed all the meat, Marcus turned to see a clothed setup that consisted of nothing but protein. Someone had gone out of their way to actually fix a turkey with all of the trimming, and Thanksgiving was more than five months away. Not believing his eyes, Marcus had to let go of Gracie's arm to take a closer look.

"Baby, somebody must have gotten my grandma's recipe for all of this good food. Look at them chit'lings over there." So excited about all of the down-home cooking facing him, Marcus lent his attention back to his wife, but only for the moment.

"Baby, you okay?" he asked, licking his lips from the food he saw and couldn't wait to partake in.

"I'm good, Marcus. Go ahead." Gracie giggled. "You know I can't cook it for you, so you better get it while you can. I'm going to see if I can find Kendra."

Gracie grabbed at the seriousness of their visit to be by Dillian's wife's side. Pointing in the direction that she thought Kendra would have been located, Gracie started on her trek. Quickly locking eyes on her sister-friend, Gracie rushed to where Kendra sat. Wanting to maul her with hugs, Gracie reluctantly had to wait her turn.

Resting in a short line to console Kendra McNab, Gracie stood with her hands on her purse strap, drumming a song that had lingered in her mind from the church's service. As the walk space became clear, Gracie closed the space between her and her friend.

"I'm sorry I was no good for you at the funeral, Kendra. I guess a mixture of Dillian's death and the—well, I'm here now." She wasn't ready for anyone to know of her new secret. "I was overwhelmed." Waiting for a response, but not receiving so much as a blink, Gracie continued as Kendra stared blankly. "I'm here for you now, and whatever you need for me to do, just let me know," Gracie announced as she pressed her tresses behind her ear.

"I'm good." Without gratitude nestling in either her voice or a gesture of thanks being flown in the air, Kendra stood from her chair. "Make sure you get some food, Gracie, and take the boys some also. I won't be able to take all this food home." Concluding her same spiel she had announced to other visitors, Kendra left Gracie's side and made her rounds. Glancing back at Gracie, Kendra pasted a slim grin on her mournful face and accepted others into her space.

Not noticing Marcus walking up behind her, Gracie only felt his presence once she felt his hand land on the bottom of her back.

Food deep into his mouth, Marcus smacked the lasting effects that the food had on his taste buds. "What was that all about?" he questioned as he quickly added his hand back to the bottom of his full plate. Marcus had noticed Kendra's coldness from across the room and rushed to his wife's side.

"I don't even know," she responded with hunched shoulders. With a painful smile added to her confused face, Gracie said, "She's probably just shocked by all of this."

"Maybe you're right," Marcus said through chewing spells. "Come on over here and get you a plate. I'm going for some of that Sock-It-To-Your-Daddy Cake." Marcus started off in the direction of the desserts.

"Honey." Gracie grabbed the bottom of his bare arm.

Marcus decided not to put his jacket back on, making sure he had ample space for digging in.

"Don't you mean *Sock-It-To-Me Cake*?" Gracie overemphasized the name of the popular dessert.

Still chewing the turkey he'd stuffed into his orifice, Marcus corrected his wife as she laughed at him. "I'm just telling you what the lady told me she named her cake. Now come on before it's all gone. You know how church folks love to eat."

Shaking her head toward her husband at his description of church-reared brothers and sisters, Gracie thought only for a second longer about what he'd said. Picking up the pace in her step, Gracie grabbed for the first plate in her sight.

"Mommy? So did you say good-bye to Uncle Dillian today? Did you cry?"

"Gregory, stop asking stupid questions. Daddy!" the taller twin yelled, wanting to make sure his dad was listening. "Tell Gregory to stop asking stupid questions!" Geoffrey tattled about his brother's comment.

The six-year-old identical twins were the spitting image of their father, sharing his brown toffee skin color. But they owned their mother's almond-shaped eyes.

"Boys, it's been a long day for your mother, so don't worry her too much, okay? And Geoffrey, watch your mouth with those nasty words. I don't plan on telling you too many more times, either." Marcus peered over his dark-framed glasses as he tilted his head to make clear eye contact with his child. Loosening his Brooks Brothers tie that had been a Father's Day gift, Marcus waited on the young boy's response.

"Nah nah-nah nah nah," Gregory, the older twin by fourteen minutes, taunted his brother. He gained the maiden name of his mother for his first name, in order to hold what legacy he could for his grandfather's surname. Geoffrey was named by his grandmother, the name she would have chosen for her own son, had she been blessed to continue bearing children after Gracie was born.

"All right now, you two. Cut it out." Gracie yawned through her words sternly as she patted either side of the king-sized bed to allow the boys reign over their awaiting seats. "We did say our good-byes today. Remember what I told you last night at the wake?" she said, looking down at both sons, thinking it was good that the boys hadn't gone to the funeral after all, since her body had given way to her internal pain. Her fainting would have frightened them to no end. "We will remember Uncle Dillian for being the good man that he was, but forgetting him would be hard."

"Yes, ma'am. We not gon' forget him either, Mommy. Okay?" Gregory announced.

"We sho' not, Mommy. We love you bunches." Geoffrey ended their three-way conversation with the phrase they often used to express their love for each other. Getting the tickle fever, the boys started with their mother, and then went for each other, aggressively crossing over their mother in a way that only boys could produce with the testosterone they possessed.

"Boys! Be careful. You don't want to hurt the—" Marcus held out his hands, dropping the brush he'd started grooming his prized waves with. Wanting to grab hold of his sons from across the room, Marcus stopped his short journey once Gracie spoke.

"Uh, you don't want to hurt the tickle machine. Uh, yeah. You don't want to hurt the tickle machine, boys. Go get ready for bed, okay?" Gracie looked past the boys at Marcus.

"Okay, Mommy. Good night." Gregory started his leave from his parents' bedroom.

"Good night, Mommy. Night, Daddy." Geoffrey eased behind his brother.

When the boys were out of sight and heard going down the hallway, Gracie laid in on Marcus. "That was close, don't you think?" she asked with a distorted look, waiting on the excuse her husband was sure to throw her way.

"What do you mean? Gracie, it's not like they're not going to know soon enough. You're a month and a half pregnant, and uh, the belly does grow beyond your belt buckle, stretching past your blouse and—"

"I know that much, Marcus." Gracie threw attitude in her husband's direction, placing her hand on her clothed stomach. "But it's not like . . . I'm just not ready, okay? I'm not ready to do any explaining of any type." Gracie sat on the side of the comfortable bed. Anticipating her rise from the bed, she readied her arms by her side, lifting herself.

Already back in the threshold of the restroom, Marcus positioned his shirtless body against the wall and looked at the back of his wife's head, wondering. He thought back to the day he proposed, and knew he meant what he'd said when he asked Gracie to be his until the end. He also knew the baggage of Dillian and Kendra that he would have to accept, and he had done so up to their current situation.

When his own painful approach arose within his person, on how Dillian and Kendra had hurt Gracie from their affair years ago, Marcus took his thoughts and feelings to the only force that would help him see beyond the natural eye: God. With peace within, the years had passed, and the two that needed Marcus and his wife the most were eventually accepted by him and etched into their close circle.

Gracie had indeed grown into a beautiful woman. Sincerity rested in her eyes as well as her heart, and it all poured through her human touch. When she did Marcus the honor of bearing the twins, the undying love that meshed between the loving pair grew into the completeness that God had promised them.

Not being naïve to the fact that married couples sometimes had hurdles as tall as Mount Everest, the two stayed grounded in their spiritual walk and grew by standing on God's Word for marriage.

Accepting Gracie in his arms after she'd made her way in his direction, Marcus played his part of the wounded husband, poking out his bottom lip. He was seeking empathy from her scolding. "So I take it you forgive me for the *almost* outburst? You know I didn't mean it. It's just I sometimes get caught up in the notion of having another baby around the house. And now that things have gone the way they have . . . you know."

With her hands meeting and resting on the back of her husband's neck, Mrs. Jeffries landed a romantic kiss on Marcus's awaiting lips. "Honey, I know. But you can't get yourself off track. We had a long talk about this even before we decided to go along with it. Please don't add pressure to what has already happened. This will still be a blessing," Gracie reminded her husband as she, herself, pouted in his arms.

"Shhh. Honey, how about we don't even talk about it right now." Marcus leaned in for what he would settle for, but he wanted more than a short kiss.

"But, honey, I don't want you to keep going back and forth. I thought we agreed." Gracie wanted to continue embedding their plans into her husband's mind.

Not wanting to answer for the fear of his true feelings being exposed, Marcus held his wife tighter. "Just come and let me wash the day away from your mind."

Now clinging to his pregnant wife, Marcus placed another of his gentle kisses right through Gracie's body until it reached her soul. Engulfing her into his masculine arms, Marcus landed needy kisses onto his wife's body as he closed the bathroom door behind them.

Chapter 2

Six Weeks Later

While sitting at the recently refurbished antique dining table in the first room at the front of their spacious home, Gracie enjoyed watching her boys from the inside. Never in a million years would she have thought she'd be a mother of twin boys, identical at that. With the August view peering through the window, Gracie silently thanked God for such a blessing. Tranquil, and with the cordless phone in her hand, Gracie gave it a quick squeeze before releasing it onto the Pledge-dusted table.

"Will that be it today, Mrs. Gracie?" Jolie, the housekeeper asked, accidentally knocking Gracie out of the trance she'd placed herself in. Noticing that she'd caught Gracie in her own world, Jolie quickly apologized. "Oh, I'm sorry. I didn't mean to frighten you, ma'am," she said with her deeply-rooted Hispanic accent.

"It's quite all right," Gracie assured, noticing she had inadvertently placed her hand to her chest. Ever since the day Dillian passed away, Gracie had been an emotional wreck. "Did Marcus pay you, or should I go get my checkbook, Jolie?"

"He did," she said with a nod. "Is there anything else I can do before I go?"

Giving her elderly housekeeper a slight smile, Gracie responded, "Just make sure you come back. I don't know what I'd do without you." She leaned her head to the side and released a sincere beam toward Jolie.

The only fixation that had helped get her mind off of her ex-fiancé's passing was the news that the doctor had given her and Marcus on the very day of Dillian's death.

It had been a week before devastation came to their family, when she could no longer sleep through the night and had begun to toss and turn instead of grasping peaceful rest. Feeling weaker than ever, Gracie made an appointment for the following week to speak with her family doctor about sleep medication. Instead of prescribing her sleeping pills, Gracie received prenatal vitamins with extra folic acid and iron attached. She was indeed pregnant.

The good news alone put her in a different mind frame, since she and Marcus had actually been trying to conceive for six months. But with the news of Dillian's death coming right on the heels of their good news, Gracie wondered if Dillian had actually given his space on this earth to the baby that was growing inside of her. In her heart, she knew Dillian would give his life for a child, and in her mind, he had.

Bitter with the sweet through her mourning, she rejoiced for another chance to be an avenue to present the world another one of God's gifts. The only thing that was missing was her friend Kendra to share the news with. Kendra hadn't called, hadn't text messaged, hadn't surfaced since the day the limo dropped her off at her house after the collation at her church.

Thrown off track once more when Marcus walked into the room, Gracie tapped on the window, getting her sons' attention and mouthing her request. Letting them know that dinner would soon be served, Gracie turned her attention to her clean cut husband with the neatly trimmed goatee that she always adored so much.

"Hey, babe, have you tried contacting Kendra today?" Marcus asked.

"Yeah." Gracie reached Marcus with her perched lips, and allowed her husband to give her the kiss that he frequently gave. "Still no answer." Gracie eyed Marcus, wanting him to tell her something, anything to make her nerves settle.

"Humph. And how's my other baby doing? How is my other li'l man doing?" He spoke to Gracie's growing three months-pregnant stomach more than to her.

"Marcus, puh-leazz. Don't start that again. This had better be a girl. We need a girl *somewhere* in the family, with all this testosterone you and your boys are throwing around. Just look at them." Gracie pointed, directing Marcus to the twins wrestling in the grass. "Get off your brother, son!" Gracie screamed through the window, hoping that the boys would listen to her plea. Shaking her head, Gracie pulled her attention back to Marcus. "I thought you were pulling for a girl at first."

"I'm just saying." Marcus gave an absent minded shrug of his shoulders. "We know what we're doing with boys, and it may just be easier to keep up the testosterone around the house. Look at my boys. They're already wrestling pros." Marcus spread a proud papa's grin on his face while his arms rested on his hard-worked six-pack underneath his relaxed shirt.

"They're wrestling pros all right." Gracie stood and grabbed the back of her hair, knotting it in a makeshift bun. "I sure will be glad when those Mohawk haircuts grow out. I can't believe I let you talk me into that mess." Gracie passed her husband, pulling her sleeveless T-shirt down from inching up her growing abdomen. Rolling her eyes, Gracie walked her socked feet across the room, headed toward the kitchen, but halted.

"Mrs. Jolie cooked dinner. I'm not hungry all of a sudden, so I think I'm just going to go take a bath and go to bed. Can you get the boys and tell them to get washed up?"

"Yeah. Sure, honey. What's wrong, you not feeling good or something? You need some crackers and 7-Up?" Marcus suggested with seriousness in his voice as he pushed up the Armani framed eyeglasses on his nose.

Laughing at her husband's thoughts, Gracie waved him off and continued on her tread toward the staircase. "Marcus, crackers and soda do not cure everything when you're pregnant. I'm going to bed."

On the way up to their master suite, Gracie decided that she would try one last time to contact Kendra on the phone, and if there was no answer, she had made up her mind that she would go by her friend's house first thing in the morning, once she dropped off the boys at school. She knew that Kendra needed time to mourn, but life was already picking up speed. Literally. The last thing she wanted to do was to leave the message on Kendra's answering machine, letting her know of the pregnancy, but she was feeling as though she may not have a choice. They had planned this together.

Just as Gracie thought, Kendra didn't answer, and she returned the phone to its cradle. Gathering her nightwear and toiletries for her bathroom experience, Gracie entered the open space of her comforting rest and reading area to set her belongings down. Sitting on the side of the whirlpool tub, Gracie released the flowing water from the brass spout and sat as the water poured in, thinking about the last few years of her life.

The days grabbed at the weeks, the weeks jumped at the months, and the months mended to the years. Before anyone could look up to dwell on right from wrong, the horrible past of betrayal from friendship and courtship had meshed itself into days of old and guided love into the two couples. Gracie had grown in her walk with Christ and eventually turned to Kendra to offer support in any way she could. Common sense lived in Gracie within the friendship that the two shared, but overall, she allowed Kendra back into her personal space once again. The reestablished relationship led way to Dillian being a part of the friendship, since he and Kendra had found a union of their own.

Lord, you're an awesome God, Gracie thought as she tested herself once more. She would often search her spirit, trying to see if she was truly happy for Dillian and Kendra. Now that Dillian had passed, Gracie was glad that he'd had someone to share his last moments with. *All things happen for a reason.*

Adding a pin to her bun-styled hair to avoid getting her natural curls wet, Gracie recalled many nights over the last six years that she and Marcus had lost sleep because of the urgent phone calls—calls from Kendra or Dillian, seeking support because one or the other had been rushed to the hospital due to complications resulting from their HIV status.

Without second wind or thought, Gracie would do as she would have done for her own sister, had she had one. Just to be there for moral support was comfort to her heart, but she knew it helped Kendra and Dillian to know that she had truly been a friend to the end.

Undressing and adding herself to the warmth of the tub, Gracie started her one on one with God. "What do I do now, God? Was I really listening to you when I agreed to this? Just what am I going to do now that Dillian has passed?

What is Kendra going to do? Lord, how are we supposed to move forward?" Her eyes peered without so much as a blink as the water continued to fill the capacity of the oval-shaped tub she had submerged herself in deeper.

Wishing that the answers would surely come as soon as she'd asked the questions, Gracie closed her eyes and sank a little further into the warm, bubbly water, thinking about the days ahead that were sure to consume her.

Chapter 3

"Hey, Ken! It's me, Gracie. I was just calling to check on you and see how you are making out. I left you a voice message last week . . . and the week before that. I know you probably need your space right now, but I'm worried about you. The boys have been asking about their Auntie Kendra, and I've almost run out of excuses. Well, call me. Love ya."

Having been grateful that Gracie was in her life and loving her like only Gracie could, the scene at the funeral pushed something deep inside of Kendra that no one could see, but she certainly felt. Resting in her assigned seat in front of her husband's blue and silver casket, Kendra had turned her head as fast as the sound she had heard. When the crowd scattered and she saw Marcus fighting the summer wind, carrying Gracie to their vehicle, that very moment gave a clear understanding to Kendra. Knowing that Gracie was a strong woman and could stand up to releasing Dillian from his earthly home, Kendra knew there had to be more to Gracie's fainting. And what it was, Kendra wasn't ready for.

Yet, knowing that the situation itself had been awkward and always would be labeled so, the scene itself showed how much Gracie had once cared about Dillian, and the feeling was no doubt mutual.

As she sat hearing the preacher speak final words over her husband's deceased body, Kendra allowed guilt to build all over again. Inside the steel casket, she knew that the last touch of affection or any type of unconditional love toward her had passed away with Dillian McNab. The harsh world would be evident to her now that she was tainted and useless. Reality set in that what she and Dillian had, not many people could agree with. Now, she was all she had.

Their unique marriage had its own ups and down, yet they survived. Dillian had once been truly in love with her best friend and business partner, but had found love with an equal that shared something deeper: HIV. Sometimes the thought of Dillian's love for her made Kendra feel as though she had played a wicked game in order to have someone meaningful in her life. But with Dillian being the man that he was, she knew deep enough that it was not the case.

She felt almost obligated to express something that had only been lust to begin with. By befriending Dillian, after it was very clear that Gracie had moved on, Kendra made it her mission to give him back what she felt she had stolen from him—a chance at life and love.

In the midst of their marriage, Kendra grew to realize that her love for Dillian was without compulsion and that his love for her was sincere. Only then did she confront her own guilt and release a truth that had been semi-buried in her soul: a past that was filled with molestation, rape, then her own promiscuous lifestyle. Kendra retreated to her and Dillian's beginning together and expressed a truth she had been withholding.

It was Kendra, not the needle that he had become accustomed to accusing, that had passed the strain of HIV on to Dillian. But when Kendra began her confession, her husband completed her thoughts, revealing that her words had been no surprise.

"It has already been told to me. I know, Kendra." Dillian had grabbed for his wife's small and bitter-cold hand. Sitting together on their shared king-sized bed, Dillian moved in closer to Kendra once he saw the exasperated look gather on her face.

"You knew?" One tear found its new home on her cheek.

"No." He shook his signature bald head to clarify. "Originally I didn't, but with more tests, more talks with Dr. Johnson, and with the particular strain that I have . . ." He didn't have to say any more.

At that moment, if she could have crawled up into a shell to die, she would have. But with Dillian being who he was, he knew her next move would be to run from another problem. He wouldn't let her. That day he did what he was built to do: He held her as she cried for her mistakes of old.

That very day, Kendra had done exactly what she should have done ages ago with Gracie. She shared who she was, what she had gone through as a child, and how she'd carried herself throughout her teenage years.

Kendra found a best friend in Dillian that day. Thinking back on that very moment was when Kendra had to shake herself in order to realize that Dillian was now only a memory.

It had been six weeks since Dillian's remains had been laid to rest at Memorial Cemetery. Kendra had yet to surface from her home in Frisco to see what another month, an end of July's days, had waiting for her. As if life couldn't get any worse, Gracie had been calling daily, trying to contact her. Even though Kendra knew that Gracie was genuinely concerned for her, she had no doubt in her mind that Gracie wanted to discuss matters at hand.

Pushing the DELETE button on her phone, Kendra left her living room area and headed to her bathroom to ready herself for her treacherous HIV tablets for the day. Tightening her worn Victoria's Secret housecoat around her thinning waist with weakened energy, Kendra opened the medicine cabinet only to break down in tears as her eyes landed on Dillian's medication bottles. Thinking back to Gracie and her messages, she couldn't help but think about being alone, and her own fate of dying before her time. With her thumb, Kendra twirled her wedding ring, and she opened the gate for her emotions to surface.

"Why did you leave me, Dillian? How dare you leave me here . . . alone! You are a quitter, Dillian! You hear me? You quit on me." She screamed out a curse word at Dillian as she stumbled and collapsed on the raised, Italian-tiled bathroom floor. Curling into a fetal position, Kendra cried freely.

It was as if she had instant replay feeding footage to her mind of how she and Dillian became husband and wife. Years ago, when all chaos had broken loose after Gracie found out about her and Dillian cheating, Kendra found herself spending more and more time with Dillian. In that period in time, her heart couldn't forget that they had indeed had a fling that obviously meant something.

Neither had ever let the very words leave their vocal cords, but it had always been a thought: If the disease that linked them together didn't exist, would their worlds still revolve around each other?

One of those days, spending personal, quality time together was all it took for them to realize that their double diagnosis opened up a reserved spot for their two hearts. With no formal conversation linking them together, they started spending more time together, and eventually, one kiss led to their nuptials.

With the previous knowledge of breaking Gracie's heart because of their unfaithfulness, Kendra and Dillian both made it a point to involve Gracie with their future plans, their courting, their marriage. When Gracie told them that she knew it would eventually happen, they were relieved as she offered them her blessings. Gracie was a blessing.

With tears still rushing at a steady pace, Kendra tried to renew her mind in knowing that one day their time together would have to come to an end as it had. Dillian now rested on the other side of this universe, while she fought, trying to figure out her next move. Failing to trick her heart, Kendra allowed herself to scream from the depths of her soul.

The piercing coldness of the bathroom floor awakened Kendra out of the lethargic, depressed sleep that she had fallen into. Holding onto the toilet seat with her feeble left hand, Kendra slowly picked up her one hundred–pound body. Not stopping to take the medicine that she had become accustomed to, Kendra left the bathroom, making her way to bed in order to properly rest.

The clock, a wedding gift from years prior, read eight o'clock in the evening. Kendra had been a slumbered heap since noon. With her mind wandering to all that she'd needed to do in the day that had passed, she shrugged her shoulders. Her doctor's appointment, the pharmacy pickup, and her first appointment with a new counselor had all been neglected. Tomorrow would have to be her new start on life.

It had been one of several days she'd gone without her HIV medication, and her body had begun to respond in a negative way. From the day that Dillian's health started deteriorating, Kendra kept up her own life-changing routine in order to be there for her husband. But as soon as he plunged and the line on the machine beeped without pausing, Kendra lost her hope.

As the early days passed, she had friends there to make sure she was still on the up and up, moving to life's beat. But as soon as the dirt covered Dillian's grave, she found herself all alone and nothing mattered. Dinnertime wouldn't be the first night Kendra had forgone the last meal of the day. Today, she hadn't even had breakfast or lunch.

Settling into the middle of her bed, Kendra scrunched her nose as she received an unwanted sniff of the foul-smelling sheets and blankets that she hadn't changed in weeks. With a scratch to her head, Kendra's hand returned with a small patch of dry and graying hair, only to be flicked from her hand, landing on the vacant down pillow next to her. No longer caring about her outer appearance, Kendra no longer felt like the happy thirty-something-year-old that had been present just weeks prior. Remote control in her palm, Kendra McNab settled in for the night, not caring if she would wake for the rest of her life.

Using her thin, worn, and polish-free nails, an exhausted Kendra picked at the drop of dried ranch dressing that was stuck on the Sanyo remote until it released from the corner. She then proceeded to surf for a channel of interest.

With her eyes half open, the young widow watched the end of a weekly series and later allowed the news to lull her to sleep. Each toss and turn prevented her from finding deep rest. As her dreary body rolled back and forth through the sheets, her weight against the remote buttons prompted the channels and the volume to change on their own accord. When the volume reached its peak, Kendra searched through the blankets without opening her eyes. Not succeeding in locating the remote, she parted her lids. Just as she peeked through her tired vision, the television began blaring a sermon.

The local church broadcast had a marathon that was attended by several people suffering with major ailments who were seeking the Lord for their healing. Cancer survivors, Acquired Immune Deficiency Syndrome patients, multiple sclerosis sufferers were among some of the life-altering diseases that were called out.

Kendra immediately sat up in bed and stared at the screen through glassy eyes. Weak from not having her medicine, not eating, and failing to take care of her body, Kendra lost herself in her own grief as she envisioned Dillian on stage amongst the others. Unconsciously, tears began to flow down Kendra's dry, brittle, and cracked face.

"Di–Dillian," she spoke to the television, "I knew it. I knew you weren't gone. I knew you wouldn't leave me." She threw the warm covers off of her body. "You knew I would be here by myself, didn't you?"

No strength within, Kendra held out her puny and ash-reddened arms and ushered Dillian back to her. "Come home, Dillian. Come home with me." She stopped short when the vision she saw started walking in the opposite direction of the others.

"Where are you? Don't you dare! Don't you do it!" Kendra's voice grew aggressive as she made her way off of her towering bed and toward the television that sat more than ten feet away. Trying to kick her way loose from covers that had tangled around her legs, she pushed one of her socks from her cracked feet and slid violently onto the floor.

"Don't go, Dillian! Don't leave me." She crawled, racing at a heavy pace while losing her vision. Grabbing at her head because of the pain that shot through her temple, black-and-white vision replaced Kendra's colorful stare.

Finally, on the floor in front of the fifty-two-inch flat screen television held by its own stand, Kendra clawed at a screen she couldn't see, in a violent movement trying to find an already missing Dillian. At the point of no longer making contact with her deceased husband, Kendra's throat caught her last scream just as she began to seize.

Within the moments of her body bouncing uncontrollably, eyes finding the backs of their ducts, and her words being caught on her unstable tongue, Kendra's being took on a mind of its own. She lay lifeless in front of the television.

Leaving her ragged, scrawny body mangled on the floor, Kendra's spirit maneuvered toward the brightness that was shining above her head. Instead of the struggle of being alone, living with the disease that would isolate her within herself, Kendra figured the fight was over. Moving from her body to spirit seemed easier than the life she would have to fight to be happy in. Now having the option of staying on earth, or going to the next life, Kendra eyed the newness that her body resembled and closed her lids.

With her life form rising higher above the ceiling of her earthly home, Kendra opened her eyes only to see the heavens open to accept her.

ing Dillian. At the point of no longer making contact with her deceased husband, Kendra's throat caught her last scream just as she began to seize.

Within the moments of her body bouncing uncontrollably, eyes finding the backs of their ducts, and her words being caught on her unstable tongue, Kendra's being took on a mind of its own. She lay lifeless in front of the television.

Leaving her ragged, scrawny body mangled on the floor, Kendra's spirit maneuvered toward the brightness that was shining above her head. Instead of the struggle of being alone, living with the distance that would isolate her within herself, Kendra figured the fight was over. Moving from her body to spirit seemed easier than the life she would have to fight to be happy in. Now having the option of staying on earth, or going to the next life, Kendra eyed the newness that her body resembled and closed her lids.

With her life form rising higher above the ceiling of her earthly home, Kendra opened her eyes only to see the heavens open to accept her.

Chapter 4

With a tight grip to his left shoulder, Marcus squeezed his trapezoid to release the pain that shot through his overworked muscle. The wrestling moves that landed on his body from the boys the day before were all evident in his slow effort in getting ready for the day. He hadn't planned on staying and playing with the boys too long last night, but the love he had for his sons made him want to be around them. Even though they were growing, he loved to spoil them with attention.

After his hot shower—the second within a twenty-four hour period—Marcus stood at their bathroom mirror. He studied his daily devotion tablet that he kept in a drawer in the restroom. Before leaving for work, it was a must for him to read and pray in preparation for the day ahead. Marcus's eyes fell to Proverbs 3:5–6.

Trust in the Lord with all thine heart. Lean not unto your own understanding. In all thy ways acknowledge Him and He shall direct your path.

"Amen to that." It was just the scripture that Marcus needed for understanding why God had allowed him and Gracie to conceive if it weren't His will for their plans to go through. "I sho' 'nuff don't understand what's going on, Lord," Marcus announced as he picked up his boy brush, as Gracie called it, and tended to his waves, "but I'm giving this worry over to you."

It had taken his breath away when Gracie had first announced the whole plan of getting pregnant for a second time. When he realized how important it was to her, Marcus reluctantly agreed, wanting everything to work out to make his wife happy.

Since the day they learned that Gracie had indeed become pregnant, the two hadn't talked about anything in detail. With Dillian's passing and Gracie being three months pregnant with their child, Marcus didn't know when to jump back in and finish the discussion he and his wife had started months earlier. Since both Dillian's death and the baby had been a surprise, he knew that Gracie wouldn't be up for any conversations any time soon. Still, the plans Gracie had conjured up for their unborn weren't something he was up for either.

It hadn't been long after Gracie had brought up the subject of a baby that their lovemaking intensified, as if they were young lovebirds all over again. Not complaining about the attention that his wife's body was giving him, Marcus knew that she was on a mission. At least for the moment, he had obliged anything she wanted him to agree to.

For a short period, he put all the blame on himself, thinking it was his selfishness in not wanting her to get pregnant all over again. But when he realized his shortcoming was because of what Gracie wished for their unborn child, Marcus felt he had a right to be angry. He'd even prayed and counseled with their pastor, asking how to get his mind, his heart, and his soul ready to deal with what was forthcoming. His pastor just simply told him to take his troubles to the Lord; and he had. Unfortunately, Marcus didn't leave them.

Marcus had fasted and prayed, and asked the Lord to give him strength, understanding, and wisdom in dealing with such difficult decisions. As time passed and peace eased into his heart, Marcus felt God had answered his prayers. Realizing the love he had for his twin boys, Marcus decided that it would indeed be a gift to extend the love he held. When it happened, he was always nervous about how he would feel if and when they had actually achieved their conception.

In a selfish manner, in turn, Marcus felt that God had made a way, through Dillian's death, a place for their budding embryo. Maybe it was selfish, but Marcus found hope that Gracie's pregnancy would mean they would be able to get things back on track for their growing family. Since Gracie hadn't yet shared the news with Kendra, Marcus thought bringing the baby into every conversation that he could, would get Gracie to see things as he had.

Headed to work, Marcus jogged down the wooden staircase toward the stainless steel–equipped kitchen area. Looking around for everyone, Marcus only located the housekeeper.

"Good morning, Mr. Marcus. Eggs and bacon?" Jolie asked.

"Good morning. Uh, I'll pass this morning, Jolie. Are Gracie and the boys already gone?" he asked while pouring orange juice in his to-go cup. "I didn't hear her get up."

"Yes, sir. She said she wanted to get the boys settled into school early this morning. I believe she said something about going over to Mrs. Kendra's. Is she still sad after missing Mr. Dillian?" the housekeeper asked with a worried look on her face.

Knowing Jolie had her own fashion in speaking, Marcus understood the question the older lady asked. "I believe she is, Jolie. Well, I'm off for today. If you're here when she comes back, tell her I said to call me. I don't want to disturb them. I'm sure they have a lot of talking to do." Marcus rolled his eyes at the thought of all the girl stuff he was certain his wife and Kendra were going to be up to. "Six weeks away from each other, and you know there is a mountain of gossip that will be going on up in that house."

Sharing a laugh with her boss, the housekeeper added her own bit. "Jes, and with Mrs. Gracie being . . ."—she displayed the rest of her conversation by making a pregnant belly form in front of her own—"they will be talking for hours." She shooed Marcus with her hands and a turn of her head.

When Marcus realized what the hired help had said, he moved in closer as if ears were listening. "Did Gracie tell you she was . . . ?" He motioned the same visual belly with his hands as Jolie had, scrunching his eyebrows as he eyed her.

"No, no, no," she answered while switching her finger side to side. "I know these things. I can see these things." She pointed to her own eyes. "It's all in her face. How pretty are her face and hair?" she said in question form without asking a question. "Oh jes, it shows."

Shaking his head, Marcus corrected his housekeeper for something that she wasn't wrong about. "Just make sure you don't say anything about the pregnancy, okay? We haven't told anyone. It's a secret. A big, long, too-confusing secret to explain to you right now, so . . . so just don't say anything. Deal?"

Zipping her lips together and magically throwing away the symbolic key, she crossed her heart and put her finger in the air in a "scout's honor" manner.

"Great. Deal. Okay, well, I'm gone. Thanks for the orange juice," Marcus announced as he held his cup in the air and walked out of the kitchen.

Once situated inside of his two-year-old Tahoe, Marcus sat without cranking his vehicle. With his head resting deep into the headrest, he didn't know what not to worry about. Something inside of his being was disturbed. Marcus prayed that Gracie would come around to talk about their growing situation before they completed a decision they both had made about their baby. Marcus didn't want their decision to become the biggest mistake of their marriage.

"Lord, we need you. My family needs for you to guide us through these days of uncertainty. Lead me this day, Lord, to be the husband and father that you need me to be. Show me how to lead this family in the direction you need us to turn to. Bless our family, Lord. Amen."

With one turn of the key, Marcus started the engine and shifted his gear before maneuvering his vehicle from their concrete circular drive, headed to the college.

Life had definitely been good to him. Having dated Gracie in high school, Marcus would have never thought God would be so gracious to him, placing her back into his life after all the years apart. Better yet, he never would have imagined Him allowing her to become his wife.

Marriage was everything everyone had said it would be and then some—work, but not for the weary. Being a husband, Marcus never figured he would have to sign up for all he had. Being in love with a woman whose ex was wounded by HIV—AIDS when his cell count became extremely low— was no easy task; especially when the ex and his wife were a constant part of his life. But Marcus managed.

Right from the beginning, he stood by Gracie for all that she had to endure. With each poke of the needle, Marcus was tested as well, making sure that he and his wife would resume a healthy living for the sake of their twin boys. His boys.

Accepting Gracie's ex-fiancé and her best friend, Kendra, who started it all, Marcus was thankful to God in heaven for the life he had. And he wore that badge proudly. Even when Gracie cried for weeks after Dillian's passing, Marcus never let his esteem waiver. He knew who he was and knew that his wife loved him. He also knew that when there is true love for someone, love always remains. Sometimes it just has to be from a distance.

Whatever his wife needed, he tried to get it. What she needed him to be, he also wanted to be. That's why, with Gracie carrying their third child, Marcus wanted to hold his peace. He didn't know why, all of a sudden, he felt the way he did, but for some reason, he wished things were different. And that's also why, as soon as Gracie seemed calm enough, he planned to talk to her about how he really felt. Whether she understood and granted him the right to use his fatherly wit, Marcus could only pray for God's guidance.

Chapter 5

"Okay, Geoffrey. Help your brother with tying his tennis shoe, all right? What do I always tell you?" Gracie asked her son. "To always help my brother," the growing boy replied, slurring his words.

"And why do I say that, son?" she quizzed.

"Because I am my brother's keeper?" he answered, not really being sure of himself.

"And that goes for you too, Gregory. And please, please don't let me have to keep reminding you two of that, okay? Now, get out of my ride and get into the school before they lock you out," she joked. "There goes Mrs. Felicia, your teacher, waiting over there by the tree." Gracie waved at the twins' summer school instructor while silently thanking God for curbside check-in and check-out.

"Yes, ma'am," the two sang in unison.

"I love you guys," she yelled out the window while quickly grabbing at her rearview mirror.

"And make sure you put those ball caps on your heads. Don't be out in the sun without those hats, boys." Texas weather could be harsh.

Gracie slicked her right eyebrow down, peered out the left back window and maneuvered her Volvo SUV out of the traffic zone. Finally able to reach forty miles per hour, Gracie pressed and held down the number four key on her phone and waited for it to connect. Hearing the rings, she pressed her earpiece once for the call to ring in her ear.

When the ringing continued, Gracie knew that the only voice she would hear would be that of the voice mail. Taking in a breath, Gracie blew out her steam before she left her request.

"Not going to pick up again this morning, huh? Well, look. I'm tired of not seeing and not talking to my friend. Kendra, I miss you and really, *really* need to talk to you. I'm coming over now, so if you don't want to see me, I suggest you leave, because I'm definitely on my way, girl. Love ya."

Disconnecting the call, Gracie drove toward the McNab household. Determined to make a quick exit at the first Starbucks she saw, Gracie had mochas on her mind. She was ready to chat over coffee like the good old days.

Granted, the days of old were long gone, but Gracie tried her best not to dwell on the past. Their more than a decade of friendship had weathered a continuous storm that not many people could have survived. Picking up where they'd left off, Gracie was ready for the next unknown number of decades their friendship would last.

Letting go and letting God was always a motto that Gracie tried her best to live by. In so many instances, Gracie could have easily gotten stuck on how Kendra had burned their friendship over and over again, but for some reason, God always came to Gracie's rescue—or better yet, to Kendra's rescue. If it had been anyone besides Gracie, a conniving Kendra probably would have been pushing up daisies a long time ago.

With plain bagels and cream cheese added to her order at the last minute, Gracie set her mind in Kendra's direction and drove while taking small sips of her mocha drink.

Before nine o'clock in the morning, Gracie found herself on the other side of town, deep into Frisco, Texas. No longer having to go to either of her gyms to instruct, the only thing Gracie normally did before nine o'clock was get the boys ready for school so that their father could drop them off on his route to work. But the need to check on her friend put Gracie on a different path this morning.

Still needing to run her business with a stronghold, Gracie could do all of her managerial connections via her BlackBerry or by appointment only. The steady growth of her very own budding franchise allowed her to see what she had built and to take the personal time that she needed to appreciate it. Gracie still loved what she did, but left the workouts to the next generation.

Her career had been a blessing for her. It had undeniably taken her places she only imagined she would go. Through her hard work and dedication in the fitness arena, Gracie had opened doors continuously for herself and others. With three locations in the Dallas area alone, her latest project consisted of branches in the Fort Worth area, with thoughts swarming in her mind of breaking ground in Houston and Austin, Texas. Now with the untimely death of Dillian, her own pregnancy, and Kendra not responding to living beyond her marriage, Gracie decided to live one day at a time.

Trying her best not to be swallowed by the guilt of allowing the weeks to go by without connecting with her friend, Gracie's mind began to swirl. What if something had actually been wrong with Kendra? She figured that Kendra just needed and wanted her space, but Gracie let out a silent prayer toward her friend's home just in case there was more.

Not once had she reminded herself of the disease that Kendra was still battling on a full-time basis. She had gotten used to one or the other calling if either Dillian or Kendra had gotten sick and needed to be rushed to the hospital.

"How stupid could I be?" Gracie said loudly as she drove with her left elbow resting on the driver's door windowpane. Recalling the hard times in Kendra's life that she had eventually come around in talking about, Gracie couldn't believe she didn't recognize that Kendra may have needed her sooner than now.

"Maybe it was because of all the stuff Kendra went through when she was young. What was I thinking?" Gracie answered her own question as to why Kendra was so withdrawn. Gracie hit the palm of her hand to her forehead when she realized she could have done more. "She must think I'm just . . . ugh!" Sitting up straight in the tanned leather seat of her ride, Gracie let her sandaled foot press heavily against the rubber that covered the gas pedal in her truck.

Thinking back once again on Kendra's past, Gracie finally realized that Kendra must have been feeling isolated and alone. With Kendra always staying to herself, Gracie realized that Dillian's passing probably put more harsh thinking into her friend's silent world than before.

Being shifted around from house to house throughout her family while growing up, Kendra probably couldn't trust anyone, and would never come right out and let Gracie know that she needed help; especially if it was emotional help that she needed.

"I know, I know," she responded to an absent Marcus. With his righteous heart, her husband was always telling her to stop thinking that others could get over things as easily as she could. Today she finally got it. Today would be the day she would sit and listen to any and everything her friend wanted and needed to talk about.

Gracie pulled her car into her friend's driveway. Lifting up the car's emergency brake for protection from the small hill that her friend's house sat on, Gracie grabbed her purse and the two cups of coffee that had been placed in a drinking tray, then removed herself from the car.

Balancing the drink tray in one hand, Gracie maneuvered through her open Christian Louboutin handbag to place her keys in the side pocket. She slowed down once she felt uneasiness in her stomach.

"Come on, child. It's too early for you to even try that morning sickness mess. We were doing so good, baby." She rubbed her belly to calm the weary feeling, wishing she could unbutton the fastener of her Gap jeans. Gracie figured that the baby needed growing space.

After stepping onto the porch and ringing the doorbell a total of three times, Gracie debated whether or not to use the key that Kendra had given her years ago. Summer raindrops suddenly began landing all around her, and Gracie lifted her jacket's hood raggedly onto her head. She walked to the garage and peeked through the small inset window to make sure her friend's 4Runner was indeed inside. Seeing her friend's vehicle, Gracie began her trek to her own car to retrieve Kendra's house key.

Gracie let herself in the house and had barely made it into the center of the living area when she gasped. As she looked around the place, she suddenly knew one major reason Kendra was acting standoffish: filth. Before taking another step, Gracie grabbed at her stomach and bent over in pain. She could only watch while hot liquid splattered from the cups she held onto the light-colored carpet.

"Ouch! I don't remember these growing pains. You must be a girl," she added while rubbing the spot on her stomach. "Kendra! Where are you, honey? It's Gracie. I'm out here. Don't make me come looking for you." Gracie placed the cups on the end table, then gathered newspapers off of the floor. Cups, glasses, and bowls that were scattered on the tables in the living room would be her next mission.

"What on earth is she doing?" Making her way into the congested kitchen area, Gracie winced and held her breath as she got closer to the sink and found spoiled food. "Oh my. Kendra!" she called over her shoulder. "Kendra Kenyatta McNab, where are you at?" Gracie stormed out of the dim kitchen.

Stopping in each room on her way to the master bedroom, Gracie opened and slammed doors. She made sure she held the doorknob extra tight on the hallway's restroom door before she headed to the last entrance, just so the smell wouldn't follow her. "Whew!"

Not liking the feeling that was resting in her soul, Gracie suddenly stopped and knocked on the private entry, hoping that Kendra would answer to soothe her own nerves. But after waiting all of one minute, Gracie's impatience got the best of her and she opened the door.

"Kendra! Oh my goodness. Kendra!" Gracie ran and fell on the floor beside her friend and lifted her head in her lap. "Help me, someone! Someone, help!" No one would hear Gracie as deep as she was in the house. Looking around for her purse, she remembered that she'd left it on the sofa as she had headed toward the kitchen area.

Softly releasing her friend's head, Gracie crawled as fast as she could to the phone on the nightstand. It only took a moment to realize that the cordless receiver was missing. Pushing herself to her feet, Gracie raced back toward the living room, forgetting about her own lingering pain that was embedded in her stomach and groin area.

Dialing 911 immediately, a frantic and screaming Gracie yelled out the address to the woman on the other line while running back into the bedroom. Falling on her knees beside Kendra once more, Gracie had small hope for her friend's lifeless body. Not realizing that the cell phone had fallen from her ear, and not making it a priority to pick it up, Gracie cradled Kendra in her arms. Swaying her friend back and forth, Gracie allowed her tears to fall on Kendra's own tear-stained face.

Gracie had no clue as to how long her friend had been lying unconscious. Being that she ran a fitness center, she was trained in emergency care. Although very faint, Gracie did detect a weak pulse. Not knowing what the next step would be, Gracie sat with her friend, grateful that the emergency sirens she heard in the air became closer with each hysterical breath she took.

"Hold on, sweetheart. Hold on," Gracie cried as she eased from underneath her friend, making room for the paramedics who had made their way into the house and into the bedroom.

"Lord, help us. Lord, we need you," a distraught Gracie whispered as she watched the medics do all that they could.

Standing back far enough to be out of the way, but close enough to see that her friend was getting the best treatment, Gracie sent forth a prayer, hoping that God had His direct attention on her.

"Lord, please come in this room and save my friend's life. Please don't let her life end this way, alone. She is your child, Lord, no matter what she thinks. Save her, Lord," Gracie cried without shame as she walked out of the room behind the paramedic crew.

She was so consumed with the well being of her friend that Gracie didn't even notice the blood that trickled from her own body.

Chapter 6

"This can't be happening," Gracie whimpered through her hiccupped cries.

Wanting to get into the ambulance that escorted her friend to the hospital, Gracie listened to the pleas of the paramedics to be seen for her own issue that had surfaced out of the whole ordeal. Cradling her body with trembling hands, Gracie sat stiffly on Kendra's living room sofa—the same spot where she had sat not too long ago, comforting Kendra on the day of Dillian's departure.

"I cannot believe this. I was going to listen to her." She slowly looked up into the confused eyes of a paramedic who was trying to get Gracie's attention. Grabbing for the blanket he offered, Gracie allowed the paramedic to rest the comforting material across her heaving shoulders. As if the paramedic knew the story behind the friendship, Gracie continued her lethargic spiel.

"I knew she needed to talk," she said through her sobs. "I brought coffee." She wobbled into a full stance, trying to locate the beverage she intended for her dear friend. Gracie looked down to see the spilled coffee that embedded itself into the expensive carpet. Her balance gave way, and the paramedic grabbed for an emotional Gracie and carefully sat her back down.

She didn't know how she was going to, if need be, bury another friend in such a short amount of time; so, she did the only thing she knew to do. Gracie slid from the sofa and landed on the floor. Right in the midst of the chaotic uproar, Gracie began to call on the name of Jesus.

"Lord, I don't know how, but I need for you to give strength to Kendra. I didn't make it before she needed me, Lord, but God, please. Please let her make it through, Father." Gracie knew that she would have to gather her composure as much as she could in order to be at the hospital with Kendra, but for the moment, she knew that only the Lord with His grace and His mercy could save Kendra.

"Father, I don't know the ailment, but I do know that no other name can I call on but yours. You are the author and the finisher of our faith. It's the faith that you're the only miracle worker that has me thanking you in advance for Kendra's healing. Give her strength, Lord. Give her comfort, Lord. But most of all, give her peace in the midst of her healing. Amen."

Bowing her head and swaying softly, Gracie allowed herself mental time alone with God, before allowing the paramedics to drive her to the hospital.

Herlene Clark rested her hands in the soapy water as she finished up the last set of dirty breakfast dishes that her family had left for her. Eyeing the warm, finicky weather from her kitchen window, Herlene thought of a chore that she could do outside; anything that would allow her to enjoy the sunshine.

Herlene, knowing her day would consist of the same routine, slowly pushed herself to finish one task, just to start another. Her part-time job only required her to be available three days a week. Being that the previous day was one of those workdays, Herlene made herself slightly busy around the house. It had been a long time coming for the almost fifty-five-year-old, but she had finally found a place that had allowed stability in her own life.

Things hadn't always been as normal as they currently were for Herlene. For now, she counted it all joy and blessed the Lord for His promises. There had been times when she had cursed God for her life, but with knowledge comes wisdom, and she was ever grateful for being a woman after God's own heart.

Herlene's past was plagued with times that she'd neglected herself, her family, and had just about made all the wrong decisions that anyone could possibly make. Now remarried and raising her ten-year-old daughter, Kenya, Herlene felt she was finally on the right track and able to right some of those wrongs.

By the grace of God, in the last decade, she had finally settled down and started back where her roots took her: to the church, having a relationship with God. Even though she had found herself at the altar for the umpteenth time, Herlene made a vow and knew that she was serious and ready for the Lord to use her. And He had. Herlene had grown tired of the person she had become, and opened up her heart to God. She allowed Him to move as He wanted to. Today, she was saved and satisfied, but only by His grace and His mercy.

Being raised by both parents, Herlene was brought up in a household that showed her love beyond compare. Having both of her parents in the household to raise her and her eight brothers and sisters in the 1940s and 1950s wasn't the problem. It was the sway of the big city that tended to crowd her mind and lead her away from the Christian beliefs and teachings that her parents tried their best to instill in all of their children.

After graduation from high school, Herlene set her sights on a home outside of her parents'. That was when she left her teachings behind. Drinking, smoking, and partying became the way of choice for her and her siblings. Herlene fought long and hard to stay on the wrong path, while her sisters and brothers eventually went back to their Christian roots.

Shortly after leaving her parents' home, Herlene found out what love from the opposite sex felt like. It was the kind of love that couldn't be provided by a father or brother. It was then that she met one of her older brother's friends that he had acquired while away at college.

On a visit from the school that was known then as East Texas State University, located in Commerce, Texas, Mitch had accompanied Herlene's brother home for the holiday visit. Herlene caught a glimpse of his slanted, beaming brown eyes and fell in love. From the point of his very own introduction and the conversation that was shared between the two of them, Mitch and Herlene became a hasty, inseparable pair.

~

As the handsome, older man wined and dined her on his two-week visit, Herlene's young heart melted every time he'd give her the smile that would show off his dimpled right cheek. He was her first love, and Herlene held on tight to the affection he offered, even giving him her virginity. From what she felt, Mitch deeply loved everything about her, giving her all hope that they would indeed have a future together.

For more than two years, Mitch would become everything that she needed, until the day she had to let him know that they were expecting a child together. With her knocking on age twenty-two, no longer in community college nor working, Herlene felt that her lover would be overjoyed. With the news, she hoped he would ask for her hand in marriage. As he expressed his feelings in a different matter than what she was expecting, Herlene's world tumbled down just as fast as it was built. Sharing one of their last conversations over the telephone, Herlene's anticipated world was condemned.

"You're what?" Mitch whispered, standing with a hard force from his desk. Listening intently, he pushed his chair back into the wall.

"I'm pregnant. Aren't you happy?" Herlene responded with a wide smile on her face. "I wanted to wait and let you know when you came back in town, but I couldn't hold it in, Mitch. Oh, don't worry. I won't tell anyone until after we get married," Herlene said with certainty as she lay across her full-sized bed. Sharing an apartment with her sister, Herlene daydreamed about marrying and moving in with Mitch.

"Whoa. Hold on, Lena," he jumped in, calling Herlene by the nickname he'd given her. "You weren't on anything? I thought you were on birth control."

Ceasing from her rocking motion, Herlene raised up on her pointy elbows. Once she heard the uneasy questions coming from Mitch, attached with the strain in his voice, Herlene said, "Yeah, well, I was, but—"

"Are you kidding me? You stopped taking them?" He switched ears for his listening purposes. Holding the receiver in his hand, Mitch stood frozen in his thoughts.

"Well, when I lost my job at the grocery store, I didn't have insurance no more, and I can't get back on my parents' insurance because I'm not in school or nothing."

Rubbing the wavy, dark hair on his head in a backward motion, Mitch blew out a hard breath. "Look, you're going to have to do something about that. I–I can't do this. I can't think right now." Mitch paced his office floor, back and forth. He didn't know what to do with the news he was given. "What do you expect me to do?" he asked, rubbing his head once more.

Now sitting Indian-style in the middle of her bed, Herlene held a worried look on her face. Tears in her bright eyes, a young Herlene couldn't believe what she was hearing. Over time she had learned that Mitch wasn't a student after all, but rather a graduate. He was a student-teacher at the college. Knowing that he could easily put in for a transfer to Dallas, Herlene announced her idea to Mitch.

"What do you mean, Mitch? You can move here permanently. You don't have to stay away from us. You can move to Dallas; you can transfer." She ran her own hand down her lengthy ponytail.

"I'm married, Herlene!" Mitch looked around after hearing his voice hit a higher than normal octave. "My wife just had a baby. You don't understand." He started to whisper. "I will send you some money for . . . well, you know, but—" Closing his eyes, Mitch knew that the call would be one of the last that he would share with Herlene. Love had grown in his heart toward the young lady, but realizing his own situation, Mitch froze from the position he had placed them both in. "I have to go." And that was that.

Although she'd received the money for an abortion through the mail, Herlene hadn't remotely considered having the procedure. She was so in love with a man she thought would be her very own husband. Once she got the news that he was already attached, Herlene found herself depressed and hopeless. Instead of making an appointment at the local clinic, Herlene used the money to officially and unconsciously start her long journey toward destruction.

In the midst of putting away her hand-washed and dried dishes, Herlene felt someone tap her on her shoulder. Knocked out of her daydream, she jumped, slinging water from the sink everywhere.

"James! What in the world?"

Not giving his wife enough time to interrogate his actions, James's serious appearance slowed her down. "What is it, James? Honey, what is it?" Herlene needed to know what could have possibly put a remorseful look on her ever joyful husband's face.

"Baby, come in here. I want you to look at the news," he said as he scurried back toward the living room. Standing in front of the television, waiting on his wife to join him, James rubbed his gray beard, not knowing what was next to come. As soon as the commercial ended, the news went to its segmented newscast.

With detached emotion, the news reporter said, "In local news, sad to say, one month after burying her world class champ husband, Kendra McNab was found in her home earlier this morning and rushed to a local hospital. Doctors have yet to release a statement on her behalf, but we have learned that Mrs. McNab is in critical condition. The cause of her hospitalization has yet to be determined. Please stay tuned as we further investigate this story for you."

"Oh my God!" Herlene yelled as she slumped to the floor in slow motion. "Oh, James. Oh, James. I'm not ready for this. I haven't even made my peace, James!" she cried out, now looking deep into her husband's eyes as he joined her on the carpet.

"It's okay, Herlene. I'll take you down there. I'll take you to the hospital, honey." Allowing his wife's weight to crowd his own body, James held onto her for dear life.

Anger filling her heart, Herlene pushed away her dedicated husband of nine years. "You know that can't happen! What are you doing, trying to make me feel worse? You know she wouldn't have me nowhere near her."

Crawling a few inches away from her husband, Herlene balled up with her head touching the floor, rocking and moaning as if her soul had been ripped from her body. In just an instant, Herlene's world had turned from stable to unsteady. Her mind clouded. She didn't know what to do.

Standing from the floor, James stepped back and held tears in his eyes as he pressed his mind for an answer to his wife's problems. He knew her story before they had gotten married, but still declared his love for her. Now, he decided, was the time to help her receive closure.

Grabbing his jacket from the wall mount, James left his wife on the floor wailing. He rushed out the door, determined to mend what had been broken in his wife's life for decades.

been ripped from her body in just an instant. Herlene's world had turned from stable to unsteady. Her mind clouded. She didn't know what to do.

Standing from the floor, James stepped back and held tears in his eyes as he pressed his mind for an answer to his wife's problems. He knew her story before they had gotten married, but still declared his love for her. Now, he decided, was the time to help her receive closure.

Grabbing his jacket from the wall mount, James left his wife on the floor wailing. He rushed out the door, determined to mend what had been broken in his wife's life for decades.

Chapter 7

Marcus pushed the silver button with the red telephone imprinted on it on his cell phone and rushed out of the college gym with only his keys in tow. He'd gotten a phone call from his wife, letting him know in so many words that he needed to get to the hospital as soon as possible.

"Kendra—hospital," was all he had a chance to retrieve from Gracie's hurried communication. It was only when a paramedic got on the line and explained what was going on that Marcus knew in which direction, to which hospital he should head.

Thankful for his profession as head coach of the university, which allowed him to dress in workout gear, Marcus ran to the parking lot and got into his truck as fast as he could. In a hurry, he set his drive toward downtown Dallas. Marcus didn't have time for anything else but prayer.

"Heavenly Father, please go before me and prepare a place. I pray for healing even in the midst of transporting to the hospital. I don't know what's going on, Father, but I ask you to step in and be there for Kendra and my wife."

Marcus prayed during the entire length of his drive. With his yellow hazard flashers going, he prayed the police wouldn't make him a random check.

When his cell phone rang while it sat in the dashboard holster, Marcus looked at the screen and then placed his eyes back on the road, not even thinking about answering it. As long as it wasn't Gracie's number, he wasn't interested.

Ky, another coach from the college and his frat brother, was calling. He was more like a little brother, and Marcus knew Ky just wanted to make sure all was well. Still, Marcus knew he would only be able to focus on getting to the hospital. He had only scribbled a note to inform Ky in which direction he was headed. Now Marcus made a mental reminder to return Ky's call later. The only thing he had on his mind was getting to his wife and her best friend.

Chapter 8

Gracie couldn't believe all that had transpired in the short amount of time that had passed since awakening to start her day. The plans she'd made the night before hadn't happened as intended. When she had pulled into Kendra's driveway, the growing baby inside of her expanded abdomen moved around frantically. In hindsight, the movements seemed to have been warning signs about an unconscious Kendra within the house.

"Marcus!" Gracie yelled in her husband's direction as her vision became clear behind the tears crowding her eyes. Marcus had exited the elevator and was standing and searching for which direction to walk. Gracie watched her long-legged husband turn in her direction at the sound of her voice. She felt blessed to be the Mrs. to the Mister coming down the hall.

"Hey, honey," he greeted his disturbed wife with a kiss to the top of her head. "Are you okay?

How's the baby?" he questioned, laying his hefty hand over his wife's stomach. "Where is the blood coming from, Gracie?" Marcus's concern doubled as he noticed dried blood on his wife's clothing.

"We're fine. I guess I hit my side on something, rushing to try to get help for Kendra. The doctor said it was a surface scratch." She raised her shirt, showing him a small bandage covering her flesh. Gracie was tempted to grab an attitude at Marcus for bringing the baby into their opening conversation, but she realized that her issue could have been worse and quickly reeled in her aggravation.

"*Kendra*, babe." Gracie still thought it was necessary to redirect her husband's attention to the real emergency. She held onto Marcus as she walked him down the hall in the direction of where Kendra's rigid body lay. Stopping short of the entrance, Gracie broke into tears and leaned into her husband's broad shoulders. "I didn't know what to do, Marcus. I don't know how long she'd been there."

"Is she okay?" he asked, genuinely concerned about Kendra, but also wondering if his wife's breakdown would hurt the growing baby. In tune with his wife's mindset, Marcus noticed Gracie's stance when he'd first arrived, and made a mental note to avoid any further investigation. Leaving Gracie's side for all of a minute, a boggled Marcus peeked into Kendra's space.

"Stable," Gracie whispered, now leaning against the wall. With her eyes stuck on nothing in particular, Gracie recalled finding her friend as she had.

Her plans were to go over and try her best to bring her friend out of the funk she had dove into and stayed. Among other things, she needed to make sure that Kendra was okay mentally. Not having to endure a death in her own family, or at least none that she could remember, Gracie didn't realize how mentally challenging Dillian's death was for Kendra.

Gracie was blessed to still have her elderly parents alive and well. No one in their immediate family had passed away since she was a little girl. Even then, she was too young to remember and didn't count it as troubling. For Kendra to become depressed and standoffish, Gracie couldn't understand. Dillian's death had been a surprise to her as well, especially since he'd died from a massive heart attack instead of any illness related to his HIV status.

Years ago, when the four of them had rekindled their friendships, Gracie walked herself through the motions of letting go and letting God. It wasn't her everyday "live, learn, and let go" test of faith, but it was a "do even without understanding" test. Gracie believed she had passed. But now with things the way they were for Kendra, Gracie felt she had to question herself once again.

When people at her gym, church, and even in her own circle had shaken their heads, not understanding what she was doing by befriending Dillian and Kendra, Gracie didn't try to persuade them differently. All she knew was that God had spared her life and given her Marcus. Love was still valid to her.

While she and Kendra worked on their relationship, sketching out a plan for their own love and forgiveness, their husbands had also found a way to become closer. For that, Gracie felt she was doing God's will.

"Did you call the pastor?" Marcus asked his silent and traumatized wife while they both stood outside of the hospital room.

"Uh, no. Can you call him, honey?" Gracie said as she looked down the hall, waiting to see no one in particular.

Marcus walked down the same hall in order to have phone privacy, and Gracie turned her head in the opposite direction, looking toward a man wearing a flat-styled hat. He was walking her way. Just as she was about to turn and enter

Kendra's hospital room, that same man called out her name.

"Gracie?" he asked once again, now closer, snatching his out of season hat from his head. He knew she was Kendra's friend, because he and Herlene had seen Gracie and Kendra together on TV once, in a commercial for Gracie's fitness center. Thinking she would look even a tad bit different than what television usually made people look, James was surprised to see Gracie looking just the same.

With a puzzled look on her face, Gracie replied, "Yes. Do I know you?" She removed her hands from the door and wiped away lingering tears as she waited on an answer.

"No. No, ma'am, you don't. I'm sorry. My name is James. James Clark." He extended his hand. After consummating their meeting, James unzipped his well-worn Members Only jacket, exposing his rounded stomach. "I–I'm, well, I'm Kendra's stepfather." Seeing the shocked look on Gracie's face, James rushed to defend himself. "I don't mean no harm, but I saw the news report. Her mother saw the news report," he continued while gripping his hat, wondering what he'd gotten himself into. Reaching for his billfold, he thought he ought to show some identification since Gracie had never laid eyes on him before.

"Herlene, her mother, of course, has been estranged from Kendra. She's been wanting to contact her for years, but Herlene knew that Kendra wouldn't have it. Here you go." He showed Gracie his identification. "It's to show I am who I say I am."

Stunned, Gracie took a step back with her mouth remaining wide open. The second time around of their friendship, Gracie tried to be more of what she hadn't been to Kendra. After their initial talk to patch up what was definitely damaged, Kendra had finally broken down her life to Gracie, letting her into her world of self-worthlessness and loneliness.

Recalling specific conversations about Kendra not being in contact with her mother and the reasons behind it puzzled Gracie even more when she realized the identity of the man standing before her. Just as she opened her mouth to speak, Gracie looked up and saw Marcus coming around the corner. Silencing herself, Gracie took another step back as Marcus made his way into the one-sided conversation.

"Hello, I'm Marcus, Gracie's husband." He extended his hand to Mr. Clark, noting the vacant look on his wife's face.

"Hey, man." Mr. Clark smiled and exhaled, hoping Marcus's presence would make his awkward approach easier. Noticing that he was still holding his identification, James placed it back into his wallet.

Marcus reminded Gracie of his phone call. "I talked to the pastor, and he said that he'd be on his way up here." With his body directly to the side of Gracie's, Marcus wrapped his arm around his wife and rubbed her to produce warmth.

Blinking her eyes uncontrollably, Gracie formally introduced James Clark. "Baby, this is . . ." Her voice trailed while she wrestled with how to make the introduction. "This is Kendra's stepfather?" she announced and questioned at the same time.

Pushing his spectacles, which he wore mostly when he was worried, closer to his face, Marcus unconsciously took the man's hand and shook it again. "Oh, okay. How can we help you? Is her mother here?" Marcus looked down the hall anticipating seeing another face.

"No. I, uh, I left her at home crying . . . on the floor. Like I was telling your wife here, the two have been estranged. But I'm ready to put that in the past."

"*You're* ready to put that in the past? Oh, okay. What about her mother, Helen? What about her?" Gracie skewed her head toward the round man. "Why isn't she here? She left Kendra. Kendra didn't leave her!" Gracie grabbed for the anger that she knew Kendra held. Crossing her arms, she turned her back on Mr. Clark. She didn't want the strange man to see tears fall rapidly down her face.

"Herlene. Her name is Herlene." He talked to Gracie's back. "Yes, young lady, Herlene is ready too. As a matter of fact, she's been ready, but she knows that it won't be easy. She doesn't even know that I'm here." He rocked on his heels.

"Wait a minute," Marcus stated while taking a step closer to James. "She doesn't even know you're here? Well, how can you be so certain that she's ready? If she were ready, wouldn't she be here?" Hunching his shoulders, not understanding, Marcus gestured toward himself to make a point. "I'm just saying, the devil's hell or high water couldn't keep me from staying away from my child. And she's in the hospital and in critical condition? Oh no!" Marcus sealed the deal with the anger that was shared between him and Gracie.

With a turn, just in time to stop Marcus from producing more anger, Gracie grabbed her husband's arm. Realizing that their defense was wearing Mr. Clark thin, Gracie hoped her husband would calm down.

"Look, you have to forgive us. My best friend just lost her husband a month ago, and now she's losing a battle herself. You will have to excuse us because now is not the time for games. If Helen, Herlene, whatever her name is"—Gracie slung her arms in the air—"wants to check up on *her* daughter, then you tell her to come to room number three-oh-seven." Gracie pointed toward the number plastered on the wall. Turning to walk into the hospital room, she grabbed the tail of Marcus's shirt. She let him know that the conversation was over despite his continued reference to what he would do if he were in Herlene's shoes.

Once inside the hospital room, Marcus worried about his wife's emotional state. "You okay, babe? Now, that wasn't expected at all." Marcus stood firm, with his hands on his hips, speaking of James Clark's visit.

Standing with her back straight, Gracie rubbed her neck. "I'm fine. I just can't believe all of this is happening. Her mother?" Gracie questioned indirectly, standing over Kendra. She stood looking as her sister-friend lay in the bed in an involuntary sleep. "I don't know what Kendra would do if she knew her mother was wanting back in."

"Hmm." Marcus scratched the stubble of the goatee that he had recently begun growing. Placing himself directly behind his wife and hugging her, Marcus thought about the bad timing. "Well, it looks like we'll have to figure out what to do about that until Kendra gets past this mark. God's will be done."

"What do you mean?" Gracie looked over her shoulder into her towering husband's eyes. "We'll have to figure what out?"

"We're next of kin. We are first on the list if the doctors need an okay about anything. Had you forgotten?" Getting the understanding that Gracie remembered from the slump of her body, Marcus continued. "If Herlene comes around, we'll just have to make the decision of whether or not we feel it's in Kendra's best interest to allow her in."

"Right," was Gracie's only response.

"Oh well." Feeling his wife ease out of their warm embrace, bringing an airy breeze toward his covered body, Marcus tried to bring light into the conversation. "Where are you going? You know you need me to cover my baby up. Don't want him to be cold from this hospital air," he faintly jived once again, moving in closer to his wife.

"Oh, hush." Gracie didn't want to start in on the baby conversation. Her eyes peeping at her barely-there belly, Gracie prayed her husband would get the message that she wasn't in the mood for this conversation right now.

"Why hush? I'm not talking about you. I'm talking about *you*." He rubbed her belly and talked in a mock baby voice.

Carrying a frown on her face, Gracie wanted to stop Marcus before he started. "No, Marcus. Not now. Don't even go there."

"What are you talking about, Gracie?" He released his wife after hearing the seriousness in her voice.

"I'm just not in the mood to start in on the baby thing. I have enough to deal with right now." Walking farther into the hospital room, Gracie turned her attention toward Kendra.

As he let out a breath of air, Marcus inhaled new air in order to get his words together. "You may as well start talking about it. Dillian is gone and Kendra is in the hospital for . . . whatever has happened to her, Gracie." With his voice picking up annoyance, Marcus closed in the gap between them. "Gracie, I don't know what your problem is, but you may as well get ready to face it. We just may have to—" He regrouped himself. "You know what? Never mind! Everything doesn't always go your way! Don't you see what's going on? We made plans and maybe, just maybe this wasn't God's plan!"

Not getting a response from Gracie, Marcus's anger took over. "Still don't have anything to say?" With a gust of steamed breath leaving his mouth, Marcus threw his hands in the air just to produce the thud sound they made as they landed on his muscled thighs. "I'm leaving. Call me if anything changes."

Chapter 9

He knew he had been a bit harsh, and if he hadn't just lived it, Marcus wouldn't have believed he fired himself up toward his wife. Feeling guilty of presenting their problem at the wrong time, Marcus stood outside of the hospital door with his athletic hands deep in his pockets. Yet, when he felt the anger still brewing, he contemplated re-entering and letting Gracie have it again. Pacing around, Marcus walked away, kicking at air rocks along his path. Only out of respect for an ailing Kendra did Marcus retract his footing and continue his slow-paced walk. He couldn't believe how hardheaded his wife was being. Marcus would have never thought Gracie would linger so long on such an important issue.

Granted, he had agreed to this pregnancy; maybe because he felt he had no choice but to be all in. Or did he? Nevertheless, things had now changed. With Gracie being so adamant about the original plans for the baby, Marcus didn't know what he was going to do. He just knew things needed to be reevaluated.

Walking as slowly as possible toward the hospital elevators, Marcus wished Gracie would run after him. Besides getting some sort of affection from his wife, he hoped they could just take out time and talk, though he knew right now wasn't the most appropriate time. He at least wanted him and his wife to be of one accord about the way things would play out for their family. Looking back one last time, Marcus pressed his thumb against the white elevator button and waited.

Every time he tried to bring up plans for the baby, Gracie would cower away from the conversations. He had as much right to change his mind about the decision they had both made as she had in not changing hers; especially since he felt there was no other choice but to make the decision for the household. He was, of course, the man of the house.

Maybe that was it. He had never planted his feet firmly when it came to Gracie. All he ever wanted to do was to love, honor, and obey . . . to make her completely happy. And he did; but Marcus was now thinking his silence was the only thing that ever seemed to make Gracie happiest. A smile and a nod always seemed to soothe his wife's wants.

Thankful that the elevator was empty upon its arrival, Marcus entered, leaned against the back wall, and rambled his thoughts out loud.

"Things are definitely going to have to change." Marcus stuck his chest out, pulled his trousers up, and crossed his burly arms. "Just who does she think I am?" he spoke with confidence as the doors of the elevator slowly began to close. Sneaking a peek and looking quickly down the hall, Marcus peered at Kendra's door. When he thought he saw the door opening, his sudden macho appeal was lost as he hit the down button repeatedly in an effort to make the doors close faster, no longer wanting to face Gracie.

Chapter 10

Kendra had been another unresolved issue that Herlene had yet to conquer. She knew that she hadn't done the best she could have with her daughter, but found it difficult to let those words leave her lips. There was no way that Herlene would ever forgive herself until Kendra had forgiven her.

Her heart knew that Kendra held her responsible for the things she had to endure at such a young age. Herlene actually agreed with the hurt and anger that Kendra held for her. Time and time again she told herself that just because she was a young, single mother didn't give her a reason to leave Kendra to figure out life for herself. Herlene had basically thrown her child away, leaving her to raise herself. She was sure that was the motive for Kendra going off to college and never contacting her again.

Almost thirty-four years prior, when Herlene gave birth to Kendra, she didn't have a decent job, nor had she returned to school. She had moved in with yet another sister. Herlene's sister had recently had a child as well, and they had plans to raise their children together. But when Herlene began making it a habit of leaving Kendra with her sister while she went out to party, her sibling became irate. With that, Herlene's sister demanded that she either get her stuff together or move; especially since she wasn't contributing to the bills. Herlene's response was to simply walk through the door one afternoon after being out all night and announce that she was getting married. Her new husband was some guy she had met at the local bar three weeks prior.

Neither her parents nor her siblings could talk any sense into her. All Herlene could think about was how Mitch had lied to her, bedded her, and dumped her with a growing responsibility that she didn't know how to handle. Instead of looking for love, Herlene was looking for the "right now" to take care of her and her two-year-old child—not to mention supporting the alcohol and marijuana habit that she had inched into.

Marrying Trent, a man thirty years her senior, Herlene found out what people meant by settling down for any old thing. Receiving all the natural herb and booze that she wanted only added fuel to her heartbreak. Not loving Trent, Herlene allowed herself to believe that she was doing the right thing with having a daddy in Kendra's life. Raising Kendra to believe that Trent was her birth dad, Kendra saw firsthand Trent physically abusing Herlene for the simplest things. The more drugs they would do, the more fighting. And the more fighting, the more weed they consumed. The arguing and fighting never stopped, until Trent took his last breath.

No one in the household saw it necessary to have Kendra enrolled in any type of pre-schooling for the first four years of her life. The child, being at home alone with the only man she knew to be her father, was the one to walk in and discover her dead daddy.

Kendra was four years old on the afternoon that she went into her parents' room to wake her dad and let him know that she was still waiting for him to make her breakfast. That was when Kendra found Trent lying in the middle of his bed. He'd died of an apparent heart attack in his sleep. No one looked further to notice that the white substance he and Herlene had moved on to had caused the older man's heart to stop. Trent's death only made Herlene's world more hopeless, producing heartache for Kendra.

Years later, grateful that her dad took his fatherly role seriously enough to list her on his retired military benefits, Kendra received a monthly check. That was supposed to help with raising her. Besides the bare necessities Kendra needed—a roof over her head and nourishment—Herlene always took the remainder of the funds to smoke, drink, and party with.

The last time Herlene saw her daughter was the day Kendra was in downtown Dallas, getting on the Greyhound bus, headed to college. Herlene's own sister had called and told her that the least she could do was put down the bottle and come wish her daughter well in the start of her new life.

"Herlene, I know that's you that done picked up that phone. Just silly. Anyway, Kendra is leaving today, and since you didn't show to her dinner last night, I thought you'd want to know what time her bus was leaving." Herlene had listened to her sister's scolding, but never responded. "You know, one day you are going to wake up from this funk you've been in all these years and see how much pain you've caused this girl. All girls need their mothers, and you'd think you'd get over this *illness*, as you call it, and be a mother."

After giving the bus number and the time that it was leaving, Herlene's sister hung up the phone, knowing that her sister wouldn't respond.

That afternoon, Herlene didn't know if she was crying because she was out of beer and drugs, or the realization that she'd missed out on her daughter growing up. She finally got up from being in her rickety daybed all day and dressed herself in the first thing she'd pulled from the floor. Afterward, she went into Kendra's room, the room the child had rarely seen the insides of since she'd moved in with her aunt. Noticing the only bear that she had ever bought Kendra sitting in the middle of the twin bed, Herlene released years' worth of painful, truth-filled tears.

Hitching a ride, she made it downtown to the bus station just in time to see the line forming with those getting onboard the bus. Looking at Kendra from afar, Herlene saw her daughter looking around, searching for something, someone. In her gut, knowing that Kendra was longing for and looking for her, Herlene found the courage within to walk around the van she had been hiding in back of. Wanting to see her daughter off, Herlene stopped in her tracks once she saw a middle-aged woman run toward Kendra and embrace her in a motherly hug. It was the same hug she had only recently started daydreaming about giving her own daughter.

With one look, Herlene glanced down at her own appearance. Comparing herself to the woman who held her sobbing daughter in her arms, Herlene ran her hand over the raggedy ponytail her hair had been in for three days. Kicking dust off of her once white canvas shoes and giving the beaten teddy bear a squeeze, Herlene decided to turn and go back to the two-bedroom apartment she called home.

That was then, this is now, is what James would have told her if he were there. Peeping from her weary and cried-out eyes, Herlene wondered where her husband had run off to. She thought she'd remembered hearing the front door shut, and after crawling out of the kitchen and eyeing the hook where his jacket always hung, she knew he did, in fact, leave.

"He's probably tired of me too," Herlene sulked, throwing her back against an available wall. "What am I going to do? Lord, I done gave my life to you and you said you wouldn't put more on me than I can bear. I can't take this, knowing that Kendra is lying in the hospital, maybe dying." She shook her head in disbelief. "I did Kendra wrong. I should be the one in the hospital suffering, not her!"

Emotional on every level, the most Herlene could do was to sit on the sofa and play her life over and over in her mind. It was full of guilt and pain. There was even more that she had done to ruin Kendra's life. She had deeply scarred her daughter.

Not having a constant figure in her life, Kendra had become defiant toward Herlene after all she'd seen her mother do. Years after Trent's drug-induced death, Kendra's early preteen years brought more distance between the two. Never having a close mother-daughter relationship because of Herlene's steady disappearing acts, Kendra started with back-talking and doing as she pleased. And it didn't help that Herlene fell deeper and deeper in a rut by increasing her abuse of alcohol and marijuana. She ultimately traded a few daily puffs on her grass substance for a glass pipe that became the family she longed for.

Not wanting the responsibility of being a parent, Herlene, in one of her high stupors, released her duties of being the half-parent she had been to Kendra. She gave in to a man that Trent had considered a brother, sending Kendra to live with him. In reality, the only "family ties" that linked the man and Trent together were the drugs they sometimes shared. After making the foolish decision to hand over her daughter, Herlene longed for the ability to smoke herself into a miserable coma. She hid in and around drug houses for days, and it was only when an old family friend ran into Herlene on the street and asked about Kendra that the lady realized that Herlene had given her only daughter away.

"She's where?" The scowl on the woman's face was so deep it looked permanent.

"Crow got her," Herlene said nonchalantly. "That girl too sassy for me. I told her to go stay with him."

Not wanting to believe the words that came out of the addict's mouth, the family friend pressed for answers. "Stay with him where? Where is she, Herlene?"

"Man, shoot." Unsteady on her feet, Herlene swayed. As if the lady was getting on her nerves, she showed all the signs of a crack rock's lover. "Why you asking me all these questions?" Herlene wiped her running nose with the backs of her gloved hands, and then scratched the sides of her face. "I owed him some money. You got some?" She stretched her eyes, hoping that money would be given to her.

"No, I don't!" the lady snapped while pulling out her cell phone, connecting her call with one of Herlene's siblings. "You'd better get down here, now!" she screamed as she closed her ear with her other hand. Warding off the frantic noise that Herlene was making, acting like a wounded mother, the friend spoke into the phone. "I really don't know what's going on, but your sister talking about she let Kendra go stay with Crow. Now, you know that don't sound right." Herlene made a move to try to flee, but the friend clawed her arm in a death grip.

When Herlene heard the words come from their family friend, she realized what she had done and fell to the ground. "He took my baby! He took my baby!" She had the nerve to act as though she'd played no part in the matter. Crying about the sick payback that she agreed to, Herlene gave her brother and her friend the directions to the molester's residence in order to save Kendra.

With a police guide, Kendra's maternal uncle showed up at the house with the intention to take his niece home with him. Not wanting to pour salt into an open wound, and hoping to save his sister's life, no one offered the information that Herlene had deliberately given Kendra away for a drug payoff.

When Crow couldn't produce Kendra, saying that she was there but ran away, God still showed Himself to be faithful. To everyone's relief, the young girl turned up at a friend's home just a few days later. Grateful that Kendra had been rescued, the family continued to praise God, though evidence was found that the child would be scarred forever. Kendra escaped from Crow's home, but not before he had forced himself on her.

Thinking back, Herlene wished her family members had made the decision to turn her in as well. Any mother that could give her own daughter away to a man for him to have his way with her didn't deserve a second chance. Even with the blow of her daughter being assaulted because of her doing, it had still taken another twelve years before Herlene would accept that she had a serious drug problem and needed help.

Shoulders bouncing uncontrollably, Herlene lay on the sofa and swayed in misery. She could very well see why Kendra didn't want anything to do with her. Right before her only child's eyes, Herlene had fallen victim to a broken heart. She had allowed Kendra to be raised on other people's problems, leaving a lifetime of heartache and pain—leaving Kendra clinging to her very own life.

Chapter 11

Marcus tried to get the unnecessary argument out of his head that had developed between him and Gracie at the hospital. He figured he'd give her the rest of the afternoon and night to calm down from all the commotion that was going on. After that, and without wavering, they would need to figure out something. All Marcus knew was that God was trying to get their attention, and Gracie wasn't listening.

Marcus had purposely left all of his belongings when Gracie made the frantic call about Kendra. Now that he'd left the hospital, Marcus drove back toward his office at the college to get his briefcase and to finish up some paperwork he had left unfinished. Pulling into the deserted parking lot, Marcus made his way toward the hushed campus that usually rang with voices intertwined as one.

Upon leaving the hospital, his initial plan was to head to school to retrieve the twins. But Marcus thought better of it once he checked himself and knew his sour attitude was still lingering. Putting in a call to Jolie, Marcus made plans for the housekeeper to attend to the boys for the rest of the evening. He didn't know if Gracie would make it home or not, but he knew he needed time alone. Not prepared to stay home, nor wanting to go back to the hospital and be around Gracie, Marcus decided to just remain wherever the wind blew him.

He pulled the SUV forward, straightening the wheel before reversing his truck into the open parking space. Gathering his keys from the ignition, Marcus chose to shut and lock the door before answering his cell phone that was ringing hysterically in its holster.

"Hello?"

"Hey there, Brother Marcus. How's it going? Pastor Regis here."

"Pastor Regis. How are you doing? Fine, I hope." Marcus was relieved to hear his mentor's voice. Needing someone to talk to was way past necessary once he'd left the hospital. Marcus had dialed his pastor earlier to inform him about Kendra, and Pastor Regis had promised to call back.

"I'm doing well," the preacher replied. "I'm just leaving the hospital after checking on Sister

Kendra, and thought I'd call you to continue our conversation from earlier. You're not asleep, are you?"

Halting momentarily from his walk toward the college fitness area where his office was located, Marcus pushed his keys into his jogging suit pocket before continuing his strut. "No, Pastor, I'm just running into my office, getting the rest of my things before heading back home." He didn't really know if he'd get there anytime soon. "How did things go at the hospital?"

With his own day scheduled full of office work and member visits, Pastor Regis pulled up to his home and turned off his ignition. He wanted to give Marcus his undivided attention. Pastor Regis sincerely felt for the young husband and father. With the decision Marcus would have to make about the imminent birth of a newborn, Pastor Regis knew that with Kendra's added illness, Marcus was stressed during this trying time in their lives.

"Well, Brother Marcus, we are praying for God's complete restoration. We know that God can do all but fail, and that's what we're praying for."

"Right, right." As Marcus passed the contract janitor cleaning the hall directly outside of his office, he nodded in silent acknowledgment.

Marcus didn't want to take his attention off of his pastor once he entered his office, but his mind was divided. Thinking ahead, he quickly gathered his belongings and wrote his cell phone number on the whiteboard. That was just in case anyone needed to get in contact with him the next day. A feeling of fatigue flashed over him, and suddenly, Marcus's strength was leaving him. He felt stressed.

"Are you there?" The pastor's voice rang in Marcus's ear.

Marcus had been busily gathering his things, but breathed a sigh of relief as he headed back out of his office. "I'm sorry, Pastor. Yes, I'm here. I'm walking back to the car now, and you have my undivided attention."

"Oh, if need be, you can call me back."

"Nah, that's cool. I'm here now, and I want to talk." Marcus clicked the unlock button on his car key.

"Okay. If it's a good time for you, it's a good time for me. What's on your mind?"

"Well, Pastor Regis, I just really don't know what to do at this moment . . . about the situation, you know." Marcus had filled his pastor in on how he felt God was trying to get his and Gracie's attention.

"Are you praying, Marcus?" Pastor Regis asked in his baritone voice as he held onto the last syllable of the young brother's name. "Have you been fasting and praying?"

"Yes, sir. But I'm not—well, I don't want to say I'm not getting the answer that I'm looking for, *but* I'm not getting the answer, the fulfillment that's letting me know that what we did was okay. Our getting pregnant was not right!" Marcus rambled. "We did it for all the wrong reasons."

"Are you looking through your eyes, Marcus, or are you asking God to lead?"

Nestled back into the comfort of the SUV's warm leather seat, foot on the gas pedal, Marcus skipped the vehicle through the streets. He passed the street lights that were trying to hold him back from the freedom he was looking for. Marcus opened his mouth to answer, but paused to push the play button on his stereo. Once he heard Dewayne Woods' "Let Go and Let God," Marcus let out a breath before answering.

"Maybe I'm looking through my own eyes. As a matter of fact, I know I am. Maybe because I never wanted to do this anyway but thought that's what I was supposed to do, Pastor. I mean, I want to be the husband that Gracie wants, but sometimes I feel she puts me in a predicament where she only wants me to answer one way. I . . . I don't know how I let her get me into this." Tears sprung from Marcus's eyes. "Pastor, this is not where my heart is. I can't do it."

"Isn't it too late for that, Marcus? Have you—"

"I mean, when Dillian died . . ." Marcus cut in. As soon as he spoke his deceased friend's name, Marcus began feeling that he hadn't fully mourned Dillian's death. With tears racing down his cheeks, Marcus fought to finish his statement. "When Dillian died, I . . . I felt that it was a sign that what we were doing was wrong." The tears from his eyes and the wetness coming from his nose were all trickling down his face. "It's like, you know, I wasn't raised to do something like this. I've always heard about it, but I can't just willingly do it."

"Brother Marcus, just because you weren't raised to do it, you can't let that persuade you. You know that Dillian was sick. You can't let that be a factor in this."

Violently, Marcus shook his head. "I know he was sick, but he actually hadn't been sick from his HIV status in a while. His medication had been regulated; he'd been doing great for years, and then all of a sudden—bam! A heart attack! You can't tell me"—he hit the steering wheel with his fist—"that our deciding to get pregnant didn't have something to do with everything that has happened."

Feeling that he needed to calm one of the most admired brothers of his church, Pastor Regis started in. "Marcus, are you almost home? I don't want you driving upset. Do I need to meet you somewhere?" Pastor Regis placed his hands on his own key ring and was one second from cranking his idle car. "Marcus!" he called when he didn't get a response. "Brother Marcus? You need to tell me something, son."

"Pastor, I'm okay. I'm going home." Somber words left Marcus's mouth. Exiting the highway, he felt weak from the pain that he held inside. "I just need to know how to let go. I don't like the feeling, Pastor Regis. I mean, tell me. Tell me . . . how do I let my wife give our baby away? How do I step back and allow my wife to give our baby away . . . to Kendra?"

have something to do with everything that has happened?"

Feeling that he needed to calm one of the most admired brothers of his church, Pastor Regis started in, "Marcus, are you almost home? I don't want you driving upset. Do I need to meet you somewhere?" Pastor Regis placed his hands on his own key ring and was one second from cranking his idle car. "Marcus?" he called when he didn't get a response. "Brother Marcus? You need to tell me something, son."

"Pastor, I'm okay. I'm going home." Somber words left Marcus's mouth. Exiting the highway, he felt weak from the pain that he held inside. "I just need to know how to let go. I don't like the feeling, Pastor Regis. I mean, tell me. Tell me . . . how do I let my wife give our baby away? How do I step back and allow my wife to give our baby away . . . to Kendra?"

Chapter 12

She hadn't moved. Gracie had remained in the same chair for the majority of the treacherous day, a day that wouldn't end anytime soon. Now that early evening had found its way into the hospital's setting, she knew that her night would be just the same as her day—without Marcus.

Midday, Gracie had called Jolie and asked for the cooperative housekeeper to gather a change of clothes for her, due to the temperature in the hospital, which was quite chilly. She figured Marcus would drop the boys at home and make the short trip to the hospital and bring her warm apparel for an evening stay. When Gracie hadn't heard from her husband to inquire of the time he'd be by the hospital, she was surprised to know that Marcus wasn't the one picking up the twins.

"Mrs. Gracie, he called and told me to pick up the sweeties. Didn't you know?" Jolie asked, not knowing of the indifference between the couple.

"Ah, it must have slipped my mind, Jolie." With squinted eyes, Gracie slid in a quick reply that was more like a lie toward her faithful guest. Although she was more like family, Gracie didn't want to bring Jolie into her and Marcus's bickering. "If you can bring the clothes up to the hospital, Jolie, I'll meet you downstairs so you guys won't have to come inside."

Thankful the opportunity had given her a chance to kiss the boys good night, an exhausted Gracie now sat with her jeans and light sweater being the only soothing she felt. Having tried repeatedly to call Marcus, Gracie could only figure that her husband was more upset than she realized. When she called his office earlier and Ky told her that Marcus hadn't returned to school, Gracie knew for certain their argument wouldn't be resolved overnight.

Frustrated that Marcus would, on more than one occasion, try to persuade her to turn back the hands of time, Gracie wasn't trying to back down. All that mattered now was that her husband had made an agreement with her, but now he wanted out. Knowing in all actuality she wasn't ready to add to their own family, Gracie knew if she went forward with releasing their baby to Kendra, Marcus would never let her live it down.

"It's always me. The finger has to always be pointed toward me," she spoke to the silent room as she rocked in the chair and abruptly turned off the wall-mounted television. "Ugh," she angrily whispered as she slapped her hands to her lap and ultimately allowed her throbbing head to rest in her hands.

Not having the energy to speak directly toward God, Gracie only had energy to think about everything that had happened thus far. Taking her thoughts back to the day she had told Marcus about her idea, there was no evidence, none that she could remember, that would indicate his indecisiveness. But now . . . now things were different.

Now that Dillian had passed, Gracie felt she was made to look like the bad person, since she still wanted to be a blessing to Dillian and Kendra. She couldn't, for the life of her, understand why Marcus would bring indecisiveness into a plan they had already manifested. The life she was carrying was everything *but* a play toy.

She recalled cooking him a wonderful meal and asking Jolie to chaperone the boys to a day at the zoo so they could have the house all to themselves. Before he could even fully digest the serving of food that he ultimately savored, Gracie had gotten up from her seat and closed the distance between them.

"Honey, I was thinking . . ." She took in a breath and held it in for a moment as she stood behind his chair. "We are still unsure when we'd like to add to our family . . . but"—she gently massaged her husband's overworked shoulder blades—"what if we were to be a blessing to Dillian and Kendra?" Before he could even gather his opinion about the idea, Gracie recalled planting kisses and remnants of love on her husband's neck and shoulders.

Never once did she remember him throwing a fit and being downright against the whole arrangement; especially since they had cut their mealtime short and showed each other love in the most glorious way.

Now, standing and walking toward the hospital's window, Gracie held on to her own attitude about her husband's new change of mind. What Marcus failed to realize was that Gracie hadn't so much as acknowledged the baby she was carrying. Because she had put her mind in the frame of carrying a child for someone else, feelings for the growing baby were just the opposite. As long as the pregnancy was healthy, that was all that mattered to Gracie.

"If he didn't want any parts of this, he should have said something. I ain't stuttin' Marcus. He'll get over it, just like with everything else."

Gracie made up her mind while peering out into the blackness of the night.

The wife's body does not belong to her alone, but also to her husband.

A scripture out of I Corinthians 7 popped into Gracie's thoughts. Wanting to make herself believe that the scripture only pertained to the sexual nature of a marriage, Gracie waved off the slight guilt and busied herself by wiping dust bunnies off of the windowsill. Slapping her hands together to rid the grime, Gracie wanted to discount the idea that God had placed that scripture in her heart to dig deeper into her situation.

"Well, anyway"—her fingertips tapped her belly—"even if that were the case, it's too late now," Gracie announced with the roll of her neck. "This baby is here now. This baby belongs to Kendra and Dillian"

Because of the darkness, she could see her friend's image reflected in the window, and it startled her. Collecting her thoughts and pushing Marcus and his behavior as far away as she could, Gracie turned and placed herself beside Kendra's hospital bed. Gently placing her hand on Kendra's body, Gracie bowed her head and prayed, thinking that her own problems would solve themselves.

Gracie made up her mind while peering out into the blackness of the night.

The wife's body doesn't belong to her alone but also to her husband.

A scripture out of 1 Corinthians 7 popped into Gracie's thoughts. Wanting to make herself believe that the scripture only pertained to the sexual nature of a marriage, Gracie waved off the slight guilt and busied herself by wiping dust bunnies off of the windowsill. Slapping her hands together to rid the grime, Gracie wanted to discount the idea that God had placed that scripture in her heart to dig deeper into her situation.

"Well, anyway"—her fingertips tapped her belly—"even if that were the case, it's too late now," Gracie announced with the roll of her neck. "This baby is here now. This baby belongs to Kendra and Dillon."

Because of the darkness, she could see her friend's image reflected in the window, and it startled her. Collecting her thoughts and pushing Marcus and his behavior as far away as she could, Gracie turned and placed herself beside Kendra's hospital bed. Gently placing her hand on Kendra's body, Gracie bowed her head and prayed, thinking that her own problems would solve themselves.

Chapter 13

With the fresh cup of ground-bearing coffee in her hand, Herlene walked out of the vending machine section on the third floor of the hospital. Coffee not really being her thing, she had to think of something quick once she walked through the hospital doors with James trailing.

James had come home only to find her still in the same mode of hopelessness. When he saw his wife sitting, badgering herself, he demanded she get herself together because he had somewhere to take her.

"Go where, James? I don't feel like it."

"Woman, get up. I've prayed with you, I've cried with you. Heck, I married you for better or worse, but I'm tired of seeing you suffer. I'm tired of you beating yourself up for the mistakes of your youth!"

"I wasn't that young," she fought back, sitting on the edge of their sofa. "I was almost forty when the girl went off to college . . . probably drank myself crazy by the time she checked into her dorm room. Who knows? I was an adult, James." Knowing that she actually had drunk herself into a frenzy that night, Herlene felt better keeping it to herself.

James shook his head while breathing heavily, not knowing what else to say. Leaving the living area, he went into their bedroom and found a pair of slippers for her to put on. When he returned, he grabbed Herlene's light sweater and purse from the wall mount and walked over to her, standing directly in her path. He was determined one way or another to put an end to the misery she had been harboring for years.

It wasn't like he hadn't tried before to bring her around to at least write a letter or do something. But now he was determined. James felt that Kendra needed to know that her mother took full responsibility. It hadn't set well with his conscience then, and it surely didn't now that Kendra's new home was a hospital room.

"Are you going to put it on or what? It's time." He stood with nothing left for her to do but push her hefty arms through the sweater sleeves.

It wasn't until they were more than five blocks away from their house that James told Herlene where he'd been and where they were headed. In the back of her mind, she already knew.

"Are you crazy? I can't go up to no hospital. I don't have no right up there. James Clark, you better turn this car around right now!" Tears flowing from her face, Herlene prayed today wouldn't be the day that her husband would start listening to her.

Yanking her face from him toward her own window, Herlene sat, closed her eyes, and prayed silently, thanking God for James's courage to make the move she had wanted to make so many times.

Who knows what I'm about to experience right now in my life, Lord, but you? No one. Please go before and prepare a safe place, an accepting place. Just to touch my daughter, Lord, just to hold her hand is what I'm in need of. I know I don't deserve it, but you are my Father whom I serve. You said to follow you and you would give me the desires of my heart. Besides serving you, Lord, this is my one desire. Thank you, Father.

When she opened her eyes, they were sitting in the hospital parking lot.

Now, the third floor vending room was the only thing separating Herlene from her daughter. *Her daughter*. Kendra. Turning the corner from the elevator, Herlene's eyes immediately drew in the door that held her daughter's body behind it.

They'd known who Gracie was from the commercials and the news footage regarding her workout centers. Some years back, when the television stations started showing her commercials and threw in Kendra's photos as one of the trainers, Herlene had once again found tabs on her oldest daughter. Instead of waiting to hear about Kendra through her one sister that still stayed in contact with Kendra, Herlene had at last found a direct avenue to her daughter. From that moment on, anything having to do with Full of Grace Fitness Spas held Herlene's attention even more.

The year that the local African American newspaper covered a conference that the fitness center held, Herlene read the article in its entirety. From what she'd learned, a local celebrity, Gracie's boyfriend, had made an announcement about his HIV status. She gathered that they were no longer together, and the photos placed a timid Kendra closer to Dillian than to Gracie.

It seemed that whenever Herlene wasn't looking for information on Kendra, information would come to greet her. In the engagement and marriage section of the newspaper years later, Herlene ran across an announcement of Kendra and Dillian's engagement. Not long after, the commotion that went on at the wedding was reported in the newspapers as well.

She mourned for weeks at the thought that her baby had been given the sentence that Dillian held. Before it was all said and done, she prayed for Kendra and Dillian and even sent them an engraved clock for their wedding gift.

Now the faces that had held her attention on television and in the newspaper held her attention as she stood in the doorway. Dazed that she would actually get another chance to touch her daughter before she parted this life, Herlene blinked, becoming aware of her surroundings. When she felt James touch the small of her back, she inched her way to the middle of the room.

"I'm Herlene, Gracie." She walked timidly toward where Gracie sat, not taking her eyes off of a bedded Kendra. Realizing that her daughter looked the spitting image of herself, Herlene allowed her tears freedom to roam from her eyes, and didn't try cutting corners with Gracie. "I'm Kendra's mother. If I had the opportunity right this minute, Gracie, I'd let her know how sorry I am, and that I know that I've caused her all the pain that she's ever felt. But I can't, so I'm telling you." Moving in closer, she looked Gracie directly in her face, not bothering to clear her face of her pain.

"I can't make excuses for what I did. I wasn't there for my child in her childhood, her teenage years, or even in her college years. I wasn't there for her to learn how womanhood should be handled. I skipped out on it all. But I've paid for it, and seeing my daughter lying in this bed—" Tears built the pain in her throat, choking her to stop speaking for the moment. "I'm still paying." Herlene held onto information about how she always played the "should've, could've, would've" role with herself. "Please let me just spend a little time with her."

Looking back at James to make sure he was still close, Herlene continued. "I don't want to, but if you want me to leave after this visit and never return, I'll do just that. But please let me just hold her. I just need to hold her one last time before I leave this world."

Not saying a word since announcing to Herlene that it was okay to come in, Gracie's entire demeanor changed. When she saw it was James returning with his wife, Gracie had put her guard up and added the angriest look to her face that she could conjure. But in an instant, something changed.

At first she felt helpless, not having Marcus there to help her make a decision they had talked about together. But it was something about the demeanor of the older lady that gave her gut a soothing feel. It was God.

Discernment was a gift that God had given Gracie, and she saw the sincerity, the hurt, and pain that lay upon Herlene. Listening to the woman's plea, Gracie stood and clasped her hands together. The tears in Herlene's eyes were real, and Gracie couldn't help but allow her own tears to slide from their ducts.

"It's fine. Kendra is my friend, and I'll take the bullet for this one. You all can visit, but I'm not leaving her side. As long as you're okay with that," Gracie added while wiping away her tears, "then you can stay as long as you need to."

Hearing the relaxed tone in the young woman's voice, Herlene responded, letting her shoulders fall from being strained together. "I don't *need* to, Gracie. I understand what you're saying, but it's important that you know that I've finally come to the point in my life where I *want* to. I'm sure Kendra's filled you in on me not being who I was supposed to be in her life, but I've grown up. I'm sorry. I want to apologize to Kendra, but I can't. I just want to say I'm sorry for all of the years." She turned and stared a longing stare toward her daughter.

"You can talk to her," Gracie said as she closed in the space between herself and Herlene. Taking the elderly lady by the arm, she walked her around to the side of Kendra's bed, where she would be able to access her daughter better. "The doctor said that many patients tend to still be able to hear what's going on around them, even though we don't think they can."

Rubbing Gracie's hand that was on her arm, Herlene held her hand in place and asked the question she'd been waiting to ask: "What's her diagnosis? What's wrong with her? What happened?"

"It was an aneurism." Gracie looked back at James, wanting him to come closer when she felt Herlene's grip loosen. "Whoa!" Gracie hollered just as Mr. Clark slid the vacant chair under his wife.

"Oh my goodness," Herlene spoke weakly. "People don't usually make it through those, do they? Oh, James." She held out her hands toward her husband for comfort. "James, it's too late. It's too late."

"Mrs. Herlene, you have to be strong. We have to be strong for Kendra. That's what the doctors have been telling us." Gracie explained in detail all that the doctor had educated them on concerning Kendra's condition.

Nodding her head, indicating that she understood Gracie's advice, Herlene scooted the chair closer to Kendra's bedside and started her long-awaited visit. "Ken . . . Kendra, it's your mother. It's Herlene, honey." She looked around, seeing her husband's and Gracie's eyes landing on her. She wished she could be alone with her daughter, but Herlene, thinking that her time may be limited for seeing her daughter alive again, put down her pride and opened up.

"Baby, I'm sorry, so sorry that it took me so long to get here." She wiped her face with the backs of her hands. "I don't know what's going on with your body, honey, but I'm praying for you, Kendra. I'm praying for your complete recovery. I–I know that you probably don't want me to be here, but . . . but Ken, I need to be here, sweetie. I don't want to leave your side." Taking a breath, Herlene looked up at Gracie, then back at a sleeping Kendra. "I'm *not* going to leave your side ever again."

Chapter 14

Before Marcus knew it, he'd made a detour and had been sitting at the sushi bar at Benihana for more than two hours, thinking and sulking, trying to remember how his marriage had jumped from him and Gracie making plans together, to his agreeing to everything she wanted without question. Just when he had made up his mind that the only thing to clear his psyche would be a drink of liquor, someone tapped him on his shoulder.

"Marcus?" the voice asked with a question behind it.

To find out who had spotted him at the wrong time—a time of feeling full of worthlessness, Marcus turned completely to his left. "Michelle." Her name fell slippery from his lips before he could find the masculinity in his own voice. Instantly his heavy eyes went to the length, the strength, and even the color of her hair. It was the same hairstyle he had been asking Gracie to wear. But Gracie was adamant about not putting too much heat to her hairdo. Sitting, eyeing Michelle's hair that fell past her shoulders, Marcus, for a second, wondered how the hair would feel between his fingers. "H–hi. How are you doing?"

"Good, good." There was a brief pause as she stood farther away, peering around the room, wondering if her eyes would land on Gracie. "Obviously, not as good as you," she said as she pointed to his wedding band, while shooting out a stale laugh.

"Oh," Marcus replied as he looked down at his traditional gold band. It held an inscription around the inside that simply said *Paris*. Both his and Gracie's rings had been adorned that way to remind them of where their lives together began. "Right. Still going strong." He managed to let the words exit from his mouth before turning and grabbing his glass of cold water that sat on the bar, just past the alcoholic beverage that had been placed in front of his appetizer plate.

In hearing the doubt in her ex-boyfriend's tone, Michelle arched her eyebrows, slightly turned her head, and stepped in closer. "Is Gracie here?" She wanted to confirm, even though her inkling told her that she was in the clear.

"No, no." He scooted from his seat and sat in the one that now had become vacant to his right.

"Here, have a seat. Wait, are you with someone?" He turned to take a look around the restaurant for Michelle's companion as he pushed his eyeglasses up his nose.

"I'm alone. Just coming to pick up a to-go order, but I guess I can eat here now, huh?" She took the seat, flirting with her eyes.

As she got situated, Marcus took notice that Michelle's black-tinted and blow-dried hair bounced on her shoulder, swaying with her every move. *Still beautiful*. He noticed that the last six or so years had truly been good to his ex—at least to her body. Shaking his head, Marcus tried to focus on their chopped conversation.

"I'm not as lucky as you, I guess." Michelle picked back up on the marriage conversation while taking off her coat and folding it across legs that were graced in silk panty-hose.

"Hmm. Luck, eh?"

"Well? Where is Gracie anyway? Out on a Wednesday night, eating alone? Didn't you two have a child?" she asked, already knowing the answer to the latter question.

"Oh, did we ever. Twins. Gregory and Geoffrey. My boys." He thought about his sons before continuing. "Gracie's actually at the hospital. We had an emergency. Her friend, Kendra. Oh, I almost forgot. You know Kendra." He took another drink of water.

"Know *of* her." Michelle aimed her arched eyebrow toward Marcus. "And that's right," she remembered, "I did catch that report on the news. I'm sorry to hear the news, and my condolences on losing Dillian." Michelle sincerely shared her sorrows.

With his hand, Marcus warded off the commiseration. In many ways, he felt as if his marriage had died with Dillian. *Maybe that was it*, he secretly thought, wondering if his allowing Gracie's ex to constantly be in their lives had actually damaged their marriage.

"It's okay." *Or is it?* He had actually agreed to impregnate his wife for the purposes of giving the child away like some kind of holiday gift. Before he knew it, he bypassed the water and grabbed the liquored drink that stood alone.

"I never did get to apologize about all of that, you know," she blurted out as she made contact with the waiter. Michelle took a moment to order an appetizer from the menu, and then her gaze returned to Marcus.

Without hearing a sensitive tone in her voice, Marcus decided to take it for what it was worth. "No problem. Hey, that was in the past. And now we—are—here," he announced in a sliced response. "So, you say you haven't married? What's the hold-up?" He tried his best not to look down at the legs that peeked through the slit in her skirt. A pencil skirt like the one Michelle wore would be perfect on Gracie if she'd just try one on. But Grace was a woman with limited skirts and dresses. Marcus always pressed his wife to show off one of her best assets, but to no avail.

Michelle studied his face with seriousness as she received the dished appetizer from the waiter. "Well, after you dumped me, I didn't take it so easy, and I've just sort of, I don't know, just been to myself." Traces of the soy sauce dripped as she applied it to her half-shelled oysters, and she licked her fingers clear of it. Hoping that Marcus paid close interest to her every move, Michelle took a chance and licked her lips in a seductive manner.

"Oh, I see." Grabbing at his growing goatee, Marcus was sidetracked as Michelle grabbed for his hand and held it close to her bosom while she talked.

"I just want you to know that I forgive you for breaking things off with me like you did. I know . . . I know I did dig kind of low to try to keep you near me, but all and all, I'm sorry, Marcus."

"Uh. That's no problem, Michelle." Marcus returned his hand to his own person. Not really knowing what to say, or how to respond by telling her that she was out of her mind thinking he was the problem, Marcus just went with the flow, as he had grown accustomed to doing in his own marriage. “Look, I better go. The boys are at home with the sitter.” He thumbed his wedding band once again.

“Oh, well. Okay.” Michelle looked for her purse. “Here.” She dug in the side of her Louis Vuitton bag. “Here’s my card. Call me so that maybe we can do lunch.” With Marcus now standing and silent, Michelle wanted to bring him comfort. “Or not. It’s no biggie. I was just thinking we could catch up. That’s it.” She brought her hands up for defense mode.

“Right,” he said as he took the card and placed it in the back pocket of his sweat suit. Marcus approached her and gave her a quick hug. “Well, I’ll be going. It was nice to see you again, Michelle.”

“Likewise,” she acknowledged as she watched Marcus walking toward the restrooms and out of her life once more.

In his quest to keep his salvation intact, Marcus never looked back. He never even lifted his head. If he had, he would have seen his friend and coworker, Ky, walking into the restaurant to meet him. Marcus forgot that he had called Ky when he had arrived at the Oak Lawn restaurant. Seeing Michelle again had wiped all priors clear from his memory.

Ky approached the bar and looked around. "Now, where in the world—? Excuse me, miss. Have you seen a guy here? I'm suppose to meet my buddy at the bar, but—"

"Gone." Michelle threw her annoyance toward the man she hadn't even bothered to look up at.

"Hmmm, great," Ky spoke sarcastically, not knowing what had gotten into his friend to make him leave, knowing that he was on his way. "Mind if I sit? I may as well eat while I'm here." Ky arranged himself into the seat that had been warmed by Marcus. Wearing a low Caesar cut, Ky removed his ball cap and ran his hand over his head, hoping he looked presentable. With another thought, Ky wondered if Marcus had tried to play matchmaker.

"I'm Ky." He extended his hand, but retracted quickly, giving a wave when he realized that Michelle was in the middle of her meal. "How are you doing?" he asked once he finally conquered a good look at the woman in his presence. Still perplexed by his friend's disappearance, Ky was indebted to his frat brother for at least seating him in one of the best seats in the house. The view clearly gave him free range to rap to the honey that he hoped wanted to be rapped to.

"Fine," Michelle answered with no smile in her voice or on her face. Readjusting her crossed legs, Michelle slightly turned toward Ky, easing a look in his direction.

"It's Ky," he said, offering another introduction. "And your name?"

"Ky? Right. Michelle," she said as she turned her attention back to her second drink. Hoping that the guy next to her wouldn't talk her head off, Michelle wanted the company of a tall, good-looking man, even if it was a friend that had to stand in Marcus's place. *This time*, she thought to herself. Not knowing if she would hold out to see if Marcus would accept a lunch date, Michelle thought it better to busy herself with the present.

Chapter 15

She couldn't believe it. She had always practiced what she'd say and how she'd act if she ever bumped into him. She never thought that she would actually have the opportunity to be so smooth in front of Marcus. Michelle purposely turned down the volume on her car's radio, cruising Dallas's streets, headed home for the remainder of the evening. Not knowing if he would actually call, Michelle hoped for the best as drunken thoughts plagued her mind.

Having stayed and taken in a few more drinks with Marcus's friend, Michelle initially bypassed all of Ky's attempts to get to know her better. The more drinks that he purchased for her, the taller, darker, and more handsome he became. In the midst of their lengthy conversation, they laughed and joked with each other. Michelle had actually released Marcus from her mind for the moment. But now, alone in her car, Michelle replayed her day.

"I guess prayer does change things," eased from between her glossed lips, as she threw a comical laugh in the air. Thinking back on one of her sporadic visits to church, the last thing Michelle remembered praying for was for God to send her a husband made just for her. "Oh my goodness. I wonder," Michelle announced to herself through her jolted hiccups. "Nahhhh, he's Gracie's *man*." Michelle pretended as if she didn't care.

The last few years, since Marcus had separated himself from her and started his life with Gracie, Michelle had been in a funk. Seeing no promising future where a family was concerned, she dated off and on, but found no one as together as Marcus had been. When one of her friends suggested she pick up a Bible and find solace with God, Michelle did just the opposite. She picked up the Bible hoping to find a man.

She'd had a few flings here and there, a never-ending relationship with a married man, and a lot of flirtatious sessions with the men of the church, but the one thing Michelle hadn't concentrated on was establishing a relationship with God. She figured if a man didn't see her fit to be in his world, why would God be any different? *He did say that He made man in His image. If a man isn't interested in me, obviously God isn't either*. Pulling her vehicle into her uptown condo's garage, a lonely Michelle questioned a God she hadn't let dwell in her heart.

"I try to do everything right. I went to school, got my degree," she pointed out as she staggered out of her car. "I worked my way up to junior partner at the firm, but I'm still by myself." She paused for another hiccup. "I thought you were a God that I could trust. It's not like I don't go to the gym and take care of my body." Michelle slammed her convertible's door without worrying about putting up the top on her Corvette. "If you really are the God you say you are, you would have let that man be my husband," Michelle charged, referring to Marcus.

At dinner she had released all of her drunken and desperate woes to Ky, who was willing to listen for as long as she wanted to vent. Though she purposely didn't divulge the name of the man she was speaking of, Michelle was content with Ky, who gave her all the attention she needed. Ky didn't budge. He just wanted to be whatever Michelle desired. Michelle noticed his attentiveness and his concerned eyes, and she found a quick friend in Ky.

Staggering her way farther into her deep living area, Michelle let her purse, along with her briefcase, fall from her hands. The items landed where they may, and Michelle quickly shed her suit jacket, exposing her see-through, cream-colored camisole. Knowing she only had a few moments to spare, Michelle rushed into the hallway's restroom to freshen up.

She wasn't in denial. Michelle knew she had baggage and was playing a deadly game. Ever since Gracie had won Marcus over, things just hadn't been the same for her. Instead of walking the straight and narrow, Michelle's gallivanting ways had put her in more predicaments than she'd bargained for.

Ding-dong.

"I'm coming, I'm coming!" she yelled toward the chiming door, making her way out of the half bath that was mainly used for company. "Whoa." She stood still a moment longer once her drunken dizziness caught her off guard. "I'm going to have to slow down on the mixed drinks," she mumbled as she made her way to her front door.

Thinking back to the evening she'd had after Marcus's departure from the restaurant, Michelle added a smile on her face and opened her front door. The vision of a gorgeous black man stood at her door, but Ky held a questionable look on his face.

"Welcome—*hiccup*—to my home. Oh, excuse me." She waved off the unpleasant interruption as she moved aside to allow her new friend room to enter.

Only stepping in as much as he thought he needed, Ky turned to start what he believed would be a brief conversation. "Well, I'm happy you made it home safely. Thank you for allowing me to trail you."

The door shut, and with her body lingering against it, Michelle stood with her hands behind her back. She wanted to thank Ky for being so patient with her. "I don't usually get so tipsy, but I'm happy it was you I was with. Anyone else would have probably taken advantage of me." She slurred her words as she passed him on her way to her loveseat.

Knowing she was more of a threat to him than he was to her, Michelle worked hard to keep a good girl's image. "Come," she called out as she bounced on the cushions. "Sit. You don't have to leave so soon. I enjoy your company."

Scratching his right temple, Ky fought to make himself turn toward the door. "Uh, I'd better get out of here. I just wanted to make sure you made it to your home safe. I'm going to head on out." He struggled to move.

Knowing that it would take her wishing him away, or even opening the door for him, Michelle knew that Ky was there to stay. Just as she had wanted. Patting the sofa, Michelle invited an indecisive Ky once more. It was then, when Michelle saw a wide-nosed Ky walking briskly over to the comfortable loveseat, that she knew she had once again conquered someone that would stay long enough to only remember her first name.

Chapter 16

Two Months Later

Days had turned into months. With October, her favorite fall month in full swing, Gracie still couldn't bring herself to leave Kendra. In many ways, she felt she was all Kendra had left, and in that, she felt as though she hadn't been a good friend to Kendra since the very beginning. Granted, most people would say that she had a right to hold back in the friendship, especially in the trust department. And she may have even acted on that. But now things were different. Gracie's friend, her sister-friend, was barely holding on to life.

Since the day that Gracie had found Kendra unconscious in her home, there had been no defined change in her status. It was wearing Gracie thin, wondering what the future held for her comrade. And with the way things had been on the home front, Gracie was also no longer secure as her role of wife to her husband.

Gracie paced around the room, hugging her five-month growing midsection in order to keep warm. Easing up to the tray sitting in front of Kendra's sleeping body, Gracie checked the refillable jar. Five times already she had gone down to the ice machine and added new chips to the jar, discarding the water that the previous ice had melted into. This time she just took the jar into the restroom inside of the room and poured the water into the steel bowl.

Standing in front of the mirror, Gracie held onto both sides of the silver-colored piece and dropped her head. Slowly turning on the hot and cold faucets, Gracie grabbed two brown paper towels and blotted them with the warm water. Feeling nauseated, cold, and faint, she shook her head, warding off the feeling of dizziness that had crept up on her. The mounting grief made her want to scream, but instead, Gracie allowed quiet tears to beat down her face.

Gracie forced herself to look in the mirror, staring at the bags under her red eyes and the dryness of her skin. She tried to pull her loose strands of hair back into the makeshift ponytail she had pinned together, but gave up and backed her way to sit on the toilet seat.

"Oh my God. What in the world is going on? What is happening?" Peeking around the small room, Gracie's teary eyes focused on the ceiling. "Dillian's gone, Kendra's . . . here. I'm five months pregnant with *their* baby. I can't do this by myself. Help me understand all of this, God."

When she heard Him say, *Come to me, all who are heavy burdened,* Gracie knew that she had spent one too many days away from the house of prayer.

The months had been draining on Gracie, but she refused to give up on her friend. And maybe Kendra would be mad if she really knew, but Gracie was thankful for Mrs. Herlene. So far she had been the help that Gracie needed to maintain her own sanity in all the madness. Just as new tears began to flow, Gracie heard the opening of the door to Kendra's room.

"That's right. I did see some of his funeral on the news a while back. So that was her husband, huh?" the new nurse asked the other.

"Girl, yeah. Shoot. He was sick, but that man was a fine one, wasn't he?" the heavyset woman questioned with a tight expression on her face.

"I know that's the truth. So how's she doing? Anything specific I need to watch tonight?" the first nurse asked her colleague. Switching shifts, it was mandatory for the leaving nurse to fill the next shift in on all that was happening.

"No. No change. She's just been sleeping. The doctor has already made his rounds, so he won't be back until about four in the morning. She's already been turned. Oh!" Gracie heard the lady snap her fingers. "Whatever you do, make sure you do not let the family know—" *Beep, Beep, Beep.* The sounding of her pager echoed. "Follow me out here, girl. Let me go check on this new patient on the south wing."

Even after the room quieted, Grace sat on the toilet lid holding her breath, making sure she didn't make any sudden moves until she was convinced the caregivers were completely out of the room. Gracie rushed to dry her face with the sleeves of her sweatshirt. Confused, she waddled from the restroom and hurried to Kendra's bedside. Gracie looked around anxiously, thinking there would be a sign as to what the nurse was referring to before her pager interrupted. She hoped to run across a file, anything that was left behind, but Gracie exhaled when she realized she wasn't left with the piece to complete the puzzle.

"What in the world were they talking about?" Gracie questioned the air. With one quick thought, Gracie raced through the door's exit, headed to the nurse's station.

"Hi. I'm Kendra McNab's family member. I wanted to know if there were any changes in her situation. How is she doing?" she added, hoping to get a clue as to what the other nurses were discussing.

"Oh, okay. Let me page her nurse for you. I think they were doing their switch. I thought they'd gone in that direction, but I'll let her know that you would like to be filled in."

Reluctantly, Gracie agreed. "Uh, okay." She stood for a moment. "I'll be in the room," she said as she turned and walked away. Once inside of the small, private space, Gracie started reminiscing about all that had been presented to her.

Falling hard on the chair that was next to Kendra's bed—the only chair in the room—Gracie reached for the remote that was attached to the bed. With one click, she turned off the television so that she could talk to her friend. "Kendra, I'm sorry." Gracie looked down at her own hands in her lap. "Maybe Marcus is right. Maybe I've jinxed us all. I–I'm sorry." Taking in a deep breath, Gracie finally allowed her hard cry to surface. "Oh God! I'm sorry. What have I done?" she asked as she looked nowhere in particular.

"Lord, I keep getting us in the same situation time after time." Gracie recalled how her demanding spirit always pushed Marcus into corners. There had been times when she'd wanted certain furniture, vacations, upgrades, and renovations to their business and home, and the whole idea had put them in tight crunches. "Now . . . now I have this baby in me, and God, I don't even know if you told me to do this. Lord, please don't let anyone else suffer because of my selfishness. All I want to do is to help, and I get in the way. Help me, Lord."

Chapter 17

"Gracie." Marcus identified his wife by her given name rather than the pet names he'd often called her. "Don't know if I told you or not, but Dad is coming to stay in and out for a while. He said he's been thinking about moving to Dallas from Paris, and he wants to take a look around at some real estate that his realtor referenced for him."

"Fine," she said without giving a notion that anything mattered. "Shoot. Children's Church is closed," Gracie read from the posted flyer on the door, thinking that her boys were following behind her and Marcus. "Why is it closed?" Gracie squinted her eyes from the hard glare of the vaulted lights, trying to prevent her ongoing headache from getting worse. Turning to look up at Marcus, who was standing directly behind her, Gracie questioned her distant husband. "Where are the boys?"

"I was wondering why you were walking this way. The play that the children have been putting together is today, Gracie." Marcus placed one hand in his pants pocket and scratched his head with the other.

Standing in her tracks, Gracie stared a minute too long at her husband and his contemporary approach to dressing. With his Barney's dress pants and starched dress shirt, she tried to find something that would make her upset at her husband. Admiring his oversized collar and cuffs accented by his own signature cuff links, Gracie rubbed her forehead with her open palm. She didn't worry about smearing her pressed powder as she came to the realization that she hadn't been practicing Gregory's and Geoffrey's lines with them.

"Oh my goodness, Marcus, I had completely forgotten about the play." She started the short journey in the other direction, following her husband. "I completely forgot. Where are they? I haven't taught them their lines."

"It's okay, Gracie. Things have been kind of crazy with you and the baby—I mean . . . with Kendra and all. You've taken on a lot." Hoping his words didn't sound too sharp, Marcus tried to bring comfort to his wife. "I've been practicing with the boys. They're good." Marcus checked his watch. "We'd better go ahead and get to the sanctuary so we don't miss anything."

With energy slowly seeping from her body, Gracie lifted her Hermes bag that hung by her side. "Thanks," she said, acknowledging the way Marcus had stepped in.

Things between them were okay, but not as good as they had been in the past, and for some reason, Gracie knew that it was all her fault. Entering through the door that Marcus held open for her, Gracie sighed when she saw the children at the front of the church arranging themselves for praise and worship. Even though she adored the children and their praise style, Gracie couldn't wait for them to start and finish so that the Word could be brought forth.

Praise is what I do . . . when I want to be close to you; I lift my hands in praise.

Not hesitating, Gracie placed her designer bag on the pew and continued to stand to her feet and help the kids raise their praise. Falling in with the ambiance of the other parishioners, Gracie lifted her hands and ushered in the Holy Spirit.

Gracie knew it was her fault that Marcus was standoffish, keeping his distance. She beat herself up for what she'd been doing to her marriage. She'd gotten them in a predicament that only God could get them out of. Hoping that her husband didn't make any drastic decisions, Gracie started praying even more after she'd found a card he'd received from his ex.

While doing laundry last week, Gracie had found an old tattered business card of Michelle's. The woman who had tried to ruin everything between Gracie and Marcus had reappeared, or so it seemed. She didn't know for certain that Michelle had resurfaced, but Gracie knew that she'd found the number in her husband's pants pocket, and that was enough to raise red flags. She had noticed how Marcus had been occupied on his cell phone, chatting away at his convenience, never letting her know who had told him the joke that had made him laugh so.

After church, she had planned on asking him about the new activities that had been going on in his life. Feeling overwhelmed and defeated in spirit, Gracie took her seat before praise and worship was over and prayed in silence.

I've been going through so much with Kendra, this baby, and now Marcus. Lord, if you don't help me, I don't think I can make it. I love my husband and I don't want to lose him. Help me, Lord. Help me. I'm tired and getting even more weary. Please strengthen me.

It was Pastor Regis's voice that took over once the children completed their praise session and their fall play. With Marcus's help, Gracie stood to her feet once more and bowed her head to receive the prayer that the pastor prayed before he started his sermon. She inhaled as she and the others were told to open their Bibles. The subject for the lesson: *Help Me, Lord.*

When the senior pastor of the congregation asked his members to turn to Isaiah 40:29, Gracie knew that God had indeed heard her prayers. It was up to her to listen.

The pastor read from the New King James Version. "The Word reads: *He gives power to the weak, And to those who have no might He increases strength.* People, read the rest with me," Pastor Regis urged.

"*Even the youths shall faint and be weary, And the young men shall utterly fall. But those who wait on the Lord shall renew their strength, They shall mount up with wings like eagles, They shall run and not be weary, They shall walk and not faint.* Amen."

"That's it," Gracie mumbled as she took her seat, straightening her back as much as she could. She was ready to hear the message.

"You say something, honey?" Marcus questioned as he leaned in earshot distance to his wife, never taking his eyes from his mentor.

"No. I was just talking back to Pastor." Looking at the side of her husband's face, Gracie tried to see if she could spot any uncertainty, any unfaithfulness with Marcus.

Knowing that she didn't want to lose her husband to Michelle, or to anyone else for that matter, Gracie grabbed his hand, gave it a squeeze, wanting to hold on. When she felt Marcus loosen his grip, Gracie sat back and gave her undivided attention to the front of the church.

The pastor continued. "There are times when we try to do *all* that we can, *all* the time. You know, we want to be the mother, the father, the sister, the brother. We want to be the lawyer and the judge, the nurse, the doctor . . . and I'm speaking about all at one time, saints." He talked toward the congregation, wanting them to follow where he was going. As he heard a few say "Amen," he continued. Gracie sank deeper into her seat, knowing without a doubt that the message was for her.

"We want to solve our problems, your problems, the church's problems, and the world's problems, but then when we realize that we are just one person, that we only have enough room to finish one task at a time, we get backed into a corner and don't know what the next best thing to do is. Confusion then sets in. It plays with our minds, our marriages. It plays with our hearts, our emotions, and even our future. What do you do?" Pastor Regis asked in a long, drawn out slur.

"It was Donnie McKlurkin who summed it up best. You just stand. But even before you stand, saints"—he pointed upward—"you look to the hills from whence cometh your help, and you simply state what He is already waiting for you to ask. Help—me—Lord."

With tears curving her pregnant, inflated cheeks, Gracie raised her hands in praise, clutching a Kleenex and mouthing those exact words. *Help me Lord.*

Not only did Marcus raise his hands, but he stood. He raised his praise to worship God. The sermon was just what they both needed, and even though he knew it was a good lesson for Gracie, he wouldn't deny that his soul had been blessed.

Before closing his eyes to enter into the holy place that God had available for him, Marcus shot a glance at a sniffling Gracie. He felt sorry for his wife, but only because she brought on so much worry to herself. He knew if she hadn't already thought about what predicament she'd placed their family in, her time was nearing. Even if that were the case, he knew deep enough they still had bigger fish to fry. Unfortunately, he knew he'd also be a part of that frying.

Suddenly, thoughts of Gracie and any convictions that might come her way exited Marcus's mind. Thoughts about his own lashing from the Father entered, and he fell into God's worship space.

With all the time Gracie spent at the hospital over the past months, being there for Kendra, Marcus had shared his bed with the twins more than he had with his own wife; so much so that he'd started sleeping on the couch and letting the boys play Twister amongst themselves instead of using his face for their next foot placement.

Their conversations were no longer short and sweet, but nonexistent and sour. It had come down to Marcus or Gracie not agreeing on a conversation that the other had found important, which always left them both defeated.

When the choir started in with a low-tuned classic by John P. Kee, Marcus swayed and silently prayed for God's saving grace to come into his heart and the heart of his wife. He prayed for an open line of communication and for a fix to the problems that were too big for them to handle on their own.

Asking forgiveness for stepping into tainted waters, Marcus held his eyes tight, only willing to open them after he had cleansed his heart and forgiven himself first.

At home after service, Gracie felt the calmness that let her know that bringing up Michelle would only bring more separation, so she decided to venture onto new territory. "So your dad is coming when?"

The doorbell rang just as Gracie finished her sentence.

"Today. Right now, is what it looks like." Marcus walked toward their nine-foot, double-coated front door. "Hey, Dad." Marcus greeted the man from whom he had received his height and good looks. Looking more like his father's brother than his son, Marcus inherited the eye shape and color of the patriarch of his family. "Come on in."

"Hey, son. How's it going?" Marcus's father asked as he slapped his oldest son on his broad back. "Where are my grandboys? And don't tell me they aren't here."

"Yeah, Dad. They're here," Marcus answered.

Standing directly behind Marcus, Gracie chimed in. "Hi, Dad, how are you?" Gracie edged herself on her tiptoes in order to kiss the older, sophisticated man. "So you're moving to Dallas, eh?" Gracie stepped back in a flash as she heard the footsteps running through the house. "Slow down," she said, but dared not get in the way for fear of being trampled upon.

"Granddad, Granddad," the boys yelled out once they landed their sights on their father's dad. "What you bring us?" Gregory and Geoffrey knew their grandfather oh so well.

"Boys, that is no way to greet your granddad," Gracie said sternly as she held onto the small sections under her rounded belly that used to be her hips.

Seeing her father-in-law open his mouth, Gracie knew that he would defend the boys. She threw up her hand, turned, and walked away. "I know, I know. They're all yours. Oh, Marcus, since Dad is here, I'm going to run to the hospital and check on Kendra, if that's okay?"

"Sure." Marcus knew that it would allow him time to talk to his father.

Gracie, thinking the same thing, hoped that Marcus would listen to anything his father had to say. Knowing he had gone down the bumpy marital road, Gracie hoped he could enlighten Marcus and eventually help their marriage.

Chapter 18

Tests had been run throughout the months of Kendra being stable in her coma. Though nothing had changed for the better in her condition, nothing had gotten worse. Per the doctors, there was nothing that they could do. Kendra's break from her comatose state was entirely up to her. And even though the patient hadn't a clue that her mother had become a fixture by her bedside, Herlene had stepped up to the plate and helped Gracie with taking care of Kendra. For the time being, all questions and attitudes had been pushed to the back of Gracie's mind. She had allowed Herlene free reign in her daughter's life.

The two had even put themselves on a rotating schedule, making sure that family was there at all times. For Gracie, it was killing two birds with one stone. Not that she was outright avoiding her husband, but she and Marcus hadn't fully recovered from their ongoing disagreement regarding their surrogate parenting. And now that she didn't know if her husband was having an affair, Gracie figured that the more she was away, the better.

She and Marcus had yet to sit down and come to some sort of an agreement. He had been so upset with her that he wouldn't even give her the time to say what she had finally come to realize. Gracie knew that she had gotten them into the mess, but Marcus wouldn't let her voice it to him.

At her every attempt, his response was, "Okay. You were wrong. Now what?" When Gracie could not come to a conclusion of what to do, Marcus would storm off from her and place himself a good distance away.

Feeling despair, Gracie had no one to turn to, since her parents were still living in Paris, enjoying their elderly enriched lives. That was partially the reason that Gracie had reluctantly become closer to Herlene over the weeks. When things around the house still hadn't calmed down between the two concerning the baby, Gracie almost blurted out her information willingly.

"That man of mine!" Gracie hollered out as she closed her cell phone. She removed her folded wind jacket from her arm as she walked through the hospital room's door.

Calling Marcus at home, Gracie had asked what he would like for dinner. He'd nonchalantly replied, "Doesn't matter," and hung up shortly afterward.

Already putting on her own outerwear in anticipation of Gracie's arrival, Herlene slowed her movement as she noticed how upset Gracie had become. "Honey, what's wrong? Marcus upset you?"

"Huh? Uh, yes, ma'am. I just don't know what to do. He hasn't been talking to me. He's been short in conversation . . . and I know it's my own fault, and I think—" Gracie let out a sigh as she took a hard seat and bawled. Before she could get out that she thought her husband was cheating on her, Gracie thought twice. She definitely wasn't going to bring up the business card that she'd found in her husband's pocket.

"Gracie, Gracie. Calm down, sweetheart. All of the crying isn't good for the baby," Herlene pointed out as she rushed over to a hysterical Gracie, kneeling down beside her.

"What do you mean? How did you know that I was pregnant?" Gracie looked down at her midsection and realized just how much her pregnancy had progressed.

Unattached to the unborn child, Gracie hadn't even shared her news with anyone outside of her immediate family. She knew she had consciously sauntered over any talk about being pregnant.

When anyone would bring up the subject, Gracie would detour to another conversation. Caught off guard with Herlene's mention of the pregnancy, Gracie let out fresh tears. *No more running,* was all she could think about.

"Gracie, I'm old, but not so old that I can't see." Herlene held her knees, hoping they wouldn't give out on her, as she stood upright. "Were you trying to hide your pregnancy?" she asked without waiting to receive an answer. "Honey, you're married; you don't have to hide the fact that you're pregnant. You and Marcus have two beautiful boys." Wondering why Gracie would try to hide her pregnancy, Herlene jumped to conclusions all on her own.

"Does he know?" Herlene closed the space between them and tried, without success, to whisper. "Girl, is this Marcus's baby?" Herlene added as she stood and placed her hands on her hips. "Girl, I know you ain't gone out there and did what I think you done did. Oh my Lord! Marcus is a good man, Gracie. He was a nice boy and has grown into a nice young man, and you just done went off and—"

"Mrs. Herlene, Mrs. Herlene, calm down." Gracie couldn't help but smile as she watched the older woman go off on her. "It's nothing like that." She waved her hands toward Herlene, trying to cool her down before the woman bopped her a good one upside her head. "Marcus knows that I'm pregnant. That *we're* pregnant. It's just that—well, my hormones today . . . Don't mind me."

She stood and hugged Herlene, reassuring her that she was okay. "I'm sorry to upset you. Here, put your coat on, and you are officially off duty." Gracie helped the sturdy lady readjust her outerwear.

"Whew!" Herlene fanned herself. "Well, tell me something then."

Looking down at her belly and finally rubbing it in public for the first time, Gracie realized that her body had caught up with the months. Her five-month pregnant belly had finally rounded out. "Mrs. Herlene, do you have time?" Gracie looked up with new tears crowding her face.

"Oh, honey. What's wrong? What is it, Gracie?"

Not knowing where to start the heart-filled story, Gracie jumped in while she still had the nerves. "They had been trying to have a baby, at least for the past year or so." Gracie sobbed into the Kleenex she had snatched from Kendra's nightstand, stopping only to blow her nose. Gracie never looked up.

"They? Who are they, Gracie?" Herlene walked back toward her new friend.

"Dillian and Kendra." She let out a breath and knew it was time for her to get the burden of messing things up off of her chest.

"But, honey, Kendra and Dillian were . . . uh, well, Kendra is infected with HIV. How was that possible for them to bring another life into this world?" Herlene leaned closer to Gracie and held her hand as she retained a puzzled look on her face.

Knowing that the lady wasn't current with all the technology that ran rampant in the world, Gracie figured now wasn't the time to break down the facts of new age medicine, but gave her some simple facts.

"There are ways, Mrs. Herlene. The doctor would use the same in vitro procedure as he would with any other couple. It took them a while to find a doctor that would even try it because the doctors knew they both were HIV positive, but because of Kendra's low viral level and the possibility of transferring the virus to the baby was low, a doctor finally took their case. I don't know all of the details, but that was it for the majority. Anyway"—she cleared her throat to continue her miserable story—"it never happened for them. The procedure never produced a baby."

Glancing into Herlene's eyes, Gracie hoped the lady wouldn't judge her, but she continued. "It was me. I thought of the big, bright idea that it would be wonderful." She threw her hands in the air. "I thought it would be wonderful if I would just have a baby for them." She stopped and looked into Herlene's pained eyes. "No strings attached. I thought that Marcus and l could get pregnant, go through the pregnancy, and hand the baby over to Dillian and Kendra."

Herlene sat still, not knowing in which direction to point the conversation. Her heart fell from its holding place, and Gracie could see straight through her.

"I know. There's nothing much to say. The worst part was that Marcus never really wanted to participate, but I didn't give him an option. Then Dillian passed, and now Kendra . . ." Gracie's throat squeaked from the cry that eased its way out. Too embarrassed to share with Herlene how she now thought she had pushed her husband into the arms of another woman, Gracie just sat and waited on a response.

Herlene jerked, realizing she hadn't said a word, nor moved. As she now moved closer to Gracie, Herlene ushered the crying woman onto her shoulder. "Wow, Gracie. I don't know what to say." She rocked, but as soon as she started, she stopped. "First," she said as she pushed Gracie's head up so that she could look into her eyes, "only an angel could even think of being a blessing for someone else in their time of need and want. You ought to be happy that God has made you the person that you are. You're a forgiving woman and a serving person, Gracie. Not many people, not many at all could do half of the things that you've done."

"I wanted to help Dillian and Kendra, b–but I wound up hurting my own husband because of it. I wasn't thinking about his feelings at all, Mrs. Herlene."

"Yes, I won't lie to you, you crossed the line. Asking your husband to give up his own flesh and blood?" She stood up and armored herself with motherly wit. "When you're married, you are one. Look, I know I don't know a lot, but I can tell that Marcus loves you and those boys." Getting a second wind, she continued. "Nonetheless, Marcus married you for better or worse. Honey, this is that worse. You've made a decision, really, without him. You're going to have to give Marcus time to clear his mind, but he'll bounce back."

"But he wants this baby. He wants us to keep this baby as our own." Gracie looked up at Herlene for an answer.

"And what do you want me to say? It's your baby, Gracie. Seriously, what can Kendra do with and for that baby right now, in her condition? We don't know when or if she'll wake up. With the Lord's healing, she will, but even still, she'll have to go through therapy." Sitting back down, Herlene eased her voice to comfort her new friend. "I know this must be a rough spot for you, Gracie, but you need to seek ye first the kingdom of heaven, sweetheart."

Shaking her head, Gracie knew that what Herlene was telling her spoke volumes of what she was already feeling. Engraving a smile on her face, Gracie sat up tall in her chair and acknowledged what she had to do. "You're right. I'll get it together. I got us into this, and with God's help, I'll get us out of it." She took another Kleenex from Herlene and blew her nose.

"Now, that's sounds much better. Honey, let me pray with you." The two bowed their heads as Herlene prayed.

"Heavenly Father, we come to you for comfort on behalf of Gracie. Lord, I ask that you give her strength to go through whatever it is her heart is going through right now. We are asking that you come in, Lord, and make all the wrongs right. We are asking for your will to be done in her and Marcus's life. This is a couple that you planted, dear God, and we are asking you to see them through this battle that is not theirs. We ask you these prayers, in your name, Father. Thank God," Herlene concluded. "Amen," they spoke together.

"Call me any time you need to talk about it, you hear?" Herlene leaned her head down, making eye contact with Gracie.

"Yes, ma'am." Giving her nose another blow, Gracie thought about what Kendra's mother had said earlier. "How do you know Marcus was a good boy, Mrs. Herlene?"

"Huh?" Herlene stiffened and scratched the top of her head.

"Yeah." Gracie laughed and danced her hands in the air as Mrs. Herlene had. "When you called yourself going off on me, you said he was a nice boy and has grown into a nice young man." Gracie replayed the event with the hand and neck movements to match. "How do you know he was a nice boy?"

"Oh," Herlene responded with a straight face, "girl, I was just hyped up, as you young folks say. Don't mind me. Look, let me get out of here." She rushed her words. "Everything is fine with Kendra. The doctors did their rounds, and there are no changes. Let me go before James starts blowing up my pre-paid phone, knowing good and well I ain't gon' pick it up. I'll see ya, baby. We'll talk later, you hear? Kiss the boys. See ya." She said it in all one breath, and then raced to get out of the closed-in room. Herlene didn't even look back to see the look of confusion on Gracie's face.

Once outside of the room, Herlene stopped and caught her breath. She couldn't believe how stupid she'd been to open up her mouth. It was bad enough that she had previously spilled her guts to Gracie, letting her know most of the wicked things she had done in her lifetime. If she opened up the can of worms that not even she wanted to relive, she'd regret it. She didn't know how long she was going to be able to keep her past in the past, but she was sure going to try. Herlene made a note to watch her mouth and not let the cat out of the bag any more than she already had.

Easing herself behind her steering wheel, Herlene couldn't shake the headache that had landed right between her eyes. With tears streaming down her aged but blemish-free face, Herlene thought that this part of her past wouldn't find her. She didn't doubt that Kendra would question her once they mended their relationship, but she had no idea that her past would present itself right in front of her.

Before she even realized what she was doing, and instead of pulling her car inside of her home's two-car garage, Herlene had made her way to the other side of town—a place where she wouldn't be spotted. Parking her vehicle in the first available parking space she saw, Herlene pulled her key out of the ignition. Grabbing her purse, she headed inside of the corner liquor store.

Chapter 19

"So what's really going on?" Marcus's dad asked, sitting on the sofa directly across from his son. "You know, the same-old same-old. Just trying to maintain. How about yourself, old man?" Marcus sat with his ankle lying across his knee and his back deep into the soft brown leather sofa. Having changed out of his church attire into jersey sweat pants and a top, Marcus relaxed as he positioned himself to watch football on his flat screen.

"All right now. I saw a few gray specks across your edges. Looks like you catching up with me." The older man peeped at his son to see if he'd hit a spot. When he saw Marcus run his hand across his forehead, he knew he'd hit him where it hurt—in the waves. "That's what I thought." He laughed.

"Aww, okay. I see how you doing it."

"But seriously, son, why do you have the attitude with Gracie?" Pops stretched one leg out on the sofa he'd been sitting on. "It ain't like I didn't notice, so don't even try to say it ain't so. I know you're not still harping on her being pregnant?"

"I told you that you had feminine ways. Just nosey," Marcus joked while grabbing at the remote to turn the volume down just a bit. In one motion, he dropped his leg and sat with his elbows touching his covered knees. "Since you must know, Dad, I'm really, really disgusted with myself. I'm disgusted with Gracie. I just can't get it out my head that I let her get us in this predicament." Having previously talked to his father about his and Gracie's situation, Marcus was comfortable picking up where he had left off.

"You still stuck on the baby thing. I thought you all got over that. She's pregnant, and your friend, Kendra, is in a coma. Problem solved. The baby stays with y'all." Pops didn't move. "It's not like it's an artificially inseminated baby. You two made this baby from your own union. What is Gracie saying?" He looked at Marcus and saw the seriousness.

Marcus held his head down. "She tries to talk, but I don't even want to talk to her. She was so into giving this baby away, and then when everything happened, I tried to get her to see that this baby is meant to be with us. She wouldn't talk about it. But now . . . now she wants to talk, and I couldn't care less."

"Well, you better start caring, because she's getting bigger. This is real, son." Pops held a grimace on his face as he witnessed a hard tackle on the surround sound television system. "Ouch!"

Looking up at the screen, Marcus didn't let the replay affect him as he debated whether or not to tell his dad the rest of what had been going on in his life. Before he could talk himself out of telling on himself, it slipped. "I saw Michelle."

Slowly taking his eyes off of the screen, the older Mr. Jeffries zeroed in on what his son was admitting. "*Michelle*, Michelle?" When his son nodded his head, Mr. Jeffries found himself sitting up in the same position as his son. "Marcus."

"I know, Dad. I already know, but I did." He was referring to calling and visiting Michelle days after their first encounter.

With his eyebrows arched, Mr. Jeffries questioned Marcus further. "Did what?" When he didn't get a direct answer, he scooted to the edge of the sofa and asked again. With a deeper tone in his voice, Mr. Jeffries said, "Did what, Marcus?"

"I–I saw her at a restaurant one night, and she gave me her card. It was all innocent. Nothing happened . . . that night." Taking a look at his father to witness his expression, Marcus carved his eyes back into the rug placed over their wood floors. "But I called her because Gracie started spending all her time at the hospital. I was trying to get Gracie to see that our baby belonged with us. She wouldn't listen." Marcus wanted and needed to place the blame somewhere besides with himself.

Now standing, Mr. Jeffries got angry. "Boy, what in the world is wrong with you? You have a wife and kids. And if you haven't really let it sink in, you're about to be a father . . . again. Didn't I teach you enough? Didn't your mother divorcing me teach you anything?" Never getting over his own mistakes of letting his family down, Marcus's dad was furious at himself as well as his son.

Marcus strained his neck to look up at his father, who was now standing directly over him, and he found himself fighting to hold back his tears. But the dam broke. "I know, Dad."

"Obviously not, Marcus. This ain't no game, man. You don't do stupid stuff just because your wife ticks you off." Realizing that the twins could be listening, Mr. Jeffries lowered his voice. "Yeah, Gracie was out of line for asking you to get her pregnant for her friend, but son, you obliged and helped her make that baby. You can't blame Gracie for all of this. And you sure as heck can't add another bad factor to this equation."

"But—"

Sitting down on the chocolate-colored ottoman that completed the family room's ensemble, Mr. Jeffries tried to calm down in order to help his son. "Son, I know we really never talked about it, but what I did to your mother, to you, to my family period, I regret. What I did is the reason why she's been happily married to that . . . Jerry, for almost twenty years," he said with a slight grin.

"Johnny," Marcus corrected.

"Yeah, him. Whatever his name is." The older version of Marcus rolled his eyes.

"You mean my great stepfather?" Marcus joked as he wiped hurt from his eyes.

"Exactly. Your great stepfather. He's lousy at dominoes, but a great father." He brought seriousness back into the conversation. "Do you want Greg and Geoffrey to have a great stepfather because of your silliness?" Marcus shook his throbbing head, and Mr. Jeffries continued. "I hurt your mother, Marcus, because of selfishness. We weren't in the same situation as you and Gracie. A child wasn't in the mix, but there is no reason either way. It's for better or worse, man."

Knowing that he had come close enough to making one of the biggest mistakes of his marriage, Marcus sealed his eyes as tightly as he could. He wished he could take back his decision to have ever picked up the phone to call Michelle.

"About time," she'd answered, after seeing his name pop up on her caller ID.

"Hey. How's it going?" Marcus had pulled out of the college parking lot headed nowhere in particular for lunch. "Just thought I'd give you a call and check on you."

Automatically, Michelle knew she had a chance. As far as she was concerned, for him to even call meant that he was open for whatever she had to offer. "I'm good. Where are you? Why don't we meet for lunch?" She'd wasted no time.

Only thinking about his decision for a split second, Marcus agreed. Even when she suggested that they meet at her apartment so they'd only take one car, his decision didn't detour.

As they arrived at Michelle's apartment complex at the same time, Marcus trailed behind her. Curving through the maze, he drove until they were in front of her condo. Anticipating Michelle joining him in his truck, Marcus relaxed his stare as she yelled out to him.

"Wait just a minute. I need to get something from inside." Walking off, just to turn back once more, Michelle tapped on his passenger's side window. As Marcus let the window down, she waved for him to follow. "You may as well come in. You know how I am with time."

Only as his foot crossed the threshold did Marcus question himself about his own intentions. Watching Michelle walk, his eyes were glued to her legs. The way she walked with authority, making her heels kill the concrete, Marcus could only envision her backside that had been hiding behind her pea coat.

Since it had been a while since he'd been in her world, Michelle had moved on to bigger adventures. Even though she stayed in the same complex, she had relocated to a different location, a three-bedroom abode that offered her space for an office, a master suite, and a guest room.

Missing in action, Michelle called out from her bedroom. "I'll be out in a minute. Make yourself comfortable."

"Sure," was all he could muster as he sat on the closest piece of furniture available. Pulling his trench coat up for the give, Marcus was still peering around the contemporary room when Michelle walked back into the space. As if by choreographed design, thunder rolled through the sky just as Michelle sat by Marcus on the loveseat.

"Are you really hungry? I can make us a quick meal, some sandwiches, if you'd like. I have turkey and Swiss cheese, Dijon mustard. Is that still a favorite?" Michelle asked as she sat closer than needed. "It looks like the rain has picked up even more." She peered out the window at the dampened streets.

"Yeah it has." He turned to look directly in her eyes. Wondering if she had been thinking the same thing, Marcus tried to break his stare. He realized he didn't win as he opened his mouth and stammered out a, "M–mustard. D–Dijon mustard is s-still my favorite."

"Don't worry." Michelle had grabbed his chin as he'd tried to look away. "I'm not thinking less of you. I don't have any questions about your life at home. I'm just happy that you're here now." Thinking that she would actually wait to see what could be processed between them, she fought against it. Michelle moved in close, placing her lips on Marcus's soft mouth.

Not pushing her off, nor giving a fight, Marcus had only thought about the sandwiches that Michelle was to make as he felt her hands removing his coat for him. Allowing his ex-girlfriend supremacy over his body, Marcus only held his arms out to let the outerwear be removed. In a split second, he had thought back months on how freely Gracie had given her body to him. It was all in order to fill her womb with a child, but now, recently, she didn't have the time or the desire. At the time, he couldn't remember which it was, but only thought how Michelle was willing. Willing . . .

In full mode, Marcus had grabbed the sides of Michelle's face and forced his mouth harder onto hers. Michelle, keeping her face intact with her ex, kept the rhythm going. She then stood to ease her clothing above her waist, returning to her seated position on Marcus's lap. With his hands, Marcus had grabbed for her hips that housed no fabric. That was when the lustful passion between the two amplified.

"Marcus!" Mr. Jeffries called out, interrupting Marcus's memory from almost three months prior. "Boy, do you hear me? You're going to have to fix this. Whatever it is you think you're doing, you need to stop it. I'm telling you." The older man, now standing to his feet again, shook his head back and forth in a confused manner. Not knowing how else to get his point across to his son, he figured the truth was good enough.

"It ain't no good being out here by yourself as an old man. All I do is go to the college to teach and back home. Ain't nothing for me out there." The senior Mr. Jeffries sang his plea toward his son.

Knowing that everything his dad told him was the truth, Marcus hung his head once more. He clasped his hands together and placed them behind his neck. Marcus knew that he'd have to lose Michelle's number and come clean with his wife. On top of that, he had to get his family back on track. Marcus cried as he thought about his actions and the dilemma he'd placed his family in.

Chapter 20

It had been hours since his chopped conversation with his father, and all Marcus had energy for was to shoot a few hoops. Marcus had hated sharing such an intimate detail with Pops, but he knew his father would keep his secret, as well as point him in the right direction. Besides, he was too embarrassed to share his shortcomings with anyone else but his father. Telling Ky, Marcus knew, would taint his image and the respect that the young man held for him.

Pops was right. It had been a while since he'd shared with Marcus the mistake he had made himself, causing his once happy marriage to die. Mentally, Marcus had tried to block out the past as well, but now, because of his own betrayal, life was way too vivid—even the past he had pushed to the back of his own mind.

Shooting baskets, perfecting his lay-up and even having a one-man dunking contest, Marcus allowed his aggression to be placed on the hard dribble of his Spalding basketball. With the fall's sun and the wind on his back, thoughts of his betrayal and even the betrayal of his father entered his mind. Marcus couldn't care less about the sweat that broke out down his face. Hoping it meshed with the tears of internal pain that bled through, Marcus used all of the energy he had to try to bury his past.

It seemed as though his parents had argued ever since he could remember. Being young and not knowing there could be rules in a marriage, Marcus told his dad one night about having been approached by a strange woman who was asking questions about their family. The arguing between his parents intensified. It seemed that his mother had been listening in on the conversation that was only meant for his dad. Because of him, or so he thought, all that had been buried seemed to have resurfaced and landed on his young, weak shoulders.

"I haven't fooled around with anyone, honey." Marcus's dad had tried his best to calm down his wife. "I don't know what lady Marcus is talking about," he tried to argue.

"You know dang-on well who he's talking about—that floozy you had the fling with, the affair, whatever you want to call it." Out of disgust, Marcus's petite but feisty mother swung her arms in the air, allowing them to fall and slap her full-figured hips.

"Baby." Her weary-eyed husband sighed as he tried to comfort his wife.

Peeping through the keyhole in his parents' door, Marcus would never forget the look on his father's face or the stained tears on his mother's caramel-colored cheeks.

"Don't baby me! I thought you were through," she beat into the older Jeffries' ear as she backed herself into the corner by their shared closet, daring him to come closer. "You said that was over years ago. I believed you."

Mrs. Jeffries tilted her head as if she wanted her nightmare to remain in her dreams. Pushing into his chest, breaking their closeness, Shirl Jeffries wanted to be finished with their marriage.

"I forgave you because I didn't know. You made a fool out of me, and I didn't even know about it." Shirl swayed as she released her pain of only learning about her husband's affair after it was over. "But it won't happen no more. I want you out." Her pain climbed through her throat as her veins stretched through her even and toned skin.

"Out!" She pointed at their bedroom door, which made a young Marcus scurry on his knees through the hallway that led to the room he had shared with his younger brother until he went off to college.

Even though his dad packed bags to leave the house that night, his parents still didn't divorce until years later. Through the years, he'd tried to tell himself it wasn't his fault. He needed to believe that he wasn't the cause of his parents' divorce; and he even got himself to believe it wasn't, for a while. For some reason, never laying eyes on *that* woman again, he figured if he hadn't shared what happened that day at the bus stop, his family would still be together.

"Would I even be in this mess if I'd just kept my mouth shut?" Marcus's adult mind questioned himself as he fought the light wind while dribbling to half court. Trying to find another place to lay the blame for his disrespectful rumble with Michelle, Marcus took off at a fast speed. Taking only three hard dribbles before throwing the ball toward the backboard, leaping up almost as high as the goal, Marcus grabbed for the orange ball before it had a chance to land, then pounced it into the net.

With both feet firmly landing on the ground right beneath the net, Marcus placed his hands on his knees as his gaze followed the bouncing ball. In no hurry to run after the threatening object, Marcus closed his eyes and welcomed the same wind that had fought him. Remembering the questions he'd asked no one in particular, he answered, "It's your own fault, Marcus. You can't even blame Gracie for this one."

Losing his balance and not fighting to keep it, Marcus found himself on the ground. Sitting with his knees bent, all Marcus had energy for was to sit low and look high. All he had to do now was wait. Remaining a man after God's own heart, Marcus knew that it would be sooner rather than later that he would have to reveal what he'd done.

same wind that had fought him. Remembering the questions he'd asked no one in particular, he answered, "It's your own fault, Marcus. You can't even blame Oracle for this one."

Losing his balance and not wanting to keep it, Marcus found himself on the ground. Sitting with his knees bent, all Marcus had energy for was to sit low and look high. All he had to do now was wait. Remaining a man after God's own heart, Marcus knew that it would be sooner rather than later that he would have to reveal what he'd done.

Chapter 21

"I'm tired." Michelle had finally allowed her thoughts to leave their holding place. In the midst of rubbing her slightly swollen feet and ankles, Ky slowed his pace and looked into Michelle's gaze.

"Just lie there, Chelle." He used the shortened version of her name that he considered a pet name for intimate purposes between the two. "We don't have to go anywhere tonight. I'm good." He gave her an effortless, clean smile, hoping that his craving to constantly be in her presence showed. Though it had only been two months, Ky didn't stray from what his heart felt.

"No, Ky. I'm–I'm tired." She looked up, back into Ky's eyes, just as whole teardrops fell freely from hers. Hoping that he would grasp exactly what she wanted him to define, Michelle knew she would have to elaborate.

"What's wrong, Michelle?" Ky straightened his back, halting the impromptu massage all together. "Baby, what's—"

Avoiding his question, Michelle couldn't hold in her emotions any longer. "I didn't really want to be bothered with you. I just . . . I just planned on one encounter with you, Ky." Michelle kept her sights on the striking bachelor who held a unique cleft in his cheek. "You are so sweet. I don't want to hurt you, and I know you probably won't want to further this friendship, but . . ." Her words trailed off.

"But what, Michelle?" He inched closer, removing her feet from his lap. Ky brought his body inches from the woman for whom he had fallen hard. "How do you know what I want, Michelle? It's you who won't let me in. I adore you." He made his true feelings known. His butterscotch skin oozed with goose bumps, visually showing his undying ache for Michelle.

Cradling his face with her hands, Michelle brought their foreheads to greet. Motionless, she allowed who she had become to be revealed. "I've done a lot of bad things, Ky." Accepting the kiss he placed on the tip of her nose, she continued her spiel before he interrupted her or she lost her courage. "I'm not a saint. At times, I've only gone to church because I was looking for a man." Her eyes tightened shut, now embarrassed about the person she was. "I've lied, I've cheated, and at times, didn't care about any of it. I've even seduced a married man."

Knowing that people had pasts that they were not always partial to, himself included, Ky didn't know what to say. He liked Michelle, maybe love was a closer description, but he didn't know how to take the news. Not wanting his facial expression to change, Ky just sat until he knew what to say or do.

There was a deep contemplation on Michelle's part. She didn't know if she had said too much, but she knew that there wasn't a choice. She had to tell Ky all that had transpired since their two-and-a-half-month meeting. Her going to church with him for the last few weeks had made a difference in the short amount of time. But like she heard Ky's dad, the preacher, say, "Once you've been born again, it's hard to fool the Holy Spirit within you."

Michelle had felt the twinge, the pull that people felt within when they were in the process of crossing over into a personal relationship with God. With Ky still having his own struggles but fighting to become a man after God's own heart, he'd led by example, a life one can live in the presence of the Lord.

"A change." She let the words that best described what she felt leave her lips.

"Huh, baby?" Ky was still confused.

There was no holding back. Michelle knew she had to put it all on the table. She had to be transparent—a word that she had learned would grant one freedom from worldly destruction. "There's a change in me, Ky," Michelle announced. The change only started when she began to know God.

Agreeing with a nod, Ky said, "I know, honey." He held her close.

"There's a change . . . in here." For the first time outside of her doctor, Michelle let someone know of her pregnancy. Rubbing her stomach that no longer belonged only to her, Michelle came to grips with the child that had been placed in her womb. "I'm pregnant." She reluctantly let the admission slip through her lips. Right then, she freed herself from her own bondage.

Ky shared no thought past what Michelle had just told him. And although it had only been two and a half months since they'd been in each other's lives, Ky didn't let what Michelle had just shared crowd his feelings. "We . . . we're having a baby?"

Stroking the back of Michelle's hair, Ky kissed an open space on her face and shot from his seat, ready to celebrate the news he'd been given. Right as he was set to kick off a one-man celebration, Michelle stood beside the man of her dreams. Confused as to how he could even still consider loving her with the news she had just shared, Michelle shook her head. The boisterous cry she released put a halt to his own happiness.

"Honey, what's wrong? I don't understand. Aren't we supposed to be happy?" He followed her as she walked away from the living area, planting herself in front of the bay window fully decorated with an assortment of chocolate- and turquoise-colored throw pillows.

Ky had been raised by both parents and five older sisters. Women and emotions were a duo that he'd become accustomed to over the years, yet a pregnant, crying girlfriend was always a new adventure. "Is it just hormones, or is it—"

"I d–don't know," Michelle was able to stammer out through her truthful, weary tears.

Half relieved to know that Michelle was just as confused as he was, Ky wanted to hold the woman who would bear his child. Maybe she would do him the honor of being his bride. If so, the child they were having would only be the beginning of their offspring.

"It's okay that you don't know. I think your doctor will have to put you on some vitamins or something to regulate—"

"No!" Michelle was upset in a flash. "That's not it, Ky!" With Kleenex tissues dangling in her hand, Michelle blurted out what she figured would cut all ties between the two of them. "I don't know if the baby is yours."

As if the moment of a lifetime had just passed him by, Ky dropped the shoulders that had, for the moment, held up his proud chest. "Whoa," he said between head nods. "Wait. So . . . your baby"—he pointed at Michelle's midsection, still covered with a size medium Marciano blouse—"may not be my baby?" He tried to do the math, but knew right away that he wanted Michelle whether the child was his or not.

Unenthusiastically, he said, "I'm still here, Michelle." He threw up his hands. "Unless, of course, you are still with the father, or want to be with the father?" Ky waited.

She shook her head from side to side. "I'm not. I can't be." The hope that Ky really did love her sobered Michelle.

Returning to their former embrace, Ky allowed his stature to crowd Michelle's person. "Fine. We'll figure it out. We . . . we will." He thought of what to say in order to fill in the deadpan of not knowing. "We'll just get in contact with him to see what he wants to do, Chell. Okay?" Resting his chin on the top of her head, Ky closed his eyes extra tight before asking the question he knew wouldn't be easy for any man: "Who is he?"

Chapter 22

In the middle of switching her volunteer hospital shifts, Gracie readied herself to leave as she heard singing coming from the doorway. "Miracles and blessings, Gracie," Herlene sang as she made her way into the hospital room. "How are you, dear?"

Her widened eyes and loudness set the mood in the hospital room before Herlene was even settled. Gracie just figured her friend was a morning person and thought no further as Herlene started to sing once more.

"Well, I guess I better say good since you're coming in here all chipper." She hugged her friend's mother. "And who is this that you have with you?" Gracie asked as she knelt down and offered her hand to Kenya.

"This is Kenya, my youngest daughter."

"Hi, Kenya. It's nice to meet you, sweetie." Gracie waved a hello in James's direction after she released the girl's hand, and then turned her attention back to Kenya when the child spoke.

"Hi, Mrs. Gracie. It's good to meet you too," the ten-year-old announced. The wide smile on her face resembled that of her much older sister.

"She's so proud," Mrs. Herlene added. "I finally talked to her the other night about everything, and she begged to come and see Kendra." Herlene put her hand over her mouth as if she were whispering. Not realizing everyone in the room heard her, Herlene continued, "I didn't want to, but"—she looked back at her husband—"James said it wouldn't hurt. He said it may even help." She laughed as if a joke had been shared between the two.

With her eyebrows crunched, Gracie wondered why Mrs. Herlene was so happy, but drew her attention to Kenya as the girl spoke again.

"Yeah. I wanted to come see my sister because I've never met her. We have lots and lots of pictures at home of Kendra when she was little like me, but I wanted to see her for real."

"That's nice, Kenya. Kendra would love that," Gracie said before she actually stopped to think whether her friend would be happy about the whole family reunion. "Well, let me leave you all alone. Um, Mrs. Herlene, can I speak with you in the hall for a minute before I leave?" Gracie started the short walk, rubbing her back as she made her way out the door.

"Sure." Herlene walked toward Kenya and gently rubbed her chin. "Honey, listen to your daddy while I go outside with Mrs. Gracie. I'll be right back, and then you have to get ready so Daddy can drop you off at school, okay?"

"Okay, Mommy," Kenya replied.

When they passed the threshold of the hospital's door, Gracie swiftly turned on her heels as if she were a soldier. "You okay, Mrs. Herlene?"

"Yeah, Gracie, I'm fine. Uh, I was late taking my blood pressure medication this morning. Shhh, don't tell James, though." She quieted her voice, knowing it had been weeks since she'd actually unscrewed the medication cap. More recently, she'd unscrewed the cap on a bottle of liquor.

"Oh, okay. You better keep up with that." Gracie eased her mind. "Here." She placed a single key into Herlene's palm.

"What is this to?" Herlene asked with a desperate look on her face.

"Mrs. Herlene, I can't pretend that I don't know what all happened in Kendra's life . . . because I know. I know how my friend has ached for a mother. She's longed to be a part of something that meant something." With her eyes filling, Gracie allowed a deep breath to enter into her lungs. "When you talk about seeing all the good, bad, and the ugly, I've seen it all. I've been a part of that with my friend, and now, Kendra is on the brink of crossing from this life. I don't want her to, but God knows best." Remembering the key she'd given Herlene, Gracie continued as she held on to the older woman's closed hand. "This key is to Dillian and Kendra's home. I've only been back once, but I feel it's time that you find out who your daughter is. Find out what she needs and what you have missed out on. I trust you, Mrs. Herlene." She tilted her head to get a reaction from the older lady.

"I don't know what to say. I don't know if she wants me to." Herlene openly cried, being knocked out of her drunken stupor.

"I'll worry about that later. I'm talking about the now."

Shaking her head in an agreeable manner, Herlene took the keys from Gracie and cuffed them to her heart. She bowed her head and silently thanked God.

"Thank you, Gracie. My mom told me that whenever I got myself together, I'd get my daughter back in my life. She didn't live to see this, but I know that she is playing a part in it. I won't let you down, Gracie."

Hugging Herlene was all Gracie had strength enough to do. She'd known the lady for only a short while, but in the midst of becoming friends, Gracie realized that all of Herlene's baggage had started from a broken heart and progressed. She had an inkling that there was more to the story than just Kendra's real dad breaking Herlene's heart. Gracie was sure that that was what had put Herlene on a warpath of destruction, but she didn't push the lady to revisit the hurtful truth. In due time, she felt, Herlene would open up.

Upon re-entering the hospital room, seeing both daughters and her husband—her family—Herlene allowed the tears to resurface. Hearing Kenya singing Yolanda Adams's "Still I Rise" to a sleeping Kendra, Herlene perched her shoulder on the wall and just rested there. She'd always wondered why Kenya picked such adult songs to sing, even with solos that she performed at church. Herlene had always said that Kenya had indeed been on this earth once before.

Grateful that God had allowed her to be sound in her mind, body, and soul to witness a time such as this, Herlene sat back quietly and enjoyed the meaningful words that flowed from her youngest child's mouth to her oldest child's soul.

short while, but in the midst of bonding friends, Gracie realized that all of Herlene's baggage had stemmed from a broken heart and progressed. She had an inkling that there was more to the story than just Kendra's real dad breaking Herlene's heart. Gracie was sure that that was what had put Herlene on a warpath of destruction, but she didn't push the lady to revisit the hurtful truth. In due time, she felt, Herlene would open up.

Upon re-entering the hospital room, seeing both daughters and her husband—her family—Herlene allowed the tears to resurface. Hearing Kenya singing Yolanda Adams's "Still I Rise" to a sleeping Kendra, Herlene perched her shoulder on the wall and just rested there. She'd always wondered why Kenya picked such adult songs to sing, even with solos that she performed at church. Herlene had always said that Kenya had indeed been on this earth once before.

Grateful that God had allowed her to be sound in her mind, body, and soul to witness a time such as this, Herlene sat back quietly and enjoyed the meaningful words that flowed from her youngest child's mouth to her oldest child's soul.

Chapter 23

Herlene was ever so grateful for the new start that Gracie had allotted her, but days passed before she used the key that had been passed along to her. She wanted to make sure that God was pleased with the decision. Herlene spent the empty time trying to fast and pray that God would give her the answer she was looking for. Between listening and waiting for God's answer, the liquor bottle had become her excuse as to why she wasn't worthy of a thousandth chance.

Her courage to fight her old demons came as Kendra's doctor entered her room one afternoon. Not knowing the extent of the wedge between Herlene and Kendra, he asked for the mother to bring in a pair of personal pajamas for her daughter. Herlene figured that the time had come. She could have easily gone to the nearest department store and bought Kendra an outfit, but being that she listened to God when He spoke, she knew that her answer had indeed come.

Herlene asked Gracie, who was now six months pregnant, to arrive for her shift a little earlier than normal so she could make her way over to her daughter's home. Herlene drove across town in the direction of homes that she only dreamed of for herself. Admiring the scenery on the drive to her daughter's house in far North Dallas, a glad feeling swept over Herlene as she praised God for keeping her daughter all of the years she was unable to.

Herlene had fought a battle to regain who she rightfully was. One heartache had caused so much damage in her soul that she took what Mitch had done to her years prior and let it reign over who she was and what she was meant to be. She knew now that she had been serving the wrong god. "It's all about you, God," she sang out as she drove.

Her life had traveled down the road of drinking uncontrollably to abusing street drugs to using the hardcore substance of crack cocaine. No matter what, Herlene still couldn't run from what one person had done to her. But it wasn't until she had really, truly given her life over to God that she realized that she had done it to herself.

"So what if he left? So what if he abandoned you? There is a different approach to putting that behind you and moving forward," she had shared with many of the young, single mothers at her church who had found themselves in the same predicament she had been in. Herlene had finally allowed her life to be on display in order to be a living testimony for others.

From the directions that Gracie had given, Herlene knew that she would be well pleased on her daughter's blessed living. Not familiar with driving on the toll way, Herlene exited I635, the Preston Road exit, and headed on a slightly longer route into Frisco. With all the winding roads that led up a small hill, Herlene let out a relieved sigh when she pulled her car in the curved driveway. Turning her key counterclockwise, Herlene sat and admired the outside of the home.

"It's now or never." Throwing her eyes toward the roof of her Ford Focus, Herlene prayed. "Lord, give me strength and wisdom. Oh," she almost forgot, "and thank you, Lord, for your son, Jesus."

It took twelve missed calls from her husband before Herlene stirred from her sleep. Having been in the deepest drunken sleep ever, Herlene's body oozed into the comfort of the unfamiliar sheets.

"I'm up, I'm up!" There was a groggy stir in her throat as she reluctantly sat up. Through blurred vision, Herlene reached for her phone on the nightstand. "Hello?"

"*Hello? Hello?* You have the nerve to answer the phone with *hello*? Do you not know that you *ain't* at home?" James dove into his wife through the line with much concern in his tone.

"James?" she responded.

"Don't James me. Do you have something you need to tell me, Herlene? Last time I talked to you, you said you were on your way home." Pacing the kitchen floor, looking at the percolating coffee pot, James didn't know how to calm himself.

"What time is it?" Herlene asked while looking directly at the clock that she'd given her daughter and Dillian for their wedding. Even though she didn't attend the wedding, she wanted to be a part of her daughter's day. She didn't even know if Kendra knew it had come from her, but seeing the clock on display was thanks enough for her. Holding her hand up to her head, Herlene needed to gather her composure.

"Let me call you back, James. I must have fallen asleep last night over here at Kendra's." She hung up without saying good-bye. Herlene reached out and touched the clock with her index finger, and as she felt the early morning tear falling, she wiped the coldness from her face.

Taking in a deep breath, Herlene looked around the room and inhaled. The previous months caught up with her thinking, and she suddenly became sick to her stomach. Jumping up from her seated position, she made her way into the bathroom.

"I've got to stop this," Herlene spoke into the porcelain commode as she heaved most of the brown liquor she had consumed the night before.

It was last night that she realized that her reconciliation with her daughter was only one-sided. Herlene began feeling sorry for her daughter and angry with herself. For that, she only found solace with the bottle. As fast as she could, Herlene ducked her head once again into the toilet and released her half-empty stomach's content. After wiping her mouth with the back of her hand and flushing the commode, Herlene slowly made her way back into the master suite.

She had jumped way off track, and Herlene knew that she would have to face the pain that had knocked her backward once again. Now that Kendra had somewhat been placed back in her life, so had the thoughts of Mitch. Not doubting God, Herlene knew that He had once purged her old doubt, and would not hesitate to do it again. Raising her hands despite her liquor-induced headache, Herlene praised God for the very moment. She stood and looked around the room, then took her time gathering her items in preparation to leave.

The night before, as she headed over to Kendra's, Gracie had warned that Kendra's home would probably look a mess. That was an understatement. She had stopped at the dollar store to get cleaning equipment, then headed right over to Kendra's house with plans to stay until things were tidy. Gracie had told her the entire story of what had gone on. Once she walked in the disarrayed home, she believed it even more.

When she had initially walked inside Kendra's house, the story on how Gracie had found Herlene's daughter raced back into her memory. Kendra's best friend had filled Herlene in on how Kendra's bout with depression since college had made her like millions of people: one prescription away from losing it all. Through the tears, Gracie had told Herlene of how more than once, she'd walked into their dorm room and found her friend on the brink of death due to self-inflicted injuries. Gracie told Herlene that it was her name—Kendra's own mother—that was on constant replay out of Kendra's mouth each time she tried to harm herself, and Herlene fought not to give up hope that the future for her and her daughter could be bright.

Nothing made Herlene feel right inside until she made up her mind that she'd had enough. She'd had enough of giving up and was ready to take responsibility for not being the mother she should have been. When Gracie offered her Kendra's house key, Herlene knew it was time. She was grateful that she'd made that decision.

Now, sitting in the middle of her daughter's freshly made bed, Herlene looked at the work that she'd completed. Starting from the front room, Herlene had cleaned her daughter's entire house. It had been past midnight before Herlene finally fluffed out the goose down blanket that now lay on her daughter's bed. The air smelled of burnt oranges, the mirror had a clear glare, and the ceiling fans housed no dust. All the work she'd done made her proud to say that she'd finally put in time for her child. Time *with* her child still lingered.

Finding wine in her daughter's house last night, Herlene made it a point to indulge herself as she cleaned throughout the night. She had laughed through her drinking spell as she ran across photos of her silly-acting daughter, and cried when she saw her daughter's diplomas. Herlene was saddened that she hadn't made an effort to help mold Kendra into a woman. She had missed too many of her daughter's important days: high school graduation, college graduation, and even her wedding. Even when Kendra finally revealed her HIV status to her family, Herlene hadn't been there. She gasped at the thought that she hadn't been there for Kendra when she needed her most, and it was at that moment that Herlene put aside the glass she had been sipping from and began drinking straight from the bottle.

Herlene knew with all of last night's doings, there was nothing more important than for her to slide from her sitting position to kneel beside the bed. Intending to rest on the side of the sleep space until she got wind to put on her shoes to leave, Herlene prayed to rid the past.

She only wished she were sober from last night's drunken stupor. Having consumed a whole bottle of wine and two half pints of liquor that she had stashed away on her person, Herlene felt the feeling that she only experienced when God tugged at her. She knew that shame would soon crowd her mind, but Herlene placed her hands together and prayed. She started by praying for her daughter, then for strength, forgiveness, and boldness. Herlene needed God in order to go through what she knew would no doubt creep into her present.

"Lord, I've always said I needed your help, but God, I now know I have to want it in order to receive it," she managed to say in between her hiccups and crying. "Lord, I've let my Kendra down so many times. I'm ashamed to even go down memory lane, but you know. That girl saw me strung out, drunk, moving back and forth from man to man. . . . I–I just haven't been there for her, and I'm tired of it. Right now, she needs me more than even I know." Herlene opened her eyes for the first time since she'd started praying. So full of grief and badgering herself, Herlene couldn't find any more words, and she started to moan.

She knew that if she couldn't say another thing verbally, God knew her heart. Finding strength once more, she continued. "I didn't think I could do it, but she was stronger than me. She wanted to go to school; I didn't help her. I wouldn't lead the way. I was too into myself and what I wanted and thought I needed. Please, Lord, forgive me for forsaking my child the right of having a mother. I'm alive and well, and yet I didn't give her the desires of her heart—a mother's love."

Thinking back on Kendra, Herlene looked at the ceiling through her bloodshot eyes. When she looked up, it was as though she could look God right in His eyes. "I mean it, Lord. If you'd please give me another chance to be a mother for Kendra, before you take . . . well, Lord, I'll be forever indebted to you," she concluded as she remained leaning against her daughter's bed.

With her head pounding, Herlene thought about the whole scenario of Mitch being brought to her present. "Mitch. Oh, Lord, what have I done? I've ruined too many lives. Let them forgive me."

Swaying, waiting on something, anything, Herlene heard the small voice, knowing it wasn't her own. Racing to her feet, she headed swiftly to the living room in search of her purse. Herlene couldn't wait to get home. She couldn't wait to share with James what the Lord had spoken to her heart . . . what He'd told her to do.

Chapter 24

"Are you kidding me? Are you freaking kidding me, man?" Ky spat anger from his vocals as soon as Marcus and Gracie stepped foot out of the vehicle. Ky had been trying to get in contact with Marcus for days. When he realized that Marcus had taken a few days off from classes, he made it a point to show up at the Jeffries's home.

The smile that Gracie had reserved for Ky quickly dissipated when she heard pure venom. "Oh my Lord, Marcus," she called out to her husband when she saw Ky running up to him with closed fists. Gracie ushered the twins toward the house, hoping to keep their young eyes from what was to come. She tried to match their steps with hers as she ran with the key in hand toward their awaiting door. Keeping the twins focused on getting inside, Gracie grimaced as she heard, rather than saw, a punch land.

Not knowing what could possibly be going on, a worried Gracie made sure that Gregory and

Geoffrey went deep into the house. She filled the living room space with their bodies. With one swipe, she picked up the cordless phone, dropped her purse, and made her way back to the front of the house.

Peering out of the window, a worried Gracie hadn't a clue what had gotten into Ky. She knew that Ky always looked up to Marcus as a big brother, but with the scuffling the grown men participated in on her front lawn, Gracie stood on the verge of calling 911. Only when she noticed that both had become short-winded did she feel safe enough to move toward the cracked front door.

Flushed and holding the bottom of her protruding belly, Gracie opened the door a tad more. She wanted to find out what the commotion had been about.

"Man, wha–what is up w–with you?" Marcus made sure he kept his distance to avoid another round of fist throwing.

"You know! You know what's up! You tell me, mister. I–I hope you find someone that's for you," Ky said in a mimicking tone. "I'ma hook you up."

"Huh? What are you talking about, Ky? I haven't hooked you up with anyone." Marcus tried to recall if he had, knowing good and well that he hadn't. It had been an ongoing joke in the office. People were always saying they were going to hook Ky up with someone.

"Michelle! I'm talking about Michelle. I thought I found my wife. I thought the baby could possibly be mine! She loves me, Marcus," Ky ranted in no particular order. "You snatched it all away." He charged at Marcus once more after lingering on the thought that he might not be Michelle's baby's father.

"Ugh! Ky, man . . . whoa! Whoa," he pleaded, pushing Ky off of him once more. Not aware of Gracie's presence at the door, Marcus wanted to understand what was going on. "First off, Michelle who?" His mind worked faster than he could speak. "Wait, I never said anything about hooking you up with Michelle." Marcus added worry lines to his forehead. He couldn't believe what was actually happening before him. Hitting his forehead with a dirty hand, Marcus was reminded of meeting Michelle at Benihana's. "Ky, that day was the first time I'd seen her in years. I called you to the restaurant because I was having issues with my wife, my baby—" His mind snapped to what Ky had said earlier. "Wait—a baby? What?" Marcus moved in slow motion.

"That's right, man. When you saw her at the restaurant, that wasn't your last time seeing her, was it? Was it, Marcus? Michelle's pregnant, and guess whose baby it is?" Ky shook his head in disgust at his friend, the friend he thought to be the family man that he wanted to be one day. "I thought better of you, dude."

Seeing Ky turn to leave, Marcus knew that he had to make him understand. "You don't know the story, Ky. You don't know the truth." Marcus turned in the direction of the noise coming from the inside of the house. Not knowing if it was his wife, Marcus continued. "Man, I haven't seen Michelle in three months."

With Ky looking in the same direction, and Gracie visible to only him, he continued his spiel. He didn't really want to throw the situation in Gracie's face, but Ky needed to get the hurt off of his chest. "Yeah, whatever." He faced his mentor once more. "And I don't know you either." He lingered a second before heading back to his vehicle. Snatching his baseball cap that had fallen to the earth, Ky didn't look back before he drove from the premises.

Gathering as much composure as he could, Marcus slowed his steps the closer he got to the front door. His wife's shadow showed before he actually laid eyes upon her.

"Gracie," was all Marcus could spring from his tongue before he saw tears in his wife's eyes as she treaded as fast as she could from his outstretched hand.

Chapter 25

"Hello, Michelle." Marcus was disheartened when he heard the voice answer on the other end of the line.

"How are you, Marcus? It's good to hear from you," Michelle added, hoping to start fresh. She knew that she couldn't take back all that had transpired since last seeing Marcus, but she hoped to make up for all of her wrongdoings. "Look, Ky told me what ha—"

"You're pregnant?" he had whispered into the phone as if there was a recorder in his truck. Marcus couldn't stand seeing his wife in pain. The way he saw Gracie walking away from him, right after Ky had left the scene, kept playing over and over in his mind. If it were the last thing to do, he wanted to get a clear understanding of what Ky was talking about.

"You told Ky that you're pregnant by me, Michelle? Do you know that man came over to my house and made a scene in front of my wife and children? What type of game are you playing?"

Alone in her office, sitting behind her glass-topped desk, Michelle stood and walked to her office door and slammed it shut. "Marcus, please!" Michelle countered, trying to display the generous feeling that arose from her soul. "First off, you act as though I've made you do something." She breathed heavily, not wanting to retreat to the side of her that she now considered to be laid to rest. "Look, Marcus, before this gets any deeper than it already has—"

"Any deeper and we'd be stepping in it, Michelle!" Marcus knew there was no arguing over the truth. "Can you explain to me, in clear English, what Ky was speaking of? How do you even know Ky? What did you do, start following me again? Don't you think you put me through enough—my family through enough—for a lifetime?"

"Marcus, please, it's not that serious. I didn't plan to have a baby. And I know it's hard for you to believe me, but I–I'm sorry."

"Sorry? What is sorry going to do? What is sorry going to do for my wife, who had to hear Ky saying that you're pregnant by me? My wife is pregnant with our child, Michelle!" He held in the masculine tone of his voice, though it screeched from his throat. Pressing the brake as fast as he could, Marcus snatched his truck from the busy road as he felt his stomach churn. Grabbing the door handle, Marcus pushed the door until it swung open. Releasing his stomach's contents onto the ground outside, he took his time in regaining his composure.

He felt as though he'd aged in a short amount of time. Marcus leaned in onto his driver's side seat. He blindly searched for his cell phone that had hit the floor once he stopped the vehicle. "Are you saying you're pregnant? By me?" he said with closed eyes and a sour taste in his mouth. "That's all I need to know."

A pacing Michelle halted as she responded to Marcus's question. "I–I . . ." Michelle stammered.

With no energy left for a physical or verbal fight, Marcus found enough strength to ask just once more. When there wasn't an answer, Marcus recalled the actual events of the day. "I just want to know if you're saying it's my baby, Michelle. We didn't actually have sex." He finally pulled himself upright in his seat. "I can only recall you sitting on my lap."

"With no underwear on, Marcus. With your privates exposed, Marcus. It doesn't take much."

"But I pushed you off of me."

"Yeah, but not before. Look, Marcus, I'm not trying to play any games with you. I know it's hard for you to even listen to anything I have to say, but I felt that the truth had to be told. I'm seeing Ky, and there is a chance that he's my child's father. Then there is always that chance that you are as well." When Marcus didn't respond, Michelle worked on showing the new her.

"I've gotten saved, Marcus. I've made plenty of mistakes, and I'm truly sorry for putting you in the middle of my mess. All I can say is that I wish none of this had happened. But we're here now."

Dropping his cell phone, Marcus knelt down, but felt too weak to even pick up his four hundred–dollar communication port. Not wanting to believe the conversation he'd just had, Marcus wiped the sweat beads that had suddenly appeared on his face and aimed his attention at finding a way out of the position he'd put his family in.

Not since his parents' divorce had Marcus found himself crying, pouring out his soul through so many tears. "Lord, what have I done?" Marcus asked God once again as he sat in his truck. "What did I do? What in the world did I do?" he asked the dark night that stared back at him.

Marcus had been driving around Dallas/Fort Worth all day, and still hadn't reached a conclusion. Now that night had fallen, he still didn't want to venture home. He didn't know how he would ever be able to look into his wife's face.

"How could I just act as if nothing happened, God? I cheated on my wife—got someone pregnant. Gracie doesn't deserve any of this." Marcus ran his hands roughly over his head then added his hands back to the steering wheel. "I'm not *man* enough to tell her how I feel about *anything,* but then I cheat on her?" Marcus's anger toward himself mounted. Just when the tears crowded his ducts blurring his vision, his compact disc changer skipped to the next disc in the chamber.

A live recording of Bishop Paul Morton's worship song, "Bow Down and Worship," rang through his speakers. Knowing that his crying surely wouldn't stop any time soon, Marcus pulled his vehicle off of the road once again. Throwing the truck's gear into park, he sat. With the car still running, Marcus brought his hands to the bottom of the steering wheel and allowed the words to soak into his thinking.

"I do need you, Father. I needed you b–before this mess," he cried out. "Lord, I've tried it my own way. I've slipped, I–I've fallen, God."

Bow down and worship Him. . . . Enter in.

Adding his face to the steering wheel's middle, Marcus rocked his body back and forth. As the music reached its threshold of praise, Marcus had no choice but to be obedient to the Spirit and praise God.

"Forgive me, Lord. I bow down to you, Lord. I've prayed and cried. I've prayed and cried. But I just haven't fully trusted you, God." There was a burning in the pit of his chest, and before he knew what he was doing, Marcus threw his hands in the small space above his head. "I–I've stepped out on my marriage, Lord. Cleanse me, Father." Not being able to control his emotions, Marcus opened his mouth, only to find nothing escaping. Not being able to come up with the words that were heavy on his heart, he hummed his sorrows away. Releasing his tears until the feeling of God's presence filled his heart, Marcus praised God for the forgiveness he hoped to receive.

Chapter 26

She needed more than energy. All of her prescribed iron pills wouldn't be able to help her out of bed. Pushing the number two on her cell phone, Gracie having Jolie on speed dial was the only thing left that she wanted to do before falling into bed fully clothed.

Holding her composure was what she did until Jolie came to pick up the boys, taking them for an overnight stay at her own home. As soon as the front door was locked and the alarm was set, Gracie let out a long, drawn-out, merciless cry, right where she was in the foyer.

Slugging her way up the wooden staircase, she realized all of her lingering doubts had come true right on top of her manicured lawn. Recalling the business card she'd found in her husband's laundry, Gracie could only think, *Marcus did have contact with Michelle.* What type of contact he had, Gracie still couldn't believe.

Never in a million years she would've thought Marcus to stoop so low. Yes, he was against her having a baby, their own child, for someone else . . . and yes, she had finally come around to realizing that her plans weren't the best. But Marcus having an affair with Michelle . . . Gracie didn't want to believe it.

She barely made it into their bedroom, and before she thrust her drained body onto their pillow-top mattress, she dug into the back drawer of her armoire. Bypassing all of her personals, she had to have it. Slinging clothes onto their Berber-carpeted floor or wherever they landed, Gracie searched for the card she had held onto, wishing she'd never have to retrieve it. Michelle's business card. With the piece of off-colored information in her hand, Gracie sank into her bed.

Not keeping up with time, she only rolled from one side of the bed to the other. Not caring in which direction Marcus had run, Gracie immediately blamed herself.

"Oh my God. It hurts. It hurts so bad," she cried out, drawing her body closer. Wanting to curse Marcus for turning to another woman, Gracie tried to prop herself up in bed, but with extra pregnancy weight and no get-up and-go, she just gave up.

"Just stop, Gracie. Just stop it." She cornered her own thoughts. Lying flat on her back on her favorite feather pillow, Gracie wiped her face with her left hand. Staring at her wedding band, Gracie whimpered. "Who am I kidding? Lord," she said, breathing deeply with the answer already in her heart, "did I run him away? Did I push him *that* far?" She looked at the tattered business card that had been squeezed and sweat upon.

Gracie was still the strong woman she had always known herself to be. She was never one to think women had to take all the blame for a failed relationship. But then again, she always believed right was right and wrong was wrong. Gracie had been wrong when she landed her family in the mess of the century.

Deep down, Gracie knew; she knew that what she had done was wrong. Worse than cheating on Marcus, Gracie had betrayed him in another fashion. She had allowed herself to step in between him and his position as the husband, the head of their household.

Always wanting to help others, Gracie hadn't even thought about the hurt she was causing her own family. Tears running down the sides of her face, landing in her ears, Gracie just lay in the midst of all that she had done, all that had transpired, and thought.

Guilt was all over her. Though she hoped the same guilt was riding Marcus's wave, Gracie dared ask God to pull her out of the mess she had boxed her family in. One particular song was all that came to mind.

Never one to claim singing as one of her gifts, Gracie believed by saying a few words, the Lord would hear her cry. "Precious Lord, take my hand," was all she said as she grabbed for the throw lying across her bed and then napped with the information of her nemesis ever so present in her palm.

Chapter 27

Life had progressed, and the friendship had granted a trust between the two ladies. With their own church anniversary near, Herlene and James invited Marcus, Gracie, and the twins to attend. Kenya made the mistake of spoiling the surprise that she and her mother had for Gracie.

"Mrs. Gracie, I can't wait to see your face when me and Mommy give you our gift. Oops!" Kenya turned quickly, looking up at her mother. "I wasn't supposed to tell you. Sorry, Mommy."

"It's okay, Kenya. She still don't know what it is. Well"—Herlene turned her attention toward Gracie as Kenya left the two women alone—"service is about to get started. I'm so glad you all made it." She patted Gracie on her shoulder and rubbed the head of one of the boys. Viewing Gracie's husband walking down the pew toward them, Herlene greeted Marcus. "It's good to see you again. Seems like it's been a while," she added. Although she saw Gracie regularly, Herlene knew she had indeed been trying her best to keep distance from Gracie's husband.

"Likewise, Mrs. Herlene. I don't know. You may see me more often now. Your husband said he put some meat on the grill for us for after church. It may be hard to get rid of me now." Marcus stared at the older woman.

Oh great, she thought. "Goodness, these two can't keep their mouths hushed. I told that man to keep his mouth closed until after church. Let me get on up here." She turned and made her way to one of the front pews.

Church service was an awesome experience for Gracie and Marcus, even though they were praising God for different reasons. Not often had they ventured outside of their own church home, but thus far, it was well worth it. Even though they had yet to sit and talk about everything they needed to discuss, Gracie still wanted their life to resemble what it had been for the past years. When the real talk did start, Gracie knew that the conversation would grow from one baby to two.

Marcus had tried to talk to her regarding his infidelity, but Gracie wasn't there yet. She gave him about a minute a day to even breathe the story to her, but nothing more. Every inch of her wanted to run as far away from him as she could. Because she felt that she owed her children the benefit of a household that didn't crowd them out with grown folks' issues, Gracie didn't leave. Talk was scarce, but she felt the time to confront her feelings was nearing. If Marcus had indeed fathered someone else's child, there were things that needed to happen. What exactly those things were, Gracie hadn't a clue.

Gracie had spent several weeks going back and forth, staying as far away from Marcus as she could. It had only been within the last week that her eyes had returned to their natural color from the red that her crying had turned them to. She had packed her bags at least two times, planning to leave her husband even though her heart loved him dearly. She prayed, fought, and questioned God about why their lives had been moving in the direction they had. When she thought back on the drastic decision that she'd made and coerced her husband into making, Gracie knew that she had pushed Marcus into a corner. Jeremiah 11:29 would always jump to her memory. God knew every step they were making. She just prayed He would answer sooner rather than later.

Looking through the church program, Gracie read the announcements and the service times that were offered. When she ventured to the back, where "the sick and shut-in list" was posted, Gracie skimmed the names. Right as she read Kendra McNab's name in bold letters among the others, Gracie heard an angelic voice glide through the speakers and into the air.

"The safest place . . . in the whole wide world . . . is in the will of God." Mrs. Herlene was standing in front of the congregation and belting out a rendition of a Karen Clark-Sheard song. Not stepping on Karen's toes, Herlene was creating her own masterpiece of the same melodies. She swayed notes and put them in spots that only she could. Standing, joining a few others who had felt the Spirit enter their hearts, Gracie gave Herlene her support.

"Go 'head on! Sing for the Lord," Gracie yelled while throwing her hands in the air.

Just when she thought it couldn't get any better, Herlene rounded out a few notes, dwindling down her section of the song. As the organ kept playing, the guitar arranged an entrance for the next melody. Gracie almost choked when she heard Kenya's voice before she saw her rise from the front pew with a microphone in her hand.

"Take your time, baby," Gracie hollered out as she wiped tears from her eyes, thinking about Kendra, Marcus, and the baby that she was carrying. Now, with the possibility that she would have to play stepmother to another baby, Gracie became emotional and realized she had more weight on her shoulders than she had recognized. With her arms extended and her head held back, Gracie became happy with the joy of the Lord, and released her tears and her woes.

Feeling her husband standing by her side, Gracie took her praise up a notch. She thanked God for His blessings that He poured into her husband as he stood next to her, releasing his heart out to his Heavenly Father as well.

Gracie knew she had come close to straining their marriage as she had pushed the measures to give their child away to Kendra and Dillian. Gracie thought she was doing a good deed by carrying a child for her friends. Even Dillian and Kendra thought the idea was a bit drastic. But because they desired a child and had been unable to conceive naturally, they prayed and believed that God had sent Gracie and Marcus to help them.

From day one, Gracie knew that Marcus's heart wasn't one hundred percent in it. She figured as long as he hadn't verbally said no, she could go ahead with it. Not being able to sleep at night was the thing that started to bother her. She had taken vows, and knowing that her husband felt a different way about a decision that she had made for the family had finally edged her. But by then it was too late. Way too late. They were nearly seven months pregnant, and they literally hadn't made any preparations for a newborn, because talking about the unborn child was taboo.

The boys had finally noticed changes in their mother's body. Knowing that their child, boy or girl, would be born in the next few months, Gracie and Marcus had sat the twins down to explain. Without all of the details, like the mistakes that Gracie had made, they simply allowed the boys to feel excitement about their sibling joining their family. Marcus and Gracie had finally concluded that an addition to their household was the best thing.

Now Gracie felt that with all the badgering she had been doing to herself, Marcus needed to own up to the hurt that he had thrown into their standing problem. She would have never thought Marcus would cheat. Gracie couldn't deny the fact that she had done something that would make anyone lose his right mind, but still. The pain that lay in her heart felt as though knives were slicing her heart right down the middle. Only praying to God would cure what the Jeffries had.

Gracie knew Marcus held a numb feeling as he tried to get into the service. Every step that he made, he'd shared with his pain-driven wife. Since the last phone conversation he'd had with Michelle weeks earlier, and one he shared with Gracie, he tried to be the best husband and father he could be. Not wanting anything to look or feel out of the ordinary, Marcus had downplayed his feelings about the upcoming birth of their third child. His main purpose was to make Gracie feel as relaxed as she could about everything.

He had come back around to being himself, but they still hadn't talked anything over. The brief talk that they had with the boys was the first step in realizing that they would indeed have an addition to their family. Daily, when his key still fit their front entrance, Marcus's face showed satisfaction. He figured Gracie was indeed willing to hear him out about the affair, but on her own time. In Marcus's thoughts, just knowing she had finally settled to become a mother to their unborn child was enough.

The entire church stood to their feet as Herlene and Kenya stood side by side, facing one another as they finished up their surprise for Gracie.

"When God says go," the two sang together, "you better go. Go-o-o."

Gracie couldn't have thought of any other gift that she would have loved more on that day.

Joining in with the claps and the praising of the other parishioners, the Jeffries gave their new-found friends, their extended family, a joyous handclap of praise.

"You have a beautiful home, Mrs. Herlene," Gracie complimented.

"Yeah, James. You gonna have to share your secrets on keeping your yard up like that during the winter time. Share that with a brother, please," Marcus chimed in.

Laughing a belted laugh, James was happy to have another man in the house, and was excited about sharing all he could. "Young man, young man, you can learn a few new things while you're visiting. Take out your pad and pen and take notes. And while you're at it, make sure you call the Cowboys' head coach and tell him to leave his team at home. Ain't no way they gon' beat up on the Red-skins."

"My friend, you can grill some meat, you can quote some scriptures, but football . . . let me handle that," Marcus joked around with the older, stout James Clark. "Which way is your restroom? I need to go wash up before I put a killing on your November 'cued ribs," he added while leaning over the man's shoulder.

After giving directions to the young man he had grown to admire, James turned his attention to Kenya and the twins. "Kenya, why don't you ask Mrs. Gracie if it's okay if you can take the boys into your playroom?"

"Okay. But Daddy, how many times are we going to have to keep telling you? It's not a playroom, it's just a room where I go and play. Only babies have playrooms."

"All right, all right. You win." He gave in with hands in the air, as if he were being read his rights.

Sitting at the table, waiting on the hot tea to finish brewing, Gracie brought up the morning service. "That was indeed a nice surprise, Mrs. Herlene. You have an amazing voice, I have to tell you." With the whistle sounding off, Gracie readied her mouth for the hot drink as Herlene passed her a mug. "And Kenya. I see where she gets it from. I mean, it's cute when children sing their little solos, but your girl can really sing. You know, like, some people can sing, but she was born to *sang*."

"I know. I'm blessed. I must say, yes, she gets it from me. Toot, toot!" Herlene snickered. "But you should know that," she said while taking a seat. "That's where Kendra gets her singing from. My whole family, just about, can sing. Except one of my sisters, bless her heart. She sounds like a crow crowing." The two belted a laugh at Herlene's absent sister's expense.

Calming down from the shared hilarity, Gracie jumped back on the subject. "I, well, I didn't know Kendra could sing. Hmm, I don't think I've ever heard her break a tune."

Ashamed that she had taken away her daughter's joy of singing, Herlene shared her view with Gracie. "I wouldn't be surprised. I probably drove that out of her, too, to tell you the truth. Umph, not only does she not want anything to do with me, she doesn't want to be anything like me." A film of sadness filled her eyes.

Gracie reached out to touch the woman's hand. "Mrs. Herlene, that was the old you, and Kendra doesn't know the good person that you've become. When she gets better"—Gracie looked down at the cup of tea in front of her, hoping that her words would bring Kendra back—"she will get to know you all over again. I know she will."

"I'm glad you think so. I hope so myself, but I just don't want to get my hopes up. Now that you mention Kendra, there is something I wanted to talk to you about." Herlene sat tall in her chair. "I was thinking, well, actually, I've been praying. I spoke with God about it." Herlene hesitated to reveal what God had spoken to her heart the day she had been drunk and guilt-ridden while over at Kendra's home.

"What if we get Kendra transferred home? I saw a movie once on Lifetime, and they did that very thing with the character. It was television, but I talked to Kendra's doctor about it, and he doesn't have any real objections to it." She waited.

"Hmm. I haven't thought about that." Gracie suddenly recalled the nurses talking a few months back and realized she never did verify what the staff wanted to keep secret. "You know, I don't remember if I told you I overheard some nurses saying that it was something about Kendra that they didn't want to be released to the family. Ouch!" Gracie rubbed her still belly. "This baby of mine," she remarked, and then continued what she was saying. "I think I'd look into that before we make any major decisions. I guess you'd just need to talk things over with Marcus and see what he says."

Gracie held a pained look on her face from her developing baby's kicking spells. Normally, she would be the one trying to persuade Marcus on any major decisions, but with the strain they were facing, the less she talked to her husband, the quicker forgiveness would etch itself into her heart. Or so she thought.

"Say about what?" Marcus came from the outside, where James had been putting his final touches on dinner. Pulling out a chair next to his wife, Marcus crossed his hands on the table and asked again. "Ask me what?"

"Oh, okay. Mrs. Herlene wanted to know what we thought about Kendra being cared for at home. What do you think about that?" Gracie inquired, holding a contorted look on her face from the feeling of the baby's activities.

"You okay?" Marcus asked Gracie before he continued. Getting a nod, he gave his opinion. "Well, I don't think anything will be wrong with that. We'll have to get in contact with the insurance company. See about the nursing system and take it from there. I'm for it as long as it's medically approved," he said as he scratched his nose with the back of his thumb.

With a relieved smile on her face, Herlene stood from the table. She clasped her hands under her chin and went in between the middle of Gracie and Marcus, hugging them both. "You two are just so sweet. I'm so blessed that Kendra has the two of you in her life. And Gracie, you have been such a wonderful friend throughout it all. For whatever wrong that Kendra has ever done to hurt you, I know she didn't do it of her own intentions. She had some of me in her. Since I wasn't there to point her in the right direction, charge it to me and not her."

"Oh, Mrs. Herlene." Gracie grabbed the lady's hand that had been placed on her shoulder. "I'm so past all of that. Kendra is my sister and God is my Father. It's because of Him I made it over. Ouch!" Gracie let out another pinched alarm. "Let me go to the restroom. Maybe this child is trying to tell me something."

"Okay, dear. Stop by the hall closet and get you a face towel and wet it. Put it on your forehead. You can go rest in the guest bedroom until dinner is ready, if you like," Herlene suggested.

"Yes, ma'am," Gracie called out as she left the dining area.

Once Gracie had left the two alone, Marcus decided to make himself busy. "Anything I can do, Mrs. Herlene, since my wife is playing the pregnancy to the T?"

"Ha! You men. If only you could carry the load for us." She gave him a devilish eye before heading into the kitchen area. "No, young man, you are a guest, and you can make yourself comfortable. If you want, you can go see if James needs you for anything or go catch some football on the tube."

"Oh, all right." Marcus started off before turning back. "Don't know if I've ever told you, but you look *so* familiar to me. I asked Gracie if I'd ever met you somewhere else before. She said that this is the first time that she's met you as well. Must be just a lookalike or something."

"Uh . . ." Herlene patted both sides of her hair as she always did when she became nervous. "Yes, uh, must be just a, uh, twin of mine out there in the world. You know what they say: everybody has a twin." She tried to make light of the conversation.

"Yeah. They do say that, don't they?" Marcus watched her just a few seconds longer before he was knocked out of his trance by the cell phone that began vibrating on his hip. Looking at Michelle's number, Marcus sent the call to voicemail and prayed that he hadn't started something that he couldn't finish. He had initially called her back again the day she had dropped the bomb on him about a baby, but he accomplished nothing.

"Michelle, the best I can do is offer you financial help in, well, making this problem go away," he offered.

"Problem go away? Marcus, puh-leaz. I'm not in the mood for all of your good-guy talking. You're talking about an abortion, right?" an upset Michelle verified.

"Yes, Michelle."

"It's not the money, Marcus." Michelle became serious in tone. "I've already been down that road with you before, and I'm not trying to do it again"

"That was years ago, Michelle. I'm married!"

"Well, you weren't married then!" she threw back at him. "What do you have to say about that?" Curled up on her sofa, Michelle had grabbed for her blanket and laid it across her lap. "When we were dating, it was hard enough for you to ask me to have an abortion, but I did it because it was early in our dating. I was hoping that you'd stay with me, marry me, but where did that leave me?" she asked, wanting to tell him about the abortion she had gotten after he dumped her the last time. "I'm not that same person, Marcus. Having an abortion doesn't solve everything. I'm still scarred. But better than that, I'm at a different point in my life where I'm praying that by a mere incident, Ky will be my child's father. If there is anything you want to offer, offer prayer in that direction."

From that day, Marcus had avoided speaking to the lady who could be bearing his child out of wedlock. He'd been embarrassed by his suggestion of an abortion to begin with. Feeling that the only means of saving his marriage was news that no baby existed at all, Marcus dodged Michelle. He prayed that God would surely work everything out for them. With her calling now, he only wondered what she had conjured up.

"Who was that?" Gracie asked Marcus as she made her way back into the kitchen area. Never one to question who her husband spoke to on his phone, Gracie was granted an attitude. She didn't know if he was still conversing with Michelle about *their* issue.

"Oh, just Coach Johnson. You know he's a workaholic and probably at the school creating some plays for the football team. I'll call him later." Walking up to his wife, Marcus tried to land a kiss on her cheek. Gracie walked away before his head could even level to her own, and Marcus turned and went to help James finish preparing dinner.

Not responding beyond what her husband had told her, Gracie held onto the back of the kitchen chair and found herself in a daze. She remembered what she'd heard about the U.S. Army's "Don't ask, don't tell" policy and prayed that if she left it alone, it would all go away.

She didn't know what to do. The best she knew to do was to pray, and she'd done all the praying she knew how. It was wearing her thin because she knew with her past luck . . . she didn't have any.

Herlene hadn't wanted to take the first drink, but the day that Gracie almost busted her out, asking her how she knew Marcus, Herlene got the worst headache and had held onto it ever since. It was only when she'd taken her first drink in over nine years that she calmed down.

"Lene? You in there, honey?" she heard James question through the door.

Kicking back another hot drink that her throat asked for, Herlene moaned in response to his inquiry. "Uh-huh."

"Good. The food's ready, baby. You better come on, now," he whispered and then chuckled before adding, "I believe this boy here can really eat." He let out a slight breath. Always wanting a son, James actually didn't mind if Marcus ate the whole table and then some. He just knew that Herlene wasn't far behind him on the eating scale.

"Here I come, James. Go ahead and show them where everything is." She hoped he'd leave so that she could brush her teeth, gargle, and add perfume to her thinning Juicy Couture that James had bought her for Mother's Day. "I'll be right there." She started on her needs as she heard his steps get farther away from the door.

Looking at her image in the mirror, Herlene no longer saw the strong achiever that she had worked hard to become. God was still the head of her life, but she just didn't know how to deal with her secret that would make everyone besides James know who she really was and what she'd really done. The liquor bottle had become the only comfort in knowing that she hadn't only destroyed Kendra's upbringing, but that she had also played a part in Marcus's teenage heartache.

"All things that lay waiting in the dark always find their way to the light," Herlene mumbled to herself, knowing that the inevitable would eventually happen. There is only so much life one can live before past situations resurface.

With prayer, Herlene could only hold on to the strength she hoped that God would grant her in order to pass through yet another trial. Shutting her bedroom door behind her, Herlene sang, "Lord, help me to hold out," as she put on a forced smile in order to join the others for dinner.

Chapter 28

"Dillian, Dillian? Are you still here? Dillian!" Kendra screamed out into the darkness. "I'm here, Kendra. I thought we talked about this, sweetheart. Why are you still here?"

"I don't want to leave you. I want to stay with you. There is no one out there for me. Who is going to love me, Dillian? Who is going to care for me?"

"Kendra, I'll always love you for the time that we shared, but it was my time to go. It's not your time. You are not finished yet. There is so much you have yet to complete, dear," Dillian's voice echoed. With his body becoming visible, starting with his face, Kendra cried out.

"I knew you'd come out. See . . . I can stay with you," she added while she hugged her husband's spirit without letting go.

"You have to go, Kendra," he said as he pried her away from his torso. "Your mother and father are waiting. Your sister and Gracie, Marcus, and the boys are waiting."

"She is not my mother, and I wish she'd go away! I don't have a father. Trent wasn't my father, thanks to my aunt telling me that. You remember? Gracie and her family don't need me; I'm just a burden for them." Anger spat out of Kendra's heart. "The only thing I love is the voice of the little girl. My sister, Kenya, she reminds me of myself. You know, I can actually hear her, and I just know she hears me, Dillian." Kendra's spirit walked away, excited. She recalled hearing the voice of her sister on several different occasions. "She's everything I wanted to be with my mother. She's so happy. My mother made her happy, but she never cared enough to make me happy."

"You must not dwell on that, Kendra. Your past has held you down for so long. It has gotten you here in the world that I am in, somewhere that you don't belong. I can't lie and say this isn't a beautiful life on this side, because it is. But my beautiful wife, please wait your time. Our child needs for you to survive."

"That is not our child! I was so stupid to agree with this whole pregnancy thing. It won't be our child. It won't be you." Kendra cried hysterically as she dropped her spirited body to the floor.

Kneeling down beside his wife, Dillian grabbed Kendra by the shoulders, bringing her into his arms. He wanted to whisper what he knew in her ear, but understood that he couldn't. Holding her was all he could do.

"How can I go back?" Kendra asked the darkness again. "I've done so much wrong, hurt so many people." Instantly, her mind raced back to Sean, the fiancé that she infected with her strain of HIV that she had been harboring for years before she knew she had it.

"Oh my goodness!" She crumpled.

The day on which she and Dillian had chosen to marry was a beautiful one. Gracie was her matron of honor, and Marcus had agreed to be Dillian's best man.

Everything was perfect in Kendra's thinking. Even with the two going through ultimate pain, they realized there was still hope for love and fulfillment. With Dillian in her vision, and Gracie, Marcus, close friends, and the most sought-after photographer, Paris Pix, in front of her, capturing the smile of the century, Kendra suddenly saw Sean standing on the white runner that had been perfectly laid.

"How on earth did I think I could go on?" Kendra reminisced.

"I loved you. You betrayed me," was all she heard before she actually looked up and saw the gun's barrel facing her. Dropping her fresh

flower bouquet, Kendra saw faces of the audience scatter, and behind Sean, she saw figures creeping up.

Stunned, shocked, not believing that the inevitable could actually happen, Kendra stood with her opened mouth to protest something, anything that she could. Kendra's voice lost itself in her vocal cords as she saw Sean pointing the firearm at her chest. With her heels sinking in the outside grass, she couldn't, wouldn't dare run.

"No!" Kendra's spirit screamed as the scene replayed itself right in front of her.

On the day that her wedding was to be, Sean showed up. Getting as close as he could to the front, Sean turned the gun from being aimed at Kendra. Before Dillian or Marcus could tackle him, the bullet lodged itself into Sean's temple, leaving Kendra's cream-colored dress stained with betrayals of her past.

"Forgive me, God! It was my fault," Kendra screamed. "I killed Sean. I infected him and made him kill himself! I did it, God!" With her face full of racing tears, Kendra covered the back of her head with her hands and stayed kneeling. She didn't know what to do next. It was the first time that she had released those words.

"His grace is good, His mercy is everlasting," was what she heard. Not knowing where the words were coming from, not knowing the voice that threw the passage her way, Kendra sniffled back her hard cry and listened.

"His grace is good, His mercy is everlasting," she mimicked. Kendra had often heard the words spoken whenever she visited church. As she heard them on constant replay in her blackness, Kendra started reciting the words.

"His grace is good, His mercy is everlasting," she mouthed right as the Holy Spirit hit her. Like a bolt of lightning in the depth of her stomach, Kendra, still on her knees, grabbed at her stomach as if fire was brewing inside. Trying with all her might, she opened her mouth to yell, but the only sounds that came out of her mouth were, "His grace is good, His mercy is everlasting."

Rolling on her side, tears constantly on display, Kendra knew to instantly let go and let God. For all of her "why" questions, and for all of the inconsistencies in her own life, Kendra knew that all she ever wanted was to be free of who she had become.

"God, you're good. Thank you, Jesus! Thank you, Lord. Thank you for keeping me in spite of myself. I–I've made so many wrong decisions,

Lord, but if you can forgive me," she screamed, "if you can help me to forgive myself, Lord . . ." Kendra raised her head to look toward the light that had shone down specifically on her. "I'll forever praise your name," she concluded as God purged her soul.

Chapter 29

A pastor had once said that the meantime is where God manifests His ability to be the counselor needed in order to get through whatever is needed to get through. In order to receive the love that only He can give, arms have to be held high, open, accepting God's invitation.

Kendra felt she was being held hostage in the darkness of her surroundings, even though she confirmed that God was what she needed. Timid from all that had taken place—nothing more than a dream—a nightmare was what Kendra perceived herself to be in the midst of, even though she believed God to be real in her life. With the majority of her darkened spirits lifted when she purged her heart's content, the remainder of her darkness still existed in her mind.

"Now what?" Kendra squeezed from her worn vocal cords, minus the attitude she'd owned since childhood. She was content to go in whatever

direction God had for her. In the meantime, Kendra had no choice but to wait it out.

Release it, *Kendra heard from the inside of her body, knowing it was the voice of the Holy Spirit within her.*

Knowing she hadn't been the bearer of the words she heard, and knowing she didn't have the answers herself, she figured that God had shown up once again. Without asking what to release, Kendra knew she had only scratched the surface of letting go and letting God.

With Sean's suicide still plaguing her mind, along with all she had personally ever done and gone through while they were in a relationship, chills set throughout her body. Kendra bit her bottom lip and stilled her nerves in the dark. Knowing her hurtful world started way before he'd ever entered her life, Kendra allowed her memory to speak volumes of her past, toward the present.

"But I don't know how I got this way." Kendra firmly tried to make herself believe she had nothing to do with the consequences that fell into her adult life. Bypassing circumstances in her youth that had been the catalyst in becoming the adult she was, Kendra knew in order for her to release into a reserved middle, she would have to look deeper.

Besides God, Kendra's mind could only vaguely recall someone truly trying to rescue her from all of the problems that had jump-started her life. Even though her aunt ultimately took her in and gave her an unquestionable house of safety after Kendra had been given to a neighborhood drug dealer, Kendra always felt that by not talking about all that had transpired in her life, it was like burying who she really was.

Knowing what she had to do, Kendra heard a unique voice give reference by saying, If you would just confess all your sins . . .

Instantly taking offense, she didn't catch herself before she said, "So it was my fault?" Sitting, Kendra vaulted her understanding toward what she knew now to be a safe place.

"Confess what I did? But I didn't do anything." She reverted back to being a young girl, a time when she really didn't know what to believe. There were moments when she would believe her life's damage was all her fault, but because so many people in the world had been hurt as she had, Kendra wasn't naïve in the truth that her mother not participating in her life was what brought on the hurt.

"My aunt said it wasn't my fault, so why do I need to confess?" With a somber feeling dwelling in a new space in her heart, a space

she hoped held a second chance, Kendra just listened for the answer she knew would be revealed.

The sin in holding on. The sin in not releasing hurt. The sin in not speaking the truth. The sin in not forgiving . . . *The list went on.*

Getting more aggressive by the moment, Kendra stood on her naked feet and charged all that had been thrown at her. She was adamant about receiving the answers to questions that forever plagued her adult mind.

"What was I supposed to do? Tell my mama that it was all right for her not to love me?" She held in her cry, needing to feel superior to her issues. "That wasn't my job. I was to forgive her, huh?" Kendra jabbed a finger into the darkness, not knowing if it represented night. "I was supposed to forgive her when she didn't care if I ate, drank, or even changed clothes for the day, as long as she smoked all the crack she wanted."

With the wish to see God's face, Kendra turned from left to right, backed herself into corners and lost her direction as she demanded answers. Fresh anger was brought forth, added with all the anger of her past.

"Tell me! Tell me who's gonna confess about hurting me, huh?" She felt like challenging God. "She left her child, a young, innocent child."

Kendra couldn't sustain the emotions that gave way. "I needed her." A grieving Kendra fell to her knees. "I needed my mama and she wasn't there for me." She had finally spoken what she had always felt.

Slamming her open and aged hand down on a ground she still could not see, Kendra released what she had secretly longed for but almost never openly talked about.

"I needed her. I needed my mommy, and she left me to be there for myself." She thought back on times in her childhood when she was not able to rely on her mother, sometimes for days at a time.

In a daze that would take someone physically pushing her out of it, Kendra had all the opportunity to get lost in where she had come from. Unlike other children who had opportunities to eat, shop, cook, or just spend time with their mothers, there was never a time Kendra could pinpoint a successful union. It was always "never be seen, nor heard." The more she stayed out of her mother's way, the better.

Kendra remembered learning how to do laundry about the same time she finally was enrolled into elementary school. Although the lesson did come directly from her mother, there was never love in the lesson.

After coming home crying about being taunted, and worse, being given a note from her teacher about her appearance and odor, Kendra did what only a child would know to do. She went to her mom looking for comfort, hoping maybe her mother would take initiative in finally showing her love, since saying "I love you" was never an option.

"Um, Mama," a six-year-old Kendra had approached her mother out of fear of presenting her bad news on a bad day. "My teacher sent you this letter. They say I smell." She took a step closer toward Herlene, who had a beer in one hand and a rolled cigarette in another.

Kendra wondered, hoped her mother would care just once. She waited for her mother to release the puff of smoke that took more effort in inhaling than telling her daughter that she loved her. Inadvertently holding her own young breath, a wide-eyed Kendra longed for her mother's arms to open and wait for her to fill them, to let her know everything would be all right. It never happened.

A high and drunken Herlene flung curse words toward her only daughter. A shy and sorrowful Kendra had to wonder if the language was meant for her or for the teacher who had sent home the letter.

"You make sure to tell them I said that. Okay?" Herlene had ordered.

Kendra exhaled, knowing her mother had spared her—at least that time she had.

"Now, go on in there and put some clothes in the washer. Put white clothes by themselves and then—" Herlene squinted her eyes, questioning if her daughter would be able to handle laundry. "Then put all the rest of them together."

Not knowing what else to do, Kendra just shook her head and accepted the only love she felt her mother knew how to give.

From that time on, being self-sufficient was what Kendra had to rely on in her growing up. When it was time for training bras, she would have to accept whatever her mother found and wherever she had found it. As the time came for her to understand why her body was rejecting her, releasing monthly pain, it was the other girls in her class that helped her through.

I told you I'll never leave nor forsake you. Believe in me.

Hearing the urge to confess once more, Kendra knew it was the Holy Spirit letting her know it was time to pull it together. Ready to go for what she really wanted to know—how to heal—Kendra blurted out her feelings:

"I literally ache in my soul," she said as she let the last syllable ooze from her pierced lips. With her hands over her stomach, Kendra grasped hold of the gown that flowed freely on her body. "I don't know how I made it to age eighteen. All I know—" She felt weak but knew the release of the setback would make her strong for the first time in her life.

"My mama"—she made a mental note not to whisper—"my mama hurt me deeply!" she yelled from the tops of her lungs.

"I was abandoned. I was raped . . . I was left for dead." She violently shook her head. "Oh my God, my childhood was ripped from me." Kendra pulled at the clothing placed on her body.

She couldn't help the motions her body was giving way to, making her leap off of her feet and run in place. "Help me, Lord, to let it go. I give it over to you, God! Thank you for taking care of me." Kendra praised God for the strength in verbally and emotionally leading pain from her heart.

Just as she took in account of God's greatness, Kendra recalled God being ever so present throughout her life.

"But, God, you held on to me. You never let me go. When so many other people couldn't have cared less what happened to me, how I would end up, you cared."

A smile that came rippling from the end of her soul connected to her heart, and just as fast, it set her on fire for the Lord. With a shout, Kendra danced in a worship praise once she realized that God had never left her. He had always been there.

"All I know is that when I was free . . . free to make the decisions that would take me down the right way on the forked road, I chose the wrong one." She jabbed her own finger into her chest, instead of looking for someone else to blame. "I got it, Lord. For taking how someone treated me and using it as an excuse . . . Lord, please forgive me for holding onto the past as if it were meant to be my future.

"Though my mother did forsake me, God, you were just the Father I needed. Hallelujah, Jesus!" Kendra lost herself in a praise that had her in an ultimate out-of-body experience with the Lord.

Falling to the unseen ground, Kendra worshiped God in spirit and in truth; the spirit of allowing God to regain His rightful place in her heart, and the truth for finally letting go of pain, no matter how great it was, and giving it to the Lord for Him to work out.

Chapter 30

Taking the nightshift was easy for Gracie since she hadn't been able to get any sleep. Leaving the boys with Marcus was never a worry, since she had been blessed with a man who was also a great father. Shifting in her seat, reading random scriptures from her travel Bible, Gracie's interest was piqued as she heard footsteps outside of Kendra's door. Placing her socked feet on the cold tile floor, Gracie sat with a straight back. She sat frozen as her stomach rested in her lap when the door was pushed open. She thought it was a nurse making her rounds, but when she heard a slight knock, Gracie thought otherwise.

"Come in," she whispered, forgetting that the volume of her voice couldn't nor wouldn't wake Kendra. "Marcus!" Gracie quietly yelled, seeing her bundled-up husband walk through the door at a little past midnight. "What are you doing here? Are the boys okay?" She stood in front of her husband, close enough to feel his breath.

Fanning her down to let her know she didn't have to stand up, Marcus cleared his wife's worries. "The boys are fine. Well, Gregory did hit Geoffrey upside the head with his Nike." Marcus made a check mark on his own forehead as he snatched the warm hat off of his dome. "Other than that, they're okay. Dad came over to stay with them," he answered before allowing his wife to speak. "Mrs. Jolie was there too. You know? I think Dad has a thing for her," Marcus teased.

"Stop it." Gracie tried not to show her blushing smile as she walked to the other side of the room.

Before he allowed himself to start on the reason for the midnight visit, Marcus stood in a trance. He stared at his wife, the mother of his children, and took in all of her beauty.

"So close." He allowed his thoughts to escape from his lips. When he saw the questioning look on Gracie's face, Marcus realized what he'd said and shook himself out of the trance he'd put himself in.

"Sooooo, why are you here?" She turned her back from her observant husband and started on her travel back to her warm and awaiting seat.

Right as she was about to take her seat, she felt Marcus's touch on her arm to hold her from sitting. Gracie peered at her husband, and his beard stubble and the glasses he often wore made her heart instantly flutter. She wanted nothing more but to be loved by her husband and to continue to love him until she took her last breath. Gracie knew she'd made mistakes in their marriage by being overbearing, but all in all, she wanted nothing more than for her husband to be the head of the household. She paused as Marcus closed in to kiss her.

"Now, what was that for?" she asked with her eyes still closed from the heat that was produced from her husband's touch. Not having been intimate with her husband from the day Ky inadvertently broke the news to her, Gracie longed for everything to be made right in their lives; especially the love between her and her husband.

"We need to talk." Marcus bit his lip, not wanting to stop the love that had fashioned between the two.

With a smirk, she questioned him. "And you needed to kiss me so that we could talk?" She playfully rolled her eyes.

"No. But I needed it, and you did too," he guaranteed with a goofy grin.

"Well, okay." Gracie started to walk past him toward the exit. "We can go down the hall."

"Here is fine, Grace." He called his wife by her shortened name. "We'll be fine in here."

Walking closer to the foot of Kendra's bed, Marcus sat on the cold floor and looked up at his wife, who was once again seated. "It's been hard, baby," he started with a bowed head. "It's been hard to sit back and allow you to take control over all of our decisions in the family. From the very beginning, I have to admit, I wanted nothing more than to make you happy. I see I've made a mistake. I love you, Gracie." He looked at his wife.

"Honey, I know. I—"

"Gracie, wait. Let me finish." He held up his finger. "I know you say you have it now, but I'm going to make the final decision. I heard you every time you were trying to explain and apologize, but I hadn't forgiven you yet. I forgive you, Gracie, for getting us into this predicament. I also know that I'm partly to blame." Pausing, Marcus looked down at his crossed hands, and then up into Gracie's eyes. "Dillian's dead, Kendra's in a coma, and that baby,"—he pointed toward his wife's midsection—"*our* baby, is coming home with us. You know that, right?" She agreed with a nod. "We tried it your way, Gracie, but now we are going to do it God's way."

He didn't want to, but Marcus knew he had to finish. "I guess I can't say I didn't cheat . . . because I did, Gracie. Like I told you, I saw Michelle and took her business card. I made the first call. It was me. I guess I wasn't feeling like the man of the house, and you know what? The enemy put her right in my path." Guilt showed its way onto Marcus's face. "I failed that test."

Sitting on the edge of her seat, Gracie felt tears streaming down her face. She questioned how she allowed herself to cause the man she loved so much pain just by being selfish. She didn't know how not to blame it on herself. All she knew was that she was causing Marcus's heart pain, and she no longer wanted to do so. "I'm so hurt, Marcus." She knelt beside him. "I'm sorry. I've caused you so much hurt, and I'm sorry, honey. I'm very angry at what you did, but I know I pushed you away. I'm not just saying that either." She stopped to cup her husband's face in her hands. "I really understand what I've done. This is major, and I've risked our marriage and a child's life. I'm sorry." She sealed her regret with a long and loving kiss. "But honey, I have to let you know how hurt I am behind you going to Michelle. Sharing what we had with another woman, that hurt is indescribable."

Breaking away from their embrace, Marcus wanted to continue. "Honey, I have to let you know . . . I have talked to Michelle a few more times." Marcus saw a confused look etch itself on Gracie's face. "But it was merely to state the facts. That—that if her child happens to be my child, I will have to stand up and do the right thing."

"I know," Gracie said. "I know you wouldn't have it any other way. That's just something I'll have to figure out how to deal with." Sadly looking into her husband's eyes, Gracie continued. "I had actually found her card in your pants pocket when I was doing laundry a while back." She stood and walked over to her purse and pulled out the card, handing it to Marcus. "I didn't know about the lunch, though." Gracie's face was filled with dried tears. "I guess that's all irrelevant now anyway."

Gracie knew she'd have to go into detail with her husband at a later date, but knew for the most part, her fears had been calmed. Although she had previously found the card, it was only when Ky made his appearance at their house that she took matters into her own hands.

The day she called Michelle, Gracie held back her tears, and she didn't wait for the pleasantries before she blared into the phone, "I don't know how long this affair has been going on, nor do I care; but as God as my witness, Michelle, if you come near my husband, call my husband, or even think about my husband, getting a restraining order from me will be the least of your worries."

"I–I'm sorry," Michelle whispered. "I never meant for anything like this to happen."

"Are you serious?" Gracie dared for Michelle to apologize again. "You did exactly what you wanted to do. But don't think that I will let my husband just claim this child. Your worst nightmare has come true. Oh, and please believe me, he will still remain at twenty-six hundred Eagle Lane." That day, Gracie didn't know if she wanted to stay in the marriage, but she did know that whatever Michelle's plans had been, she would cancel them.

Bringing her thoughts to the present, Gracie focused her attention back to her husband. "I'm not going to say I approve of what you've done, but I know that I pushed us in a corner. I love you, and I don't want to lose you, or what we've built," Gracie explained.

"I don't want to lose you either, Gracie. I regret even calling her, but that's over. And I want you to believe me." Bringing himself to the height of his wife, Marcus held both of her hands, wishing he couldn't feel the pain that she felt, the shame he felt. Marcus hugged his wife and hoped to comfort her against all they had gone through in such a short period of time.

"I felt you didn't appreciate me as your husband, and I felt that I wasn't given the chance to make decisions that needed to be made for our family."

"But I want you to make decisions, Marcus, and I'm sorry. I'm sorry. I don't want to look back," she said with her head buried in Marcus's chest.

Lifting his wife's head, Marcus kissed her and reassured her. "Gracie, there is nothing, nothing that will knock me off course. I'm sorry for putting us through this, but we can survive it, okay?"

Nodding in agreement, Gracie allowed her husband to kiss her again. They stood in the middle of the occupied hospital room and embraced. Finally able to bare his soul to his wife, Marcus silently cursed the devil in hell who tried to put them asunder.

Instead of going back home, Marcus decided to stay with his wife. For the next few hours, they sat talking about the baby: all of the conversations that Gracie had previously avoided with him. After a few stale conversations thrown in the air, Marcus allowed Gracie to catch a few hours of sleep and promised that he'd wake her if things changed for Kendra.

When she woke and saw that time had passed into the morning, Gracie looked around for Marcus only to find him at Kendra's bedside. He was holding Kendra's hand and praying, and Gracie made no sudden movements. She simply waited until the final *Amen* had been released from her husband's lips to greet him.

"Good morning, honey."

"Hey, babe." He stood. "You know, I'm not going to have you staying out here too much longer, being all crunched up. You and the baby need to get the best rest you can."

"I know, but I just feel like I have to be here. I can't go on doing things as usual, Marcus. I mean, Mrs. Herlene is really helping out a lot. I can't ask that lady to pull full-time here. As a matter of fact," Gracie said while looking at her Citizen watch, "she should be getting here soon."

"Yeah. I'd better get going to make sure the boys get to school on time. Are you coming right home?"

"Yes. I'm just going to give Mrs. Herlene the rundown, and I'll be right there. Why? You're not thinking about staying home from work today, are you?" Gracie said with a pleasing look on her face. She finally felt desires for her husband that hadn't been evident in the last few months.

"Don't start none, won't be none." Marcus sassed his way to his wife and laid a passionate kiss on her. "Honey, are you sure we never met

Kendra's mother before? I could swear Mrs. Herlene is looking more and more familiar to me."

Adjusting Kendra's pillow and hand-combing her friend's hair backward, Gracie squinted her eyebrows and thought. "I told you, not to my knowledge, honey. You've only seen the lady just about as much as me, Marcus. You think you know her? Ask her, babe."

"Well, I did, but she said she's never met me. I've never met her, I guess." Shrugging his shoulders, Marcus prepared to head toward the door. "Well, let me get out of here so I can go get the spunky bunch." Touching Kendra's resting hand and hugging his wife, Marcus left the hospital room.

Chapter 31

After Marcus left, Gracie hoped things were looking up for their family. Even though she still prayed and waited for Kendra's recovery, Gracie knew she had unfinished business. Alone with an ever-sleeping Kendra, Gracie didn't know if she'd ever get the chance to officially apologize to her. Not knowing in which direction God's story would end, Gracie knew she'd put it off long enough.

"From the very beginning, I should have helped you," she said as she sat in the chair she had become accustomed to calling her own. "When we were younger, I should have been a better friend."

Wanting to be real, not wanting to short-change Kendra, Gracie sat and thought about why she knew she had played a major part in their ragged friendship. Straightening the pillow behind her lower back, Gracie continued. "I never took responsibility for your pain. If I had, if I were your true friend, I would have asked more questions. I wouldn't have—I shouldn't have just patted you on your back and thought that was enough. I should have listened to you."

On a roll, Gracie felt more ashamed for all that was so very clear to her now. "Humph. You know, I don't see how you did it. I know people ask me that question all the time, on how can I be friends with you, but honestly, how could you be friends with me?" Becoming tired of sitting, Gracie stood to her feet and leaned into Kendra's bed.

"I mean, seriously, Kendra . . ." She stroked her friend's hair that had changed its texture from all the medicines, all the chemicals in her body. "I cried on your shoulder for the simplest, most selfish reasons, but when you cried, you cried because you were hurting. You needed someone, and that someone should have been me."

Not feeling worthy of wiping the tears that had rolled down her face, Gracie continued. "You were hurting. You were alone. I was your family, and I did a bad job at it. I hurt you just as much as everyone else did, didn't I?" Wishing that a response would be released from her friend, Gracie knew better. She knew she would have to believe Kendra loved her just as much as she loved Kendra.

"Kendra, I pray that your heart will forgive me. I could easily say our whole world started crumbling down with you, but if I had been a friend, even while we shared our dorm room . . ." Gracie couldn't hold it in any longer. Through sobs, she finished. "You wouldn't even be here right now."

Holding an almost lifeless Kendra's hand, Gracie released her desires. "Kendra, will you forgive me for not being all that I could be? All the friend that you needed for me to be? Please forgive me." When Gracie heard the door opening, she looked back.

"Excuse me, ma'am," a young boy with a balloon bouquet entered Kendra's room. "I have a bouquet delivery for a Gracie Jeffries," he read directly from the card.

Wiping her eyes, Gracie walked toward the delivery man. "You mean Kendra McNab? She's Kendra." Gracie pointed back to a comatose Kendra. "I'm Gracie." She pointed to herself. "Surely the bouquet is for her."

Releasing the card to an approaching Gracie, he shrugged his shoulders and waited for her to read the card herself:

For all that you have done, we present these balloons to you for lifting Kendra's spirit, even in times such as these. Kendra will be pleased. Blessings forever. James, Herlene, and Kenya Clark.

"Aww." Gracie couldn't hold her tears before the young boy was out of the door. "This is too sweet. I don't even deserve it."

Starting on her trek back toward Kendra's bedside, Gracie thought back on what she had been doing prior to the interrupted surprise, and she stopped in her tracks.

"God, you are way too much, and too good to me." Gracie shook her head about the goodness of God. Taking the balloons and the card as a sign that Kendra had forgiven her, Gracie loved knowing that God always has a way of speaking in only the way He can.

Chapter 32

On her routed morning drive home from Baylor, the hospital in which Kendra had no choice but to call home, Gracie didn't bother to turn on the car's music contraption. With all the upgraded amenities her Volvo housed, even with the XM Radio, her speakers would make her Anthony Hamilton CD seem as if he were singing live, right from her vehicle. For the headache that had been brewing on top of her mind, Gracie decided to just think of the singer's talented voice.

It was as if Anthony's song was still singing to her from the last time she had been in her car. *My soul is on fire, and I can't take the pain away,* landed right in Gracie's feeling. She knew she should have been on cloud nine about her and Marcus's reconciliation, but in actuality, she had just gone through a traumatic experience in her married life.

The day at their home, once she found out about her husband's infidelities, Gracie thought she'd taken the responsibility of her husband's wrongdoing and let it go. She thought she could just wash her and Marcus's sins away and sweep them under the rug. Gracie even felt she released his action when she dialed the other woman's telephone number. But now, driving, managing to detour without so much as thinking about it, Gracie let what so many other couples face settle in her reality. Marcus had indeed cheated.

"Cheated." She allowed the marriage-killing word to leave its internal hiding space. Gracie allowed her mind to wander, as her driving speed couldn't match that of the other cars on the winding roads.

"My husband cheated on me." Gracie tilted her head to the side, just enough to let the feeling of broken vows linger in disbelief.

Arriving at one of the entrances to White Rock Lake, on the east side of Dallas, Gracie parked her SUV and allowed her shoulders to slump. Making no sudden movements other than removing her foot from the brake, Gracie sat.

"Oh my Lord," she bellowed out in disgust, her true feelings for what her husband had done. With the unmistakable boy-hurt-girl gut feeling brewing in her pregnant stomach, Gracie's bouncy locks swayed as she bobbed her head from side to side. Releasing one hard breath, all Gracie could do was rest in her monstrous truth.

She wasn't in a hurry to get home, even though she and Marcus had sort of made plans. One side of her couldn't wait to be in the arms of her husband for the months they'd spent apart. The other side could wait until her memory permanently erased the scene that replayed over and over in her head, of Marcus pleasing another woman he had not made vows to. Gracie knew that wouldn't happen. Until the day she died, she knew that her marriage would be labeled touched, sacrificed . . . even molested.

"Oh God. Ugh." Gracie held onto the last syllable with her once shining brown eyes hidden behind her lids. Stomping her sports shoe as hard as she could on her car's mat, Gracie sealed the deal by slamming her fist into the steering wheel's middle and then hugging her own middle.

Trembling at the after effect, the thought of Michelle being pregnant with her husband's child made Gracie's knee jump at an involuntary pace. Chills dwelling throughout her skin, Gracie shook her sweaty palms as if she could wipe the slate clean.

Feeling the dirt and grime of her tainted marriage, Gracie knew she would need to have strength to get past her hurt, her emotions, and even her insecurities. Bringing her hands together in symbolic prayer, Gracie placed them on her chest.

"We've fallen short of your glory, Lord. But—" Gracie almost couldn't believe she was about to say it. "But I made a vow to you, and I won't go back. I don't want to go back, Lord."

All the hardness, all the strength, and the effort of being able to let go and move forward had caught up with her.

"I still—ugh!" She didn't want to really believe she had finally been like other women, something she always tried to convince herself that she wasn't. "I still want my husband?" she questioned, not really knowing why, but now realizing how so many women went back again and again. Gracie recognized, "Lord, I love my husband and I want to forgive him . . . for real." For the first time since arriving at the lake, she wept from her center for her family.

She wasn't the first, nor would she be the last woman who would be threatened or kidnapped by the infidelity spirit. Infidelity played with not only the husbands of marriage, but with the wives as well. It just so happened that Marcus was the one to cross the line, and it just so happened that Gracie had been the one to push him.

Cast your cares upon the Lord, she heard. *Tell your sins to flee.*

The winds were high, and though the *Morning, Texas* weatherman said the day would be lovely, the waves bouncing in the lake begged to differ. Taking this as a sign to be caught up with Jesus, Gracie opened her door and stepped out.

"I'm taking you with me, God, on this journey, on this tedious journey." She sniffed with each step as she reminded herself of the old-time church song.

Even though she wore a lightweight sweater, her chattering teeth made her realize just how cold the weather was. With pushing wind gathering strands of hair behind each ear, Gracie walked and held her rounded belly for stability.

Standing close enough to the dock's edge, Gracie held her head back and let the wind dry her tears. Opening her mouth to speak, no words escaped.

Just ask me. She heard the words once more.

"Speak to my heart, Lord." Gracie knew not to fight what God wanted. Her fighting against God's wishes had gotten her pushed into the corner in the first place.

Not caring if joggers or the park rangers were watching, Gracie only cared what God saw when He looked at her heart. Right where she stood, Gracie truly, without superficial bragging rights, allowed herself to forgive Marcus, but not before she forgave herself.

She knew everything started when the devil's light plugged itself in her mind, coming up with such a plan that would drain her marriage as much as a digital camera wore down cheap batteries. In the beginning, even though Kendra and Dillian had reluctantly agreed to accept her help, Dillian challenged her.

"Why would you want to do this, Gracie?" he had asked on a day they'd shared a quick and private lunch. Dillian had asked her to accompany him to an uptown eatery.

With legs on both sides of the fence, Dillian had tried to get truth from Gracie.

"Dillian, why do you keep asking me this?" She wouldn't make lasting eye contact. "I know how it feels to be a mother, and Marcus loves being a daddy. I want you and Kendra to experience the same," she gave as her definitive answer. There was truth behind what she had said. It hurt her to imagine Dillian and Kendra married without children, which is something they didn't desire.

"But Marcus . . ." He paused to see if his ex would interject and give him Marcus's true feelings. When he didn't see a change in the speed at which she nibbled on her panini sandwich, Dillian just spoke. "Marcus doesn't seem too thrilled with the whole idea. I mean"—he hunched his shoulders—"he's smiling and nodding his head, but I know you, Gracie. I know when you're adamant about something you don't just stop like that." He snapped his fingers. When Gracie still hadn't made eye contact with him, Dillian called her name.

"Gracie!" She finally became coherent. "What is your deal? What is Marcus really saying about all of this?" Dillian wanted to know.

Still chewing, Gracie reared back as far as she could in the upright chair and knocked her ponytail off her shoulder. Taking a sip of water, Gracie tried to figure which words to use.

"He's fine with it. He had some concerns about me being attached to the baby," she spoke, knowing it was Marcus who by then had already become attached to a child they hadn't even yet conceived. "I'm fine, Dillian. Marcus knows that now. Just stop putting so much emphasis on all of this."

"I wouldn't be asking so much, but this child is *your* child. This child is not some stranger that was left without a family. If that doesn't make you feel apprehensive, well, then me and Kendra are for it." He leaned forward on the table. "Only if you are absolutely certain, Gracie. Only if both you and Marcus are absolutely certain."

That was when Gracie stepped in and did what she wanted instead of what God would have told her if she had fasted and prayed for God's approval. Gracie had always been a strong-willed, independent, and God-fearing woman, so when she plugged her own words into sentences she knew God hadn't ordained, Gracie surprised herself.

"I've prayed about it, Dillian, and . . . and it's all right," she had said as she choked down the last remnants of her sandwich.

That day was now such a disliked and dishonest memory. She had stepped so far out of God's will, but with the Father she served, Gracie knew He had opened his hands to receive her once again.

Focusing on the lake, Gracie tried not to grow angry with herself. She knew not to put too much strain on her developed and pregnant body. Back to her reason for standing on the dock, Gracie held her hands out and allowed the winds to land in her palm as she cried to the Lord, saying, "Forgive me, Father, for I have sinned."

Chapter 33

"I am so excited." Herlene clapped as she spoke with Kendra's doctor. "Thank you, Doctor. I'm so happy. I know Kendra is happy."

"It's quite all right, Mrs. Clark. As long as the nursing schedule works out, Kendra will be fine at home, in her own surroundings." The middle-aged doctor shook hands with his patient's mother.

"Okay. I have the car loaded with the majority of the stuff. Now, what about all of these flowers and plants and things? Are they staying?" James asked his wife upon entering the hospital room for hopefully the last time. Wiping the sweat from his brow, James placed both hands on his love handles.

"Oh, James, Marcus is on his way now with his father. He said he didn't mind coming and getting all of the stuff you didn't get," Gracie answered.

"His father? Marcus *and* his father? Oh, that's nonsense, Gracie. Uh, we can get this stuff ourselves, can't we, James?" Herlene asked her husband with desperation in her voice. While rubbing her hands furiously on her lounging dress, Herlene tried to keep her purse attached to her wrist as it swung back and forth.

"Well, baby, it really is kind of tight." James took off his wool cap to scratch the top of his balding head.

Sitting on the empty bed, Gracie waved off another third trimester dizzy spell. "Mrs. Herlene, you go ahead. The ambulance is going to beat you to Kendra's house if you don't get to moving. You don't want Kendra to get there ahead of you. Marcus and Pops are probably already downstairs, and I'll more than likely leave my car here or ride with them. I don't feel too good." Gracie rubbed her belly, hoping to ease the pain. "It's no big thing, really."

"So they're coming over to the house? Marcus and uh, his father?" a sweating, stammering Herlene asked.

"Yes, ma'am. We'll be right behind you. I'm going to ride with them." Gracie sounded tired and sluggish.

"You all right, sugar? You need some soda and crackers?" James asked.

With the snap of their necks and looking directly at each other, both women laughed at the thought of James and Marcus. Like Marcus, James had thought the mixed concoction of soda and crackers would solve every pregnant woman's needs.

On the ride from Baylor in downtown Dallas, back to Frisco, James and Herlene followed the ambulance through the afternoon traffic. Sitting quietly on her side of the vehicle, Herlene held a million thoughts in her mind.

Had she been right from the start? Since the day that she met Gracie and Marcus, had she been right? Or was she making her mind replay the past? She had no idea what she was going to do, but somehow she was going to have to get the ambulance to drop Kendra off, set up whatever it was they needed to set up, and she was definitely going to have to be on her way. Dialing the nurse's number, Herlene wanted to make sure that the nurse was already at the house, or at least on her way.

She knew that James would question why she wanted or needed to all of a sudden get home. They had already made arrangements with James's sister to pick Kenya up from school, so there really wasn't a rush. Knowing that Kenya would be taken back to the sister's home until they came to get her, Herlene couldn't use their daughter as an excuse.

"Think, think, think," Herlene accidentally said out loud.

"What did you say, honey?" James looked in her direction briefly before he focused back on the road.

"Oh, nothing. Just thanking the Lord for this blessing." *Oh Lord, please forgive me for that one. What have I done?* She tightened her eyes and shook her head, feeling that the worst part of her was about to be exposed.

She had tried, with success, to kick the old habit that she'd picked up back to the curb. It had been a few weeks since she'd picked up a bottle of liquor from the liquor store, but now that she felt she was in a bind, her taste buds longed for something that would take her into another world—any world besides the one she had made a mess of.

Finally making it onto Kendra's street, Herlene turned around to look at the street behind them. *So far so good.* The road was clear, which meant that the others weren't as close as she thought they would be. Taking out her phone, Herlene dialed Gracie's cell phone number just to verify her thinking.

"This is Gracie," she answered.

"Gracie, honey. Are you all near a store or anything? I'm so thirsty for a Dr. Pepper, but of course we can't stop because we need to get Kendra settled. Do you think it would be possible for you all to stop for me and get a cold drink?"

"Ah, let me check with Pops." Taking the phone from her ear, Gracie asked her father-in-law if they could stop. "He said we can stop for you. I need to use the restroom anyway, and I do mean right this minute. I sho' hate to use these public restrooms, but when you have to go, you have to go. Have you all made it to Kendra's yet?" Not getting a response from Herlene, Gracie asked again. "Hello? Have y'all made it to Kendra's house yet?"

"Uh, oh, yes, I'm sorry, baby. We have." Herlene jumped out of the zone that she had slipped into. "Okay, I'll see you all when you get here." She hung up the phone, not believing that after all those decades, the voice she just heard in the background through Gracie's phone hadn't changed a fragment. There was no doubt she'd have to make a clean getaway before they made it to Kendra's home.

Grateful that the nurse was waiting on their arrival, Herlene jumped out and started to get the things out of the car as quickly as possible.

"Baby, why you in a rush?" James asked.

"Honey, I just forgot I was supposed to go and open up the church doors for the sewing group. Lord, my mind just went and left me."

"Well, I can solve that. I'll just call Deacon Smith and see if he can go do it for you." James tried to come to his wife's rescue.

"But I'd rather do it myself. Since the nurse is here, we can go ahead and just unload and let her get Kendra settled in. She has to apply all the tubes and get her bedding situated. Uh, we can just come back tonight. How about that?"

Shrugging his shoulders, James dared not argue with a woman with her mind made up. "Suit yourself," he answered as he grabbed suitcases to take into the house.

Watching her husband make his way into Kendra's home, Herlene looked up toward heaven and thanked God. She didn't know when it was going to happen, but she knew the inevitable was just around the corner. Her past had finally caught up with her.

Chapter 34

Gracie didn't know what to think. Throughout the day, Herlene had been acting strange, as if she was running from something. What that something was, Gracie had no idea. What she did know was once she mentioned Marcus and his father, everything about Herlene's demeanor changed. She was beginning to think that something of great significance was going on with her dear friend.

Waiting in the car for Marcus to return from inside the convenience store with Herlene's cold drink, Gracie mumbled louder than she thought about getting to the bottom of Herlene's problem.

"Whatcha say?" a partially gray-haired Pops asked while sitting in the passenger's seat. Scraping underneath his nails with a wooden-handled pocketknife that looked older than Gracie, Mr. Jeffries waited on Gracie's response. With his head pressed into his headrest, Pops waited to hear what was on her mind. "Huh?" he reminded her that she hadn't answered.

"Oh." Gracie flung her hand toward Mr. Jeffries as his voice knocked her out of deep thought. The backseat swallowing up her medium frame, Gracie apologized for her outburst. "I'm sorry. I was just mumbling to myself." She rubbed and pointed at her stomach. "Kendra's mama has been acting strange all day long, just in a hurry about everything, and that's kind of worrying me."

"Humph. Maybe she's just excited to get her daughter home." Pops thought he'd solved Gracie's problem and started back on his task. "You did say she had been trying to take care of all Kendra's business, didn't you?"

Leaning back against her own headrest, Gracie looked out the window of their Tahoe at the unusually warm November day. "Mm-hmm. Yeah, I guess you're right. But,"— the itch in her scalp intensified, leaving her digging her fingernails in to soothe the tender spot—"she just seems uptight for some reason. You just have to know Mrs. Herlene to know that she's acting different. I don't know." She shrugged, as if considering brushing it off.

With a pause in his back-in-the-day nail-cleaning option, Pops sat up straight in his seat. "What you say? You say Herlene?" Mr. Jeffries closed the army knife and was about to turn his body around. Just as he got his rigid body to cooperate and make contact with the backseat to get more out of his daughter-in-law, his son opened up the passenger's door where he sat.

"Here, Dad." Marcus laid two plastic bags full of merchandise in his father's lap. "Hold that," Marcus said as he slammed the door before his father could object.

"Boy," Mr. Jeffries remarked as he turned to face the front. "Something wrong with that boy. I ain't no woman, holding bags and stuff."

Gracie reached up and slapped his left shoulder. She made sure her father-in-law felt her playful rage.

Not bypassing the changed demeanor in Pops, and silently wondering, *Now what's wrong with him?* Gracie started to think her pregnancy hormones had been out of sync, thus the reason for her jumping to conclusions. No matter what, her mind was made up. As soon as she was face to face with Herlene, Gracie would question the older woman.

closed the army knife and was about to turn his body around. Just as he got his rigid body to cooperate and make contact with the backseat to get some out of his daughter-in-law, his son opened up the passenger's door before he sa[id]

"Here, Dad." Marcus laid two plastic bags full of merchandise in his father's lap. "Hold that," Marcus said as he slammed the door before his father could object.

"Boy," Mr. Jeffries remarked as he turned to face the front. "Something wrong with that boy. I ain't no woman, holding bags and stuff."

Gracie reached up and slapped his left shoulder. She made sure her father-in-law felt her playful rage.

Not bypassing the changed demeanor in Pops, and silently wondering, *Now what's wrong with him?* Gracie started to think her pregnancy hormones had been out of sync, thus the reason for her jumping to conclusions. No matter what, her mind was made up. As soon as she was face to face with Harriette, Gracie would question the older woman.

Chapter 35

With Thanksgiving only days away, and with a still comatose Kendra settled back into her own home, Herlene, James, and Kenya made their way over to the home. Bringing food, decorations, and everything needed to start the holiday season off right, Herlene and James busied themselves with household duties. With her mom and dad away in the kitchen putting the finishing touches on everything she couldn't touch, Kenya went to spend time with her bedridden older sister.

"Kendra? It's me, your little sister, Kenya. I wish you would wake up so that you can talk to me and play with me. I want to take you to my school so that my friends will believe me when I tell them that my sister was married to Mr. Universe." Patting her sister's hand, Kenya continued to discuss their lives from her point of view. "I know you don't think I know, but I know you been mad at Mommy for a long, long, long time." Kenya used her eyes to drag out the conversation. "But it's okay. She's a good mommy now."

Hearing her sister from the world that locked her out,

Kendra's soul responded, *Yeah, but she's a good mommy to you, not me.*

"She loves you, Kendra," Kenya responded, unaware that her sister could actually hear her. "Mommy loves you. She talks about you all the time. She's always comparing things that I do to you. I don't get mad, though, because I love you too," she said as she jumped in the full-sized medical bed. "She said when I sing, I sound just like you did when you was a little girl."

Having heard all of what Kenya had said to her over the months, Kendra knew that divine intervention was at hand. Learning more about Kenya, Kendra wanted to become closer to her sister. Over the last couple of months, Kenya had given Kendra a new outlook into her mother's life, but Herlene was still not one that she knew for herself in the physical.

You don't know if she loves me as she loves you or not. Baby girl, it's not that simple, and you'll never understand. You have a mother and a father, two people to love you—well, three now, because I definitely love you.

"If you pinkie swear, I'll tell you a secret." The ten-year-old lifted her sister's deadweight hand with her own and twisted their pinkies around each other. "Mommy and Daddy have been married for nine years."

And?

"And I'm ten." Kenya rolled her eyes around the room, landing at the door. Making sure her mother or father weren't in listening range, Kenya continued. "Daddy is not my *real* daddy," she whispered. "Mommy said he rescued her. When she was down and out, the day she walked into the church we go to now, he looked into her eyes and she was hooked. You know, that lovey-dovey stuff. Anyway, they told me all about it last year.

"Well, Mommy said that she started her life over once she found out she was pregnant with me. Daddy truly loved her, but she wouldn't really let him in her world until after I was born. She said she had to know that he wouldn't change after I came into the world. He didn't change, either. He loves me like I'm his baby." Kenya smiled. Wanting and needing her sister in her world, Kenya wished she could talk directly to Kendra, so that she could understand that there was enough love to go around for her as well.

"He'll love you too, Kendra." She left the thought in the air and started singing one of Kirk Franklin's renditions. "He'll take the pain away, I know. . . . He'll take the pain away."

"Kenya!" Herlene called out to her missing-in-action daughter.

Shocked by the tears that were coming out of her sleeping sister's shut eyes, Kenya answered her mother without taking her eyes off of Kendra.

"Huh, Mommy?"

"Girl, you better quit all that *huh* mess. See who that is at the door, please."

Racing out of the still room, Kenya ran full speed down the hall and toward the front door. Once she peered out of the window that sat on the side of the door, Kenya opened the door and let their company in.

Herlene had just left the formal living area where she and Kendra's nurse had been decorating for the Thanksgiving holiday. She then made her way into Kendra's room to check on her daughter. She wanted to make sure Kendra was presentable and looked comfortable while resting. Just as she leaned over to fluff the pillow that lay under her daughter's head, oblivious to Kendra's tears, Herlene heard Gracie's voice and called out to her.

"Hey, Gracie, I'm in here. Come on in. Kendra's decent."

"Hey there, James," Gracie called out to the older man, who had started walking down the same hall. "Mrs. Herlene, how are you doing?" Gracie waddled into the room with her maternity blouse pushed to its limit. She greeted Herlene officially with a long hug. "Kendra looks so peaceful."

"Doesn't she, though?" She hugged back. "Where are Marcus and the boys?"

"Oh, you know Kenya got the boys under control somewhere in there. Marcus and Pops are in the hallway with Mr. Clark," Gracie announced.

Herlene stopped in her tracks. *This is it*. Silent from that point on, Herlene looked down at her clothing, pressed out her blouse with her hands, and just stood. She watched the door and listened to the voices.

"You all right, Mrs. Herlene?" Gracie asked with her own hands pressed palms down on the small of her back. "You look as though you've seen a ghost."

With the response from her head bob, Herlene Clark just stood, listening to the voices as they came closer.

"Hi there, Mrs. Herlene," Marcus addressed her as he walked through the door with James following and his dad bringing up the rear. "I want you to meet my dad, Mrs. Herlene. Mitch Jeffries."

"Lena?" Marcus's father spoke as his left foot crossed the threshold of the door.

"Mitch," Herlene finally spoke, releasing years of pain in one word. "How are you?" She took a step back, almost losing her balance.

"Oh, you two know each other?" Gracie inquired as she held her stomach with a grimace held deep on her face. Walking away from Kendra's bedside, Gracie flowed closer to her husband, who was still standing by the door.

As if the past few months had replayed in his mind, Marcus's face grew into an inquisitive look. Staring into Mrs. Herlene's face, he tried to comprehend if his father knowing her was the reason she looked familiar to him.

Then it hit him. Right then and there, his own past caught up with his thoughts.

"Yes." Mitch spoke first, looking in Gracie's direction. "It's been . . . a long time." He placed his cold hands into his corduroy pants pockets. "You know my boy? And Gracie?" He thumbed back in the direction that the two were standing.

"Uh, yes." She eased closer to her husband and grabbed him around the waist. "This is my husband, James, and—" She was cut off when Kenya ran back into the room and toward Kendra's bed. "That's my daughter, Kenya."

"Hi." Kenya threw up her hand without looking, placing most of her body's weight on Kendra's bed.

"That's where I know her from!" Marcus shot, but no one dialed in to what he said as Mitch started speaking again.

"Well, how've you been?" He came in closer. "You know Kendra as well, I see," he stated, never thinking about *their* problem from years prior. Mitch only thought about the love they once had. Of course, he remembered her being pregnant with his child. After he came clean to her, letting her know that he was married, there was no reason for Mitch to believe the money he'd sent Herlene in the mail for an abortion had not been used.

While Gracie and Marcus stood close together, farther away from the others, they whispered amongst themselves. Marcus said, "She's the reason for my parents' breakup. How could I be so dumb?" He slapped his forehead and hit the wall with his fist before trying to make his way out of the room. Seeing, but not understanding rage within her husband, Gracie tugged at the tail of his shirt before he was able to escape.

Holding her husband by the bicep, Gracie didn't quite understand Marcus's anger. "But your folks didn't divorce until you were in high school," she whispered.

"I know." Marcus gave her a "don't ask, don't tell" look as he proceeded out the bedroom door.

Walking behind her husband at a fast pace, Gracie nearly ran into the back of him as he abruptly stopped. He leaned against the eggshell-colored wall with water in his eyes. "I was young and had no idea that the lady was telling the truth." With his eyes closed, Marcus released what he had never told anyone but his father.

"I was getting off of the school bus one day. I had to be about nine or ten years old." He let out a breath. "This woman, she—Herlene cornered me. She started asking me all kinds of questions. She was asking me for my name, my parents' names, and my parents' information. She had the nerve to tell me that she was my daddy's girlfriend. Her eyes were bloodshot, she reeked of liquor, and she was trying to make me take her to our house." With Gracie now standing in front of him, hugging him around the waist with her head lying on her husband's chest, she felt for her husband's pain. Gracie felt the pain of Marcus knowing his father had had an affair. "She even told me . . ." He couldn't release what he had pieced together. Looking down, Marcus cried.

As Marcus stopped talking and with Gracie now knowing that it was possible that Herlene and Mitch had had a fling back in the day, she didn't want to make James feel uncomfortable.

Wanting to break up the awkwardness of the reunion, Gracie yanked her head off of Marcus's chest. Bursting back into the now crowded room, Gracie broke into the conversation.

"Well, isn't this nice? Pops had come back in town and just wanted to ride over here with us. He'd met Kendra on several occasions and wanted to see—*ouch!*" Gracie grabbed the bottom of her stomach. "He just wanted to see her before he left going back home." Finding the nearest wall, Gracie positioned herself to anchor the pain she felt throughout her body.

"Yes," Marcus's father said, noticing that his son had come back into the room as Gracie cringed in pain. No longer worried about his daughter-in-law, Mitch reverted his attention back to Herlene. "This is such a small world. So, how do you know them again?" Mitch asked Herlene, who had tears in her eyes. In the back of his mind, Mitch already knew the answer to his questions, but he was having trouble wrapping his mind around the situation, running into Herlene again after all these years.

Looking at her husband, who stood right by her side, and then to Kenya, who was in the middle of placing kisses on her sister's face, Herlene finally noticed tears running from her oldest daughter's eyes. Making a mental note to check on Kendra, Herlene then turned back to Mitch. Thinking for just a short moment, Herlene knew there was no turning back. Her full circle would be complete, and the part of her life that had once kept her down would be over.

"Kendra . . ." She hesitated slightly. "She's my daughter, Mitch."

With one quick motion, Mitch turned his puzzled face to study Kendra's, and then quickly he turned to Marcus. Marcus had engulfed Gracie's pain as his own, with tears burning his eyes. Placing his hand over his mouth and then down to his chin, Mitch pondered if now was the time for the questions that instantly popped into his mind.

"She's your daughter? I thought—" Mitch caught himself. "I never knew you had any children back in the day, Lena." Forgetting that anyone else existed in the small room, Mitch took a step forward, confronting Herlene for all to hear. "Is Kendra your husband's daughter? Is she James's daughter?" he asked while pointing his finger back and forth, no longer acknowledging James's presence.

"Wait a minute, man." James stepped forward, gently pushing aside his wife. "What's going on here? You can't just—"

"Honey, honey. It's all right," Herlene said as she grasped her husband. Noticing that Marcus had made his way into the bedroom, Herlene knew by the look on his face that he'd figured out where he knew her from.

"No. I just need to know, James. I'm sorry, but Lena?" Mitch didn't have to replay the question. He knew that Herlene knew what he was getting at.

"It's okay," Herlene said to her husband again once he eyed her. "It's okay. Yes, Mitch, Kendra is my daughter. But no, she is not James's. She is—" She paused to look at Marcus, and then turned back to Mitch. "She's your daughter," she finally released through tears as built up hurt and pain released from her body.

"Mommy! Mommy! Look! Look, Mommy! Kendra opened her eyes for me! Look!" Kenya's voice rang out as she jumped up and down next to her sister's bed.

At the same time all the heads turned to see Kendra's opened eyes, a loud *thump* was heard, only for everyone in the room to turn again and notice Gracie lying on the bedroom floor.

had made his way into the bedroom. Herlene knew by the look on his face that he'd figured out where he knew her from.

"No, I just need to know, James. I'm sorry, but I can't." Mitch didn't have to replay the question. He knew that Herlene knew what he was getting at.

"It's okay," Herlene said to her man and again once he eyed her. "It's okay. Yes, Mitch, Kendra is my daughter—but no, she is not James's. She is—" She paused to look at Marcus, and then turned back to Mitch. "She's your daughter," she finally released through tears as built up hurt and pain released from her body.

"Mommy! Mommy! Look! Look, Mommy! Kendra opened her eyes for me! Look!" Kenya's voice rang out as she jumped up and down next to her sister's bed.

At the same time all the heads turned to see Kendra's opened eyes, a loud thump was heard, only for everyone in the room to turn again and notice Gracie lying on the bedroom floor.

Chapter 36

After all the commotion of Kendra waking from her coma and Gracie fainting in the middle of the floor, everyone scattered to make sure that both women were taken care of. Once the ambulance arrived, Marcus rode with his wife to the hospital. Herlene rode in a separate ambulance with Kendra as they took her in for a battery of tests. The doctors wanted to make sure all was well since she'd been in a coma for the last six and a half months. James stayed behind to watch all the children at Kendra's house, and Mitch used Marcus's car to trail the ambulance to the hospital, not knowing in which direction to go once he arrived.

Marcus couldn't believe what his ears had heard. Not only did his father have an affair that caused their family to split, but he'd actually had a child that he left fatherless in the world. Kendra was his sister. Later, he'd definitely have to have a talk with his father.

Out of nowhere, a memory of his own infidelity with Michelle added to his already pounding headache. He couldn't believe that he was possibly making the same mistake that his father had. When Ky came to the house and announced to him, through thrown fists, that he may be the father of Michelle's baby, Marcus had no choice but to come clean with the whole truth to his wife. Marcus prayed that his marriage could reach back to the point of trust that he and Gracie once shared. He just knew it had to be done. Pushing those thoughts aside for now, his present concern lay with Gracie and their unborn child.

Pacing the room that would house Kendra once she returned from her series of test, Herlene wrung her wet hands, not believing all that had happened in a day's time. "Lord, give me what to say, to both Kendra and to Mitch." She knew it was wrong, but besides praying, the only other thing she could think about was where she could get some hard liquor. Just as she headed to her purse to pull out a stashed bottle, she stopped in her tracks. Herlene saw the hospital bed being wheeled through the widened door.

More than anything, she wished that Gracie could be there to talk her through. Given the circumstances, Herlene bowed her head and silently prayed. She thought of Kenya and how much Kenya wanted to be a part of her older sister's life, and used that energy to start in on the healing process for the both of them.

With only a wall keeping her from her firstborn, Herlene made herself visible as the nurses pushed the bed into its place. As they locked the wheels and rearranged Kendra's pillows to better fit her, Herlene stepped forward.

"Hi," was all she knew to say. Not knowing if Kendra would be able to talk to her, Herlene waited for her daughter to respond in any manner.

Batting her eyes to adjust to the face that was looking down at her, it took Kendra three minutes to find her mother's reflection. Opening her mouth to speak, she cleared her throat before words would expel. "She 'kay?" Kendra dazedly asked, referring to Gracie.

"She'll be okay. Gracie will just need her rest." Herlene wondered if she should tell her the whole truth, and she looked toward the nurse's direction for clearance. She stepped in closer to her daughter and continued. "Gracie was pregnant, Kendra. She wanted to have the baby for you and Dillian, but—" She took in a breath. "I just . . . I just got word that she lost the baby. Marcus is upstairs with her."

Turning her head toward the spot where her nurse once stood, Kendra hoped to disguise the tears that had started to reside in her eyes. "My fault?" Kendra spoke in chopped sentences. "I scared her?" she asked, not able to make words quite sound as they should.

"No," Kendra's mother rushed to say. "No. Don't think that, Kendra. The baby had stopped developing for some time, Marcus said. That's what the doctor told Marcus. He had just stopped growing."

"He?" Kendra tried to swiftly look into her mother's face. With Herlene's confirmation, Kendra turned once more to look toward the sky that was showing through the hospital window.

"Look, Kendra. I know we need to give this time. You've been through a lot, and I want you to get your rest, but I've written down my number." Herlene held up a piece of paper with writing on it. "I'm going to place it here, and your nurse knows how to get in contact with me. If and when you want to talk to me, I'm just a call away."

Kendra ignored the one-sided conversation and inquired about her sister instead. "Ke-ya?"

Allowing a smile to dwell on her face, Herlene was glad to continue her small talk with Kendra. Knowing that she was inquiring about her younger sister, Herlene raced to fill Kendra in. "She's actually at your house. I have to go pick up her, the twins, and James, my husband."

Pushing something deep within, Kendra thought to fight against the weighted love that she had been receiving from her mother for the past months. Her life being renewed, Kendra gave in. "You don' go. Stay wi' me. Wan' you to stay wi' me," Kendra managed to get out with much effort.

"Oh—okay." Excitement, along with tears, grew onto Herlene's face. "I, uh . . . I'll just call James and let him know." Wanting to make sure Kendra really wanted her there, Herlene asked again. "You want me to stay with you, right?" She pointed to her heaving chest.

"Yes," was as much of an answer as Kendra could give before she closed her eyes and fell into her medicated sleep.

Pulling a chair by her daughter's bed, Herlene held Kendra's hand and cried for the peace she instantly felt. For the first time since she had started backward toward destruction, Herlene could feel herself gaining all the strength she needed to press forward. Making a mental note, she *knew* her first stop would be ditching the alcohol that was still tucked away in her purse.

younger sister. Harlene needed to tell Kendra in. "She's actually at your house. I have to go pick up her, the twins, and James, my husband."

Fighting something deep within, Kendra fought to fight against the weighted love that she had been receiving from her mother for the past months. Her life being renewed, Kendra gave in. "You don't go. Stay with me. Wait until . . . with me," Kendra managed to get out with medication.

"Oh—okay." Excitement, along with tears, grew onto Harlene's face. "I, uh . . . I'll just call James and let him know." Wanting to make sure Kendra really wanted her there, Harlene asked again. "You want me to stay with you, right?" She pointed to her heaving chest.

"Yes," was as much of an answer as Kendra could give before she closed her eyes and fell into her medicated sleep.

Pulling a chair by her daughter's bed, Harlene held Kendra's hand and cried for the peace she instantly felt. For the first time since she had started backward toward destruction, Harlene could feel herself gaining all the strength she needed to press forward. Making a mental note to herself her first stop would be ditching the alcohol that was still tucked away in her purse.

Chapter 37

"Baby, I'm going to fill out all of the paperwork, so don't worry about it, okay?" Marcus told Gracie as she lay in the hospital bed with the covers nestled close to her body. Nodding yes in her husband's direction, Gracie stared blankly.

"If you want to talk about it, Gracie, we can talk, but if you—"

"Not right now," Gracie finally responded as she turned her face from her husband. She wished all that she had just gone through had been a nightmare, but it wasn't. She knew no matter how many times she closed her eyes, reality would still sting. The sibling she carried for the twins was now gone. The possibility that Michelle would bear her husband's third child stung like the wind in a Chicago blizzard.

The last thing Gracie remembered was standing alongside everyone else in Kendra's bedroom. When Gracie became coherent again, she was in the hospital, having to deliver a baby to the world that was already deceased.

From what the doctors were telling her, there wasn't anything anyone could have done to save the pregnancy. But Gracie knew the truth behind it all. This one wasn't a pregnancy that was ordained by God; she had made all of the decisions herself. Figuring she started all the pain, all the turmoil, all of heartache in the first place, Gracie tried to forgive her husband even more.

"Just the price I had to pay. My poor baby." Gracie wailed freely.

Inching his way into the adjustable bed with his wife, Marcus held Gracie as she poured out her soul. "I can't believe what just happened. I thought I was doing the right thing, and now my baby had to pay for it."

"Hey, hey. We are not going to beat ourselves up about this. We will just have to accept what God has allowed. It'll take time, but we'll get through this, babe." Marcus kissed his wife's forehead and rocked her until she finally closed her eyes. Not questioning his wife allowing him to touch her, Marcus just thanked God for the moment.

"Will you forgive me, Marcus? Will God forgive me?"

"Honey. Don't do that to yourself. Don't beat yourself up over this. If you have to blame someone, blame me. I should have stood firm against this decision from the beginning. Don't worry about it, baby. Give it to God, and don't worry about it." Marcus wanted to assure his wife that he was all hers. "And you don't—"

"Not now," Gracie whispered as she snuggled deeper into her husband's arms. No reassurance on any level would help bring Gracie out of her heartache and pain. Only time would heal.

Never roaming far from his wife's side, Marcus prayed for guidance for his family and for his own path of having to have the dreaded talk with his wife. Marcus eased from the bed to allow Gracie as much rest as she needed. Once he knew that she had drifted to sleep, he headed to the hallway. Searching for a signal on his cell phone, Marcus had to call Ky.

"Hey, man. I was just hitting you back, man. You called?" he asked Ky as soon as he heard his distant friend's voice answer the line.

"Yeah, I did. I'm sorry, man. Pastor Regis called and told me." Ky didn't want to repeat what Marcus had witnessed. "How's Gracie?" Once Marcus filled Ky in about the day's unlikely journey, he reverted back to his reason for the call.

"She's sleeping now. Man, I really need to talk. There's so much that has gone on." Placing his free hand in his jeans pocket, Marcus needed to talk to Ky in person. "Can we get together right now?" he asked before he heard Michelle's voice in the background. "Oh, dude. I didn't know you had company. I can catch you another time."

"Nonsense. Michelle will understand. I need to talk to you about some things as well. You want to meet up?" he asked.

Michelle. Marcus mouthed the name. Agreeing to meet his friend in the hospital cafeteria, he shut his cell phone and walked to the nearest nurse's desk, where he reluctantly asked about the burial process for their child.

"Hey, man, I hope I didn't keep you waiting too long," Ky stated as he gave Marcus the kind of brotherly hug they used to share.

"You're cool, dude." Not forgetting all of his woes, Marcus dove in, asking Ky about his dealings with Michelle. "So you and Michelle, you're taking it to the next level anyway?"

"What do you mean, *anyway*?" Ky's grin slid from his face.

"I mean by all the stuff she did. The lies I'm sure she's telling you about how she's changed, the baby . . ." Anger rose in Marcus's voice as he described all that Michelle had taken him and his family through. Just thinking about having to bury his baby made his anger grow immensely.

"Whoa." Ky held up his hand. "I don't think you really want to go through all of that now." Ky looked around and soon saw Marcus's eyes follow, making him recall that he was in the hospital cafeteria.

"But actually, that's what I wanted to talk to you about too." Picking up the cup of coffee that Marcus had already ordered for him, he took a sip. "I know everything. Everything, I believe, from beginning to end. Michelle told me how she meant to sleep with you." He looked down, hating to even think about Michelle being with someone else. "And she told me how she . . . seduced you," he added through clenched teeth.

"Exactly! Finally, you're listening to me." Marcus felt pressure leave his head. "It wasn't as if I planned to go over there and be bothered with her like that. She seduced me, and now she's got you thinking you may be the child's daddy too."

"Marcus, don't. Man, we both know it's our own will to do whatever it is we do. You didn't have to call her, you didn't have to ask her for lunch, or pull *your* vehicle into her apartment complex. You didn't even have to go inside and allow her to make you lunch." Ky, noticing Marcus's whole demeanor changing, knew he had gotten his attention.

"Michelle has changed, Marcus." His manly eyes pleaded with his frat brother. "Ever since we hooked up that night at the sushi bar, we've been kicking it. I mean, it wasn't like she wasn't trying to come on to me the same night that I met her as well. I just let her know that wasn't what I was looking for."

As if Marcus had asked the question, Ky continued. "Yeah, it was hard for a brother not to give in, but I managed not to. Not that night anyway. Then she found out she was pregnant some time after we did become intimate."

Sitting back deeper into his chair, Marcus grabbed his cup of coffee once more and brought it to his mouth without speaking. Although the news was hard to take at any level, Marcus knew that the ultimate relief would come once the baby was delivered.

"I really wanted to just let you know that I don't fault you. I apologize for coming over to your house and acting up like I did. But I thought you were skipping out on your responsibilities. I'm not asking you to speak with Michelle, but I'm letting you know from this point what I can see. And I can see me and Michelle being together."

"What about the baby?" Marcus asked. "What if the baby is—?"

Ky didn't wait for him to finish. "We're just praying that it's not."

"I had no idea, Marcus," Mitchell Jeffries relayed to his son. "Yes, I had the affair, and your mother never got over it, but I had no idea. None whatsoever." The older man sat across from his son with a lost look on his face.

Nodding his head, Marcus didn't know why he was harboring anger against his father. Back at Kendra's house, when everything was brought to light, he had instantly found his hidden anger toward his father all over again. It had taken him years to get over his father cheating on his mother. From the feelings that he was now experiencing, Marcus didn't know if he actually did rid his heart of the same hurt his mother felt.

Not wanting to speak with his father about the whole scenario, Marcus searched and knew deep down that if his father had known that Kendra had been in this world, he'd have done everything in his power to love her as he had all of his children. Marcus had avoided his father's presence at the hospital, but now it was time to sit down and talk to Mitch about what had gone on, in addition to his own secrets.

"I understand," was as much as Marcus could get out before his own covert tears started streaming down his face. "I have enough to deal with of my own."

Grabbing his adult son's hand across the table, Mitch felt just as bad as he did years ago, when he packed his last piece of luggage and left their household. "Marcus, I hope you believe Daddy." He hadn't babied his son in ages, but his love was as strong for Marcus as the day he brought him home from the hospital. "I've done so much wrong, but I'm so happy that you are the man you are and haven't made these types of mistakes—"

"Michelle is pregnant, Dad." Marcus leaned in on the table. He couldn't risk his father praising him for being someone that he wasn't.

Mitch let his own sorrow escape through his mournful mouth as he pulled his large hands back. "What are you saying, son?" Tears crowded the bags underneath his bottom lashes. Knowing that his apologetic conversation wasn't over, Mitch gave his aching son his undivided attention.

Marcus whispered through sniffles, "I didn't want to tell you that part because I doubted that the baby was mine. We didn't go that far." He slammed his fist onto the cafeteria table, causing his hour-old coffee to splash over the edges of the cup.

Mitch had already fast-forwarded his own outcome. "So what are you going to do?"

"Ky just left." Marcus finally looked up. "*He* says they are praying the baby is his."

"Ky? And Michelle? How'd that happen?"

Pushing the invisible air away from his face, Marcus didn't want to linger. "The first night I saw Michelle at the restaurant, I had invited Ky to join me, not realizing that Michelle would stop by. I left before he arrived, but she was still there when he got there. One thing led to another, and I guess they took it from that point."

"Umph," was the only response that Mitch was secure with. "I can talk to her for you, see what's going on." Just as Marcus was about to intercede, Mitch picked up speed on his vocals. "You have enough to deal with, with Gracie . . . and the baby." Mitch seized his son's hand once more and held onto it. "I'll talk to Michelle about all of this. I'll let you know."

"Don't bother. If Ky thinks the baby is his, maybe I should just let it alone," Marcus thought out loud with a shrug of his shoulders.

"Son," Mitch said, turning his son's attention to himself, "haven't you learned anything from me?" Tears held in their place as the older Jeffries said, "Don't be like me, son. Don't let a lifetime almost slip you by before you know if you have a child or not. That child has a right to be in your life no matter what."

“Don’t compare my problem with your problem, Dad. That’s your problem,” Marcus spat out without thinking.

Getting up from the two-seat table, a boisterous Mitch towered over his son. When Marcus looked up at his lofty father, he saw the seriousness in his dad’s face and turned his eyes toward his own feet.

“I love you, son, but you know what the right thing consists of,” Mitch called out as he gave Marcus a smack on his shoulder and started on his way.

No matter how hard his father tried to charge him in the right direction, Marcus knew all decisions would be his to make. How would he be able to bury a baby that was conceived with his wife, only to birth another out of an affair?

Chapter 38

Three days passed before Gracie was allowed to go home. On her last day, she had gained enough energy, mentally and physically, to visit with Kendra, who was in the same hospital on a different floor.

"Gracie." Kendra managed to ease her friend's name from her scratchy throat. Reaching her hands out for her friend to enter into her awaiting arms, Kendra yearned for her sister-friend. "Oh my goo'ness, Gracie," she cried. With her eyes slowly regaining strength, tears fell.

Gracie eased her way toward her college friend, full of emotions as she closed in the gap between them. "Oh, Kendra, I'm so happy. I prayed . . . I–I didn't know if you were going to ever come back," she cried.

"I here, Gracie. T'ank you . . . t'ank you." They held their embrace and cried together.

When Herlene walked through the door, Gracie eased up to see who had joined them. Looking over her shoulder, Gracie stood straight and turned her attention back to Kendra.

"I hope you forgive me, but I couldn't turn your mother away." Grabbing for Herlene's hand, Gracie pulled her in closer. "She was there every step of the way, Kendra."

Nodding her *yes* gesture, Kendra said, "I know, Gracie. I know." With her hand held out, Kendra waited for her mother's touch. "It's the past. I can't 'llow it to run my life no mo'."

Turning her attention to Herlene, Kendra continued through her severed speech. "Herlene, I know I tol' you." Kendra paused in order to gain strength to continue. "But I fo'give you. I fo'give you fo' not bein' there 'cause when I need you most, you here. You here now." She crookedly raised her hand and touched her heart. "That's what matter."

Not anticipating any other visitors, when the door squeaked, the three looked in the direction of the doctor's voice. "Well, I'll be. I'm sorry I'm just getting back in town," the tall, plainly clothed doctor spoke. "How is everyone?" He walked closer, shaking hands as he made his way to Kendra's bedside. "I guess you weren't finished, huh?" Dr. Smith asked.

"No, sir." Kendra smiled, looking up at her doctor of many years.

"Good, good. I cut my vacation short," he said while leaning down, using his flashlight to visit the pupils of her eyes. "I had to come back to see it for myself. What a blessing." Putting the flashlight back into his pocket, Dr. Smith picked up the folder he had placed on the foot of the bed.

"Well, I do have some added news." He looked down at the paperwork, and then toward Kendra. "It's good news, Mrs. McNab."

"Okay. Long as it's good news, lemme hear it."

Looking back at Gracie and Herlene, he asked, "Are you sure you don't mind sharing the news with your family?"

"They fine. You can tell me," Kendra added.

"Well, when you were first brought in, when you were found at home, there were several tests that were run. Leaving no stone unturned, this one test we took had shocking results. No one in your family had shared the news with us, so we assumed no one knew." Taking a look behind him, he continued.

"We knew about your HIV status, of course, so that was a given on how to treat you." Getting a second wind, Dr. Smith continued his speech. "We didn't share the latest news because of not knowing what the outcome would be with you." He studied their faces. "We didn't want to give anyone false hope on the baby's survival."

"What is—what?" Kendra asked.

With an added grin, Dr. Smith shared the news. "Kendra, you're pregnant. Definitely with child." He halted as he saw Kendra look down at the sheet covering her midsection.

"What?" Herlene yelled. "Oh my goodness. Oh, chile! Oh, chile. I'm gonna be a nana?"

"Huh?" Gracie sounded a confused response to the news, but quickly let the past months be her recourse. Kendra had gained weight while in the hospital, but Gracie figured it was Kendra's inactivity combined with side effects from her medication that had caused her to swell.

"Pregnant?" Kendra understood as she pulled back the covers and laid a hand on her widened and stretched stomach. Knowing that her comatose body had fought and won against her years of working out, Kendra thought her midsection had just grown flabby.

"Yes, ma'am," the proud doctor announced. "You're about seven months along. We've been doing ultrasounds every three weeks, making sure all is well, and, well, all *is* well. We even know the sex of the baby if you want to know."

Trying her best to look around the doctor once he stepped back, Kendra laid her eyes on the two women who had been there through it all. Not knowing what to say, Kendra felt she didn't have to say anything once the two rushed to her side and engulfed her with feelings.

"I thought I jus' got fat, y'all," Kendra called out through a crooked half laugh and cry.

He didn't want to break up the moment, but Dr. Smith spoke through the commotion. "It seems that the last in vitro procedure that you and Dillian went through worked."

In an airy breath, Gracie spoke. "Dillian?" She stopped to bring remembrance to her departed friend with a smile. "Oh, he must have left his space open for the baby."

Closing her eyes, Kendra thanked God for her husband. She quickly recalled his spirit asking her to take care of their baby. Moving her lips as if Dillian were in the room with them, Kendra inwardly thanked her husband for making her see that it wasn't her time to leave.

Thank you, Dillian. I'll always love you.

I'll always love you too, Dillian's spirit spoke back to his wife's heart. *Take care of our baby.*

Always.

to say anything once the two rushed to her side and engulfed her with feelings.

"I thought I just got left, y'all," Kendra called out through a crooked half laugh and cry.

He didn't want to break up the moment, but Dr. Smith spoke through the commotion. "It seems that the last in utero procedure that you and Dillian went through worked."

In an airy breath, Gracie spoke. "Dillian?" She stopped to bring homage to her departed friend with a smile. "Oh, he must have left his space open for the baby."

Closing her eyes, Kendra thanked God for her husband. She quickly recalled his spirit asking her to take care of their baby. Moving her lips as if Dillian were in the room with them, Kendra internally thanked her husband for making her see that it wasn't her time to leave.

Thank you, Dillian. I'll always love you.

I'll always love you too, Dillian's spirit spoke back to his wife's heart. *Take care of our baby. Always.*

Chapter 39

The same way they traveled was the same avenue Herlene and Kendra took on their return to Kendra's home. After a week at the hospital, being certain of the miracle that had transpired in her life, Kendra was once again released to start her life anew. Nothing would be the same.

Never knowing when her and Herlene's silent conversation would spill into their present, Kendra knew that everything she had experienced had granted her a second chance; even a second chance with her mother. While riding the waves of the rocky ambulance, on one of the bumps that almost released her from her bed restraint, Kendra grabbed for Herlene's hand.

"Whoa, hold on, Kendra," Herlene suggested as she was jolted from her seat. Releasing her grip, Herlene held tight once she realized Kendra hadn't planned on letting go.

Kendra knew when they got to her home there was a possibility that a steady flow of visitors would come through. She felt she needed to at least get started on their heart to heart, no holds barred.

"Thank you, f–for bein' there for me, Herlene," was the first of what she had to say. "I really 'preciate you bein' there for me, helping Gracie and Marcus out."

With her mouth pursed tightly, Herlene knew that the inevitable had surfaced. "Kendra, you don't have to thank me for that. That's the least of what I could have done for you." She gave the thickened air a frightened chortle. "I–I mean, I know I didn't do nothing else for you, so I don't want you to thank me for something I am supposed to do."

Her eye contact landing everywhere else but on Herlene, another jolt struck Kendra. "Well, can I thank you for finally being good to *you*? I know you've changed up a lot. You look nice."

Wanting to lean in and kiss and hug her daughter, Herlene knew she had to tell Kendra about what had actually tripped her up years ago. She wanted to finally share with Kendra what had sent her on a tailspin.

"Kendra, I–I'm so happy that you're proud of me, but, but . . . I just don't want to disappoint you anymore." She placed her hands in her own lap. "You see, I . . . I, you see, when I was pregnant with you, I was with a man who I thought loved me and was going to marry me." Herlene felt embarrassed, but she knew she had to finish. "He was a married man, but I didn't know. There was no way I knew that Mitch—" realizing that she had said Mitch's name too soon in the conversation, Herlene grabbed her mouth.

Not wanting to hear Herlene down herself any further, Kendra let out what she thought she ought to share. "Herlene, I know. I heard everything. I could always hear everything you said." Kendra wanted to make sure Herlene understood her. "When I was 'sleep, I heard you. I heard you tell me the story. I know how much you loved my dad and that it must have broken your heart, but now you have James, and he loves you like you deserve to be loved." With a deep breath added to her lungs, Kendra added, "And you have me. There is no way I want us to be apart. I wish I had been strong enough while you went through what you went through, but I was a child."

"I just wish you never had to go through it," Herlene countered with easily flowing tears. "There was so much pain I put you through. My heart—I probably won't ever forgive myself, but baby, as long as you let me, I want to make up everything I wronged."

Kendra looked deep into her mother's eyes and said, "I know from this point on, it may get rough before the road actually smoothes out for us, but just promise me, Mommy, promise me that it only gets better from here."

Hearing Kendra call her by her maternal identification for the first time, Herlene allowed her tears to fall like never before. "There is no question, honey. It only gets better from here."

Once they settled Kendra back into her warm and welcoming home, Herlene brewed coffee and sat in the kitchen. Not wanting to put any distance between her and her daughter, Herlene knew she wouldn't be leaving Kendra's side any moment soon. She still couldn't believe all that had transpired, and had to keep pinching her dried skin to remind herself that she was not dreaming.

There was no doubt about what Herlene was feeling in her heart. No matter what she had gone through, God still thought enough of her to not only forgive her, but to set her free. The forgiving herself part was what she would have to work on, but with Kendra being the woman God had blessed her to be, Herlene automatically knew Kendra was already the inspiration she needed for self-healing.

Though Gracie's attempt to heal Kendra from inside out didn't develop into a plan that God allowed, Herlene prayed that the Lord would bless Gracie in a mighty way for thinking of His people. She prayed and asked God to heal Marcus and Gracie's household like she knew only He could.

Her prayers deepened when she thought of withholding years from the relationship that could have been meaningful to Kendra. If she had to do it all over again, no doubt Herlene would have been up front with Mitch and let him know her true feelings toward him and his thoughts on her pregnancy. Holding on to her emotional pain only broke her heart and the heart of the person who counted most—Kendra.

Young and thoughtless about relationships and the quality of them, Herlene realized she had lost herself when she initially lost her relationship with the sweet-spirited Savior. Though youth played a part in her lack of wisdom of being a mother and not knowing how to give her all to God first, herself, and then her child, Herlene recognized she had skipped all three steps of a union with God.

Falling back in love with Jesus was the best thing Herlene could have ever done. Even when she wanted to reconcile years prior, she knew

God's timing would be perfect when He moved and manifested His promises. Never believing things would happen in the fashion they had, Herlene accepted what God allowed and readied herself for the future that lay waiting ahead of her.

She knew she wouldn't push herself on Kendra, but she did know she would be available for whatever her daughter wanted and needed of her. Though it wasn't too late, it surely was the beginning of a mother-daughter relationship she had fasted and prayed for.

"For giving my years back, Lord, I thank you. For ordering each of our steps so that we would praise your name together, Lord, only you can be so gracious."

Sitting at her daughter's kitchenette, Herlene raised her coffee and held the sides of the warm mug. A conquering smile stretched on her face as she took in the warmth as God's reassurance and love. With a sip of the hot beverage, Herlene imagined God's love surrounding and mending her once broken heart.

"Oh, taste and see that the Lord is good," she said as she daydreamed on Jesus.

Epilogue

Six months had passed since the delivery of her baby girl, Mercy, and life as Kendra knew it would forever be different. She would be saddled with a permanent limp, but Kendra wouldn't let that minor setback keep her from living.

An HIV negative status for her daughter had given Kendra hope for Mercy to have a healthy and normal life. Still being plagued with all the bushels of medication that clouded her days, Kendra hadn't once neglected her intake. She vowed that Mercy would be her inspiration to continue living.

"I'm so happy that you made it," Kendra gleamed as she held a bubbly and growing Mercy.

"Boy, if she's not looking just like her daddy. Ain't that something?" Marcus added about his goddaughter before he took note of his cell phone vibrating on his hip.

Looking at her husband, who had been shocked by his cell phone, Gracie guided her attention back to Mercy. "Let me hold my niece before the service gets started." With her hands held out, Gracie felt Marcus stand from the church pew, but she didn't give much notice to his expressions as she sat Mercy on her knee.

"So do they do the dedication ceremony before or after the service?"

"After, so if you want, Mercy can sit with you all while I help out with the choir," Kendra added, waiting for Gracie's response.

"The choir? So you really can sing, huh?" she joked, making her friend blush through her coffee brown skin. "I'm so happy that everything turned out for the best."

"Yeah, I am too." Kendra knelt next to the pew, down by Gracie and Mercy. "I really am happy you didn't turn my mother away. I can't even believe that I'm calling her my mother."

"But she is your mother, Kendra."

"No, she isn't the mother that I hated. She is someone I love. I guess I shouldn't have let so many years get in between us."

"Yeah, maybe not," Gracie said as she playfully bounced Mercy around on her lap. "But we are here now, and that's all that matters. And James isn't that bad either, huh?"

Standing back to her feet, Kendra straightened her skirt and gave herself a once-over before speaking. "I couldn't have asked for a better stepfather." With a quick look toward the pulpit, Kendra gathered that it was time for service to start. "Okay, Mercy's okay with you, right?"

"Sure. Go ahead, girl. I can handle her. As long as those boys stay in children's church, I'm cool. Marcus"—Gracie looked to her right—"he just stepped out, but he should be right back, I guess."

Making her way to the front of the church, Kendra grabbed one of the microphones from another member on the praise team and took her position. When she looked up and saw Gracie noticing her stance, she smiled and mouthed the words *this is for you*, right before the music started.

Gracie couldn't believe that in all the years of her friendship with Kendra, she didn't know that her friend loved to sing, or even that she could, for that matter. As soon as Kendra opened her mouth, sweetness flowed through the air as she looked right into her friend's eyes and sang from her soul.

"Never would have made it. Never could have made it . . . without you," Kendra sang from the depths of her soul. She knew that God had offered her another chance to right all the wrong that she'd done. For the ultimate gift of sparing her life and giving her another chance with Mercy, Kendra made a vow that she wasn't going to look back.

Adding follow-up verses to her rendition of the inspirational song, Kendra couldn't help but notice that her father, Mitch, had made it to the service as well. He was headed in Gracie's direction, she was sure, to place as many kisses as he could on his granddaughter. Secure in knowing that Mitch truthfully hadn't known she existed in the world, Kendra was blessed by the relationship that her father promised could only get better. Smiling through her singing, a reconditioned, saved, and forgiving Kendra closed her eyes to bask in her God's presence. Never having a feeling like God had given her heart, being a mother and a lover of God covered all of her past disgraced living. Moving in the direction only God could have wanted for her, Kendra knew her future would be far better than her past.

As Marcus made his way back into the sanctuary, he added himself back beside Gracie. "Hey," he whispered to Gracie, who was standing, holding a joyful Mercy to her bosom.

Throwing him a quick smile, Gracie didn't sway from the sounds that her friend sang toward her. With tears strolling down her face, Gracie took Kendra's words into her heart.

Tapping Gracie on her shoulder, Marcus pointed Gracie's attention toward Herlene. The new grandmother stood, ready to relieve Gracie from the growing grandbaby. With his hand out, Marcus continued to stand, swaying with his wife as the song and the music ministered to their hearts. Trying his best to display a face of solace, Marcus fought to keep his own blessed tears intact.

He'd just received a call from Ky, letting him know that he and Michelle had just left their doctor's office with their own baby girl. Wanting to wait until after service, Marcus knew God had answered once again and he had no choice but to share the news. Grabbing Gracie around her shoulders, he brought his lips to the side of her face. "The baby is not mine." Marcus was ecstatic to pass along the news that his close friend had given him.

Wrapping his arms around his wife, Marcus pulled her into him as he continued to sway to the musical number. Glad that he'd shared the news with his wife, Marcus figured he'd wait until after service to let Gracie know that Ky wasn't the child's father either. Marcus rejoiced that his sin hadn't produced the baby, but he couldn't help but feel bad for Ky and Michelle, and he said a silent prayer for them as he continued his worship.

Lifting hands, praising God for all that He had done, the Jeffries worshiped along with the other parishioners. They thanked God for their right now. With all they had suffered through, Gracie and Marcus praised God for His grace . . . and couldn't help but exalt Him for His mercy.

Readers' Group Guide

1. Do you think it was sensible for Gracie to even entertain the thought of having a baby in the first place? Do you think she prayed to God before considering her own plan?
2. If you were Marcus, would you have made your beliefs known sooner? Should Marcus have even considered the pregnancy? Do you believe he prayed on the circumstance, and if so, do you believe he waited on the answer?
3. Do you believe Marcus's meeting up with Michelle was the right thing to do, even if sleeping with her wasn't on his mind?
4. Was Herlene to blame for Kendra's actions as an adult?
5. If Herlene had to do it all over again, do you think she would have tried to contact Kendra earlier? Do you feel that her finding God made a difference?
6. Should Kendra take responsibility for her

own actions as an adult? Do you believe if Kendra had a relationship with God that her life would have gone down a different road, even if Herlene had still done the things she did?

7. Do you believe Kendra should have forgiven her mother years prior in order to have bypassed all the heartache they both went through?
8. Do you believe Michelle had actually changed? How do you feel Ky will respond to the outcome?
9. Has Gracie learned a valuable lesson?
10. The friendship between Kendra and Gracie has mended. The relationship with Kendra and Herlene has healed, etc. How did God play a significant role?

About the Author

Keshia Dawn is currently working on her third novel. Residing in Texas with her daughter, Chayse, Keshia is also working to complete her degree in journalism. *His Grace, His Mercy* is the sequel to *By the Grace of God.*

Find out more about the author by visiting:
www.KeshiaDawnWrites.com

Other Works by this Author

By the Grace of God
(novel)

His Grace, His Mercy
(novel)

Keeper of My Soul
(novel)

"Stroke of Purpose"
(short story in *Triumph of My Soul*)

"Baby Boy"
(short story in *Bended Knees*)

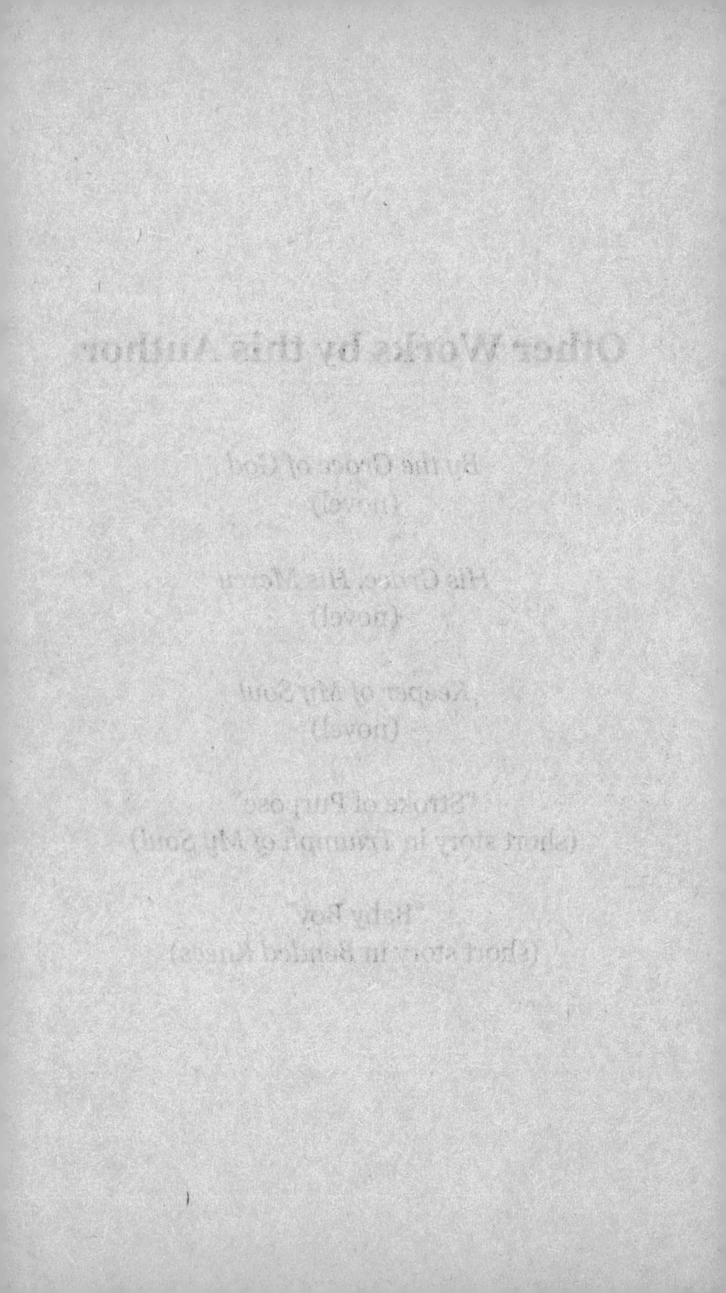

UC HIS GLORY BOOK CLUB!

www.uchisglorybookclub.net

UC His Glory Book Club is the spirit-inspired brainchild of Joylynn Jossel, Author and Acquisitions Editor of Urban Christian, and Kendra Norman-Bellamy, Author for Urban Christian. This is an online book club that hosts authors of Urban Christian. We welcome as members all men and women who have a passion for reading Christian-based fiction.

UC His Glory Book Club pledges our commitment to provide support, positive feedback, encouragement, and a forum whereby members can openly discuss and review the literary works of Urban Christian authors.

There is no membership fee associated with UC His Glory Book Club; however, we do ask that you support the authors through purchasing, encouraging, providing book reviews, and of course, your prayers. We also ask that you respect our beliefs and follow the guidelines of the book club. We hope to receive your valuable input, opinions, and reviews that build up, rather than tear down our authors.

What We Believe:

—We believe that Jesus is the Christ, Son of the Living God

—We believe the Bible is the true, living Word of God

—We believe all Urban Christian authors should use their God-given writing abilities to ho nor God and share the message of the written word God has given to each of them uniquely.

—We believe in supporting Urban Christian authors in their literary endeavor s by reading, purchasing and sharing their titles with our online community.

—We believe that in everything we do in our literary arena should be done in a manner that will lead to God being glorified and honored.

We look forward to the online fellowship with you.

Please visit us often at: *www.uchisglorybookclub.net*.

Many Blessing to You!

Shelia E. Lipsey,
President, UC His Glory Book Club